Fine, I'm a Terrible Person

LISA F. ROSENBERG

Sibylline
DIGITAL FIRST

Published in the United States by Sibylline Digital First, an imprint of
All Things Book LLC, California.

Sibylline Press is dedicated to publishing the brilliant work of women
authors ages 50 and older. www.sibyllinepress.com

ISBN: 9781960573674
ebook ISBN: 9781960573308
LCCN: 2024952259

Cover Design: Alicia Feltman
Book Production: Sang Kim

Note to Reader: This is a work of fiction. Names, characters,
businesses, dialogue, events and incidents, with the exception
of some well-known figures, are the products of the author's
imagination and are not to be construed as real. Any
resemblance to actual persons, living or dead, or actual
events is purely coincidental.

Sibylline
DIGITAL FIRST

This book is dedicated to the enduring legacy of the enchanting ghosts of the island of Rhodes. A community annihilated by the Nazi's in World War II. Their unique, beautiful, and delicious culture inspired this story and will continue to live in my heart.

Ke Sus Almas Repozen en Gan Eden
May Their Souls Rest in the Garden of Eden

Refran mentirozo no ay, [Ladino]
A lying proverb doesn't exist.

Ladino: Throughout this story you will encounter foreign language words and phrases. This is Ladino, otherwise known as Judeo-Spanish. Ladino is the spoken and written Hispanic language of Sephardim, Jews of Spanish origin dating back nearly a thousand years. Ladino is a mix of Castellano, French, Italian, Greek, Turkish, and Hebrew. The language follows the route of the Jewish people's migration from Spain after they were expelled in the mid-1500s

★ ★ ★

Rhodesli (plural Rhodeslis or Rhodesli): a Rhodian Jew, or a Sephardi Jew from Rhodes.

Related terms: Rhodes, Rhodian, Rhodiots

CHAPTER ONE

Pasa punto, pasa mundo.
A moment passes, a world passes.

★ ★ ★

It is the first post at the top of her newsfeed. It stops her cold. Leyla worries that the violent beating of her heart will wake her husband, Stephen, who is snoring like a sea monster beside her. She clenches her fist, presses it to her mouth, and exhales forcefully through her nose, then sits upright and rocks her torso ever so slightly in that involuntary way humans do when they experience sudden and severe pain. She cannot fill her lungs.

Everything she loathes about social media has delivered her to this moment. Her father, Robert Henry Feldenburg, is dead. The intensity of emotion she stifles is staggering, but Leyla knows how to contain—some might say repress—feelings (an inherited Feldenburg family trait).

In the darkness, silent and compressed, her family asleep around her, she does not shout or cry. She surrenders to the violent tsunami of shock and sadness washing over and through her. Her heart is exploding. Her ears are roaring.

Though this is a nauseating discovery, it's not as if she is unaccustomed to the lonely, bleak middle of the night. Leyla inhabits this place with regularity. An acute insomniac, she is a naturalized citizen of that middle-earth space of angst and weariness—the battleground of the chronically unrested. We call it "the dead of night" for a reason.

★ ★ ★

Each night when Leyla wakes, she pauses in hopeful hesitation, lingering in the dark sliver of not knowing, relishing the possibility that it's morning, and she's slept through the night. After checking the time and finding that she hasn't, she endures the repetitive cycle of devastation and failure—yet another night where sleep eludes her. For the remaining hours, she must suffer the nocturnal torments of adult insomnia.

First up: shame-attacks—one for every decision ever made, followed closely by fear of future catastrophes. Fear and shame are mere warm-ups for the "coulda woulda shouldas," and finally, guilt arrives to close out the night—deep, vast, excruciating parental guilt from the nightly review of each mistake, misstep, and wounding core memory she is responsible for creating in her children. The cycle repeats each night with conditional additions and subtractions of an array of abstract terrors and frets.

Her mother, Aurora, was the vexing source of tonight's restless anguish. Today was grandparents' day at the kids' school. The brainchild of some brilliant independent school development director. Invite grandparents to spend a day at school, soften them up with a few adorable songs, tug on their heartstrings with a cute side by side art project, add in a cookie or two sprinkled and frosted with their grandchild's tender little paws. Then wave them off with a hug and an aggressive solicitation for this year's annual fund, imploring them to "dig deep" to support the world's darling future leaders.

Aurora showed up late, no surprise. Leyla had given Aurora her usual false arrival time. If she needed Aurora to be somewhere that had a start time at 10:00 a.m., she'd tell her to be there at 9:00 a.m. Aurora would then arrive at exactly 10:15 a.m., thereby being only fifteen minutes late. It was basic Aurora math and time management. Somehow Aurora never caught on to the ruse.

The special assembly had already begun. Leyla, in the fourth-row center, on the watch for Aurora, was scanning the low panel of windows along the side of the gym. She saw the flash of pink sparkled sneakers first, walking toward the window.

Oh god.

Leyla looked up to the higher row of horizontal windows and saw her mother, hand to her forehead in a kind of salute, long purple sparkling nails glimmering in the sun. She was smashing her face against the glass, squinting through her oversized rhinestone-rimmed glasses, bright fuchsia lipstick smudging the glass.

Leyla shook her head with the futile hope that somehow her mother would spot her in the room, see the directional hint and comply. She did not. The security alarm went off as the children were on the first stanza of "Oh say can you see."

Aurora had shoved open the door clearly marked DO NOT OPEN EMERGENCY EXIT ONLY and entered the gym. All eyes now focused on the source of the disruption. The chorus teacher waved her baton at the kids to keep singing.

Aurora began to sing along. Still not noticing Leyla, who was shaking her head at an accelerated rate back and forth, her expression a combination of rage and panic. Aurora was belting it out with her signature off-key—way off-key—vocal skills and total disregard for accurate lyrics.

"Why so proudly we sail, to the twilight that's steaming."

4 | LISA F. ROSENBERG

Leyla now mouthing "NO."

The patrician private-school grandparents were also shaking their heads but rather in sneering disdain. The same judgmental glances and horrified side eyes followed her mother wherever she went. Well-groomed blue grey heads subtly signaling to one another, gesturing and head nodding toward Aurora, wordlessly communicating: Who is that? Has she no dignity? I mean really.

No, she doesn't, thought Leyla, and she is my mother.

The pickleball-tanned matron in the cream-colored St. John knit, directly in front of Leyla, turned to the tall even-skinned man in the grandfatherly grey V-neck sweater of Brooks Brothers cashmere and audibly snickered.

Leyla closed her eyes and swallowed hard. Never one for self-consciousness, Aurora proceeded with her performance of discordant vocal patriotism. Leyla was revisiting this episode for tonight's insomnia replay-and-review session.

★ ★ ★

Her "essential sleep hygiene strategy," which she learned about in the *New York Times*, requires preventing any light from leaking into the room. Leyla does everything possible to seal every door and window and cover every smoke detector and modem to achieve complete darkness. Stephen knows not to, under penalty of death, leave his collection of Apple devices glowing bedside. He also knows, from previous disastrous episodes, not to say anything about the absurdity of her time consuming and futile interventions. One recent comment of, "Is this really essential, sweetie?" led to an epic row and a stone-cold scowl from Leyla that lasted three days. The guy knows now to just stay out of the way.

She's tried using an eye mask for personal light blockage, but her aesthetician advised against it as it can accelerate the development of crow's-feet.

The last time she slept through the night was an anomaly. That single, delicious episode of deep, satisfying slumber resulted from a melatonin supplement, valerian tea (not too close to bedtime as that would trigger waking up to pee), "sleepy" herbs from her acupuncturist, GABA gummies, CBD tincture, lavender-scented magnesium foot spray, and a bedroom temperature of seventy-one degrees Fahrenheit. All helped along with half a bottle of Biodynamic Napa Valley Rose and two tablets of Benadryl. That was months ago, and it hasn't happened again.

Her bedtime "sleep-efficiency prep" takes nearly twenty minutes and was initially a source of much eye-rolling from Stephen. She checks the thermostat to be sure he has not adjusted it, then positions the weighted blanket on her side of the bed. She read that the DPS (deep pressure stimulation) that it provides is supposed to initiate the parasympathetic nervous system which encourages rest and recovery (a lifelong claustrophobic, Stephen hates it.) She checks her phone to see if it's on silent, checks his phone for the same.

"Leyla, give me my phone back"

Then she swallows her supplements and tinctures and adjusts her earplugs for a tight seal (added insurance against being woken up by the sea-monster husband).

The disappointment she feels each night when her strategies and interventions fail elevates her heart rate. This is discouraged by Dr. Mark Hayden's Functional Medicine Institute's "Sleep Remedy Etiquette."

Sometimes when she wakes, it's 1:00 a.m., which is so upsetting no amount of vagal breathing will soften the blow. The lack of sleep has ravaged her, not to mention the catastrophic impact on her daily "to-dos." Leyla adamantly adheres to the daily "to-do list system" of her TaskSage app.

"Just take a sleeping pill," her mother suggests when Leyla mentions her struggle with sleep.

"How can you suggest pharmaceutically altering my serotonin levels? You know I've struggled with endorphin deficiency my entire life!" Leyla responds.

"Maybe try some of that Melanoma stuff. People say it really works?"

"It's Melatonin, Mom, not Melanoma. I've tried it. It doesn't work."

"Well, then how about a little Vicks VapoRub under the nose?" Aurora subscribes to the dictum that nothing can't be helped with a little dab of Vicks under the nose. "*Mi alma*—my love—just a little dab and you will *dormie con los anjelitos*—sleep with the angels."

"Don't start with the folklore remedies, Mother. Next, you'll tell me to put garlic on a string around my neck."

"Well, have you tried it? It might work."

Leyla's insomnia arrived with the onset of perimenopause. She attacked midlife with her signature determination, dug in her heels, and "leaned into it" with her penchant for exhaustive research. She succeeded in mitigating most of the classic symptoms.

She has never had a hot flash (homeopathic Maca root); she lost weight in her midsection (NAD supplements, planking); her skin glows and her hair is thicker (chemical peels and homemade organic collagen gummies); and she has the muscle tone of a thirty-year-old (Pilates, intermittent fasting, and a strict Keto diet). She takes pride in her defiance of mortality. Still, every once in a while she does wonder how much of a difference it would make if she ate just a little breakfast. For Leyla relinquishing self-control is inconceivable. It is her sustenance. Who needs breakfast?

But she has completely lost the ability to sleep. Leyla never had a problem with sleep before. She used to brag about what a great sleeper she was.

"Not me, lean me against a wall, and I'm out," she'd say, whenever someone complained of a sleepless night.

She now thought maybe the boasting had been a mistake. Leyla refuses to succumb to the superstitious traditions of the Rhodeslis women she descends from. She thinks them provincial, the women and their traditions. Still, she can't help wondering now when considering her acute state of insomnia.

Whenever someone bragged, her grandmother Floru would say, *"Hazer y non agradecer*—Do, but don't brag. Then she'd spit on you to ward off the evil eye—the *oju malu*. Leyla spent much of her childhood awash in Floru's distinctive, nicotine-laced spittle.

Though Leyla scoffs at the absurd folkloric notion of the evil eye, she is so delirious with lack of sleep she is willing to consider it a possibility. Did she tempt the dreaded *oju malu* by bragging about her talent for sleeping?

She tries to get back to sleep each night. She turns on her Calm app and listens to the wind and rainwater sounds, forces yawns, gets up to pee, practices her NSDR (nonsleep deep rest) protocol, gets up to pee again, taps on sleep acupressure points on another app—ultimately exhausting every homeopathic, functional medicine, googled strategy, until finally giving up and surrendering to nocturnal wakefulness.

★ ★ ★

Leyla concentrates on the one sliver of glow she failed to eliminate. Is it streetlight or moonlight. Is the sun coming up? Is it morning?

Her nightly time-reveal is a precisely choreographed process. She attempts to accomplish it without arriving at full wakefulness, on the off-chance that she might be able to return to sleep. It begins with a deep breath through the nose, a slight turn of the head, and a one-eyed squint. From that position, she seeks clues revealed by the narrow gap between the shades and the windowpane, attempting to determine the time by assessing the quality of the light shining through.

She resists the urge to look at the phone. The blue light cell phones emit is a direct violation of sleep-hygiene protocol. But tonight, after an hour and forty futile minutes of the Calm app, duvet wrestling, tossing, turning, and CBD vaping, Leyla admits defeat. She takes a deep breath. Here goes, she thinks, and rolls over to reach for her phone.

"Fuck me." Her phone clock reads 3:00 a.m.

Leyla commences her nightly doom scrolling. She starts with the Dow Jones—just a quick glance at her and Stephen's portfolio. If the market is up, it fills her with a warm sense of security. If the market is down, her anxiety is nourished. Then on to a skim of headlines. The push-pull, attraction-repulsion of middle-of-the-night social-media immersion is another weakness she has identified but not overcome. She knows it's unhealthy. It does not help her insomnia, yet it is a magnetic draw during those 3:00 a.m. wake ups, high on her list of discussion topics to address with her therapist. Leyla has a long list.

She taps the blue square with the big white F for the dreaded Facebook check. Leyla professes to eschew the "pedestrian phenomenon" of social media.

"I refuse to debase myself by engaging in social media," she self-righteously proclaims when someone asks if she's seen a recent post. The truth is, Leyla is a Facebook creeper. She doesn't participate in social media, but she peeks. She never likes, posts, or comments, but she obsessively, salaciously, secretly, observes.

Social media is harrowing for her. Each viewing of the curated highlight reels of people she knows, as well as those she does not, brings with it massive doses of low self-esteem accompanied by a deluge of inadequacy. They all look so thin, fashionably and expensively dressed at fabulous events in marvelous locations (that neither she nor her children were invited to) while affectionately embracing other slender stylish people. The anxiety ignited by these surveillances is brutal.

Still, she scrolls, checking her sister-in-law, or possibly "outlaw"; she isn't sure whether her brother is even married to Acacia anymore. She hasn't spoken to Branan in years. Estrangement runs rampant within the Feldenburg family of elite grudge-holders. The Facebook photo dumps by Acacia are all the intelligence she gets about Branan's life, children, and whereabouts.

Leyla's curiosity overwhelms her commitment to sleep protocol and she persists, enduring the ego assaults of highly skilled "Facebraggers." She peeks at her ex-BFF. After thirty years of friendship to a white supremacist, Donald Trump-supporting, conspiracy theorist whom she'd spoken to daily since the first day of freshman year in high school, Leyla called it quits after an insomnia-fueled Facebook creep unearthed a comment from "exie" that included the N-word, "all lives matter," and George Soros and the Jews run the world.

She peeps to see where her current frenemies from All Friends Day School spent President's week/Indigenous Peoples' Day/spring break/summer vacation/festive holiday. The hyper-competitive social environment of her children's elite "independent" school makes for less-than-authentic social connections.

Leyla's spirit shrinks with each post of humbly satisfying second homes, sexy marriages, and high achieving, artistically *and* athletically gifted offspring with the appropriate #grateful and "feeling blessed" emojis. No matter how far she has come in life, Leyla can't shake the feeling of being an outsider, a decided imposter in the world of one percenters. These nightly online meanderings do not encourage the relaxed state needed for sleep.

Tonight's session brought an unexpected and particularly explosive dose of anguish. Cousin Sam, her father's brother's oldest son, apparently suffering so terribly from the loss of his uncle (Leyla's father, Robert), raced within minutes of his Uncle Robert's "passing" to share his "feeling sad" emoji on Facebook. Leyla realized she might be the first to see his post when she looks at the time stamp, just two minutes prior. There are no "like," "love," or "care" emoji reactions yet.

She reads through the nauseating twenty-first century spectacle—the Facebook eulogy. Charmed by the sound of their own voice, people shed the angelic light of the obituary upon their lost loved ones in exchange for sincerely perfunctory responses from distant acquaintances with tiny little animations of "like," "love," "care," or "hugs."

She swallows hard to keep down the bile as she reads. *Robert Henry Feldenburg, decorated Korean war hero* (he signed up just to piss his father off, and because he was flunking all his classes at Cal), *played football for USC* (nope, total lie, never happened, he went there for one semester after returning from Korea, and by then he was alcohol-dependent, borderline diabetic, and had diminished hearing in his right ear from carrying a bazooka. The head coach observed him for one workout on the field and sent him packing, but it was a good pickup line, so he stuck with the lifelong lie. *Devoted husband* (Hmmm, to exactly which one of his three wives, and multiple long and short-term mistresses?), *loving father and grandfather.*

"Nope, no fucking way," Leyla shudders. "Boy, would I like a shot at writing his obituary."

The Robert H. Feldenburg that she knew was a serial womanizer, thief, liar, pathological narcissist, habitual bankrupter, rabid misogynist, drunk, racist, dog beater, and the kind of father who reminded you at every opportunity that your very existence is a disappointment.

"*Este es kanyo kon loda*—He is bad through and through," Grandmother Floru had pronounced whenever his name was mentioned—followed, of course, with the requisite loogie on the floor.

I wonder if there are dog-beater emojis? Leyla allows herself to imagine the digital graphic form they might take.

Leyla hasn't spoken to, or seen, the man for over twenty years. Still, learning of your father's death on Facebook, in the middle of the night, during a humdinger of an insomnia bout, and not even having a best friend to tell, is a searing laceration to the soul.

She won't tell Stephen. How can she ever put into words how it feels to find out on Facebook that your estranged father died? Stephen would never understand, having come from the blissfully mundane stability of an intact family. No doubt he'd be supportive, but the emotion she feels the strongest is shame, and she doesn't feel up to sharing that right now.

Leyla would never lean on her sons. They are still too young, and from their births she's made every effort to fiercely protect them from what she considers to be the curse of the Feldenburg family lineage.

She's erected a solid wall of psychological and spiritual concrete between her Feldenburg heredity and her precious boys. Their identities are firmly entrenched in the world of the Rothsteins, with as little Feldenburg contamination as possible. In this one realm, she relents to the extra insurance of Rhodeslis folkloric rituals and spells.

"I thought you weren't superstitious." Stephen teased when she waved her fingers and mimed spit with a *pu pu mashallah* after their unremarkable pediatrician visits when they were little.

"You never know," she'd say, narrowing her eyes at him.

Leyla commits to doing everything within her power to

interrupt the conduit of epigenetic damage the curse has rendered upon generations of Feldenburgs. She wants no thread of connection from her children to the generational bankruptcies, failed marriages, lost fortunes, real-estate forfeitures, familial estrangements, digestive disorders, and rampant strabismus in the Feldenburg family tree.

So, tonight she lies still, overwhelmed by the devastation of finality. Though they had been estranged, so long as RHF was alive, there existed the remote possibility of his acceptance, approval, even affection. She didn't really believe that would ever happen, but if he was in the world, it was possible if not probable. Even more than that, with him gone her exquisite revenge fantasy of achieving total perfection, thereby surpassing his doubts in her talents and abilities, and then somehow making sure he knew it, drove Lyla's raison d'etre. That dream was dead now, impossible, completely, and forever. Her heart hammers as if she's swallowed a hand grenade.

There is only one person who will understand, though she understands little else. Her mother will grasp the complicated tangle of insecurity, anger, resentment, heartbreak, rejection, and loss that Leyla endured as the daughter of Robert Henry Feldenburg. No doubt Aurora will sum it up in one short, obtuse Ladino proverb.

Aurora, who exasperates her, drives her mad with daft idiosyncrasies and frustrating ineffectual habits, is tethered to her soul in what Leyla's therapist referred to as "chaos attachment." Leyla tips her head back and stares at the ceiling to wait out the torments of the remainder of the night. When the sun comes up, she will call her mother.

CHAPTER TWO

Ken perkura tiene ventura.
You keep trying you get lucky.

★ ★ ★

"H'lo," Aurora croaks into the phone. The feebleness of her early-morning greeting reveals the sixty-plus year, pack-a-day habit (now only one before bed) of her beloved More cigarettes. The fact that she has yet to put her teeth in also impacts her performance.

Her daughter, Leyla, set the volume on the phone to maximum because Aurora can only hear out of one ear. "What if there is an emergency?" Leyla had said when Aurora objected to the decibel level.

"*Ah Dio, mi alma*—Oh, God, my love—everything with you is an emergency."

The phone sits on the table at the right-hand side of the bed. Aurora is deaf in her left ear, so it does not need to be so loud. When it rings this morning, she expects to hear Leyla's brisk, authoritative voice with her endless to-do lists and scolding tone, inquiring why Aurora isn't up yet; she should go to bed earlier, she shouldn't sleep the day away, and maybe she should go for a walk, get some exercise; after all, the bike path is right down the hill; maybe expose herself to a little sunlight, eat some fruit, and address the critical issue of geriatric neuroplasticity, "And for god's sake, Mother, don't answer the phone without your teeth in."

Aurora is surprised. It isn't Leyla.

"Is this Aurora Hmans Feldenburg?" The mature female on the other end of the line butchers Aurora's name, as most people do, pronouncing it like "ham" and "mans" smashed together. When enunciated correctly, the H is practically silent, like exhaling with the mouth closed. Aurora's lifelong campaign for correct pronunciation has been focused on a name that isn't even her true family surname.

Hmans is an Ellis Island butchering of Hanan. Her father fled his home on the island of Rhodes in 1910 in search of a better life, landing at Ellis Island as Leon Bohar Hanan, fourteen years old and alone.

He spoke Ladino, a composite dialect of primarily Spanish, with a fusion of Hebrew/Greek/Turkish amalgamated over time, immigration, and persecution. The immigration officer did not understand him and did not ask twice. Leon Hanan became Leonard Hmans with a sloppy, wet, rubber stamp of U.S. immigration.

Aurora inhales deeply through her nose with her usual flourish, and with all the imperiousness she can rally at this hour, responds.

"Yesh, thish ish Rora Hmawns Felbmbrg," she responds, the H properly exhaled, and the A pronounced like a soft yawn. The absence of her front teeth compromises an exemplary execution of her name.

"Ms. Feldenburg, I am calling from Cedars-Sinai hospital in Los Angeles regarding Mrs. Esther Hmans."

"Sheeders, huh. Hoshpdal?" Aurora slurs with suspicion. "Eshdur?" she asks, revealing a hint of recognition.

"Ms. Feldenburg, I have some rather unfortunate news," the caller announces with equal parts gravitas and boredom.

Aurora knows who the woman is talking about. Esther was the grand finale in an extensive line of wives, legal and otherwise, of her long-deceased father, Leon.

"Wha happn da Eshdur?"

"I'm sorry, Mrs. Feldenburg. Mrs. Hmans passed last night. Am I correct in assuming that you are the next of kin?"

"She pasht?"

Aurora's interest is piqued. Still, she hesitates, unsure if accepting the next-of-kin designation is a good idea. Her deceased father's impressive, though clandestine, conjugal track record means she never knows how much "next of kin" is out there, and what they might owe or potentially be charged with.

At Aurora's last count, the tally of her father's wives hovered somewhere around eight. Some of his alleged wives resided out of the country and were therefore challenging to confirm. Some weren't legal marriages at all. Papa's history of matrimony was difficult to quantify and challenging to verify. Aurora is inclined to deny the next-of-kin status.

Her general policy when answering the phone is to hold back on committing to personal identification. Aurora has had more than her share of experiences with tricky bill collectors who call with all manner of ingenious schemes of verbal entrapment. One recent experience had a young man listen intently to the oral history of the Jews of Rhodes (Aurora's singular domain of expertise) before he sprang the issue of her six-month-overdue cable bill. The memory of that deceit still stings.

"Howd dju get my number?" Aurora asks.

"Mrs. Hmans's landlord was kind enough to enter her apartment after she was brought to the hospital. Apparently, your name was on a Post-it on the wall by the phone in the kitchen. Are you in fact directly related to Mrs. Hmans?"

"Yesh. She wsh married thu my father," Aurora concedes.

"Excellent, may I ask as to how you plan to handle the remains?"

"Hanel da remainsh? Da remainsh a what?"

"Ms. Feldenburg, I am referring to the remains of your beloved deceased." Aurora did not appreciate the change in the woman's tone.

"Eiff no idea. How should I hanel da remainsh?" Aurora's head begins to throb.

"Well, did she have a will, an advanced health care directive, a burial plan? Did she wish to be interred? Who will transport the deceased, to what funeral home or cremation services? Who will be financially responsible?" She rattles off an intimidating litany of considerations. Aurora is overwhelmed. This is just not her thing.

The administrative details of adult life are not an area where Aurora Hmans Feldenburg excels. She briefly considers referring this woman to Leyla. Leyla has the dominant gene of administrative efficiency, whereas Aurora's is distinctly recessive. She refrains. Leyla moves so fast, too fast for Aurora. Leyla is swift and brutally efficient.

Aurora has always been confounded by how bossy her daughter is. Leyla is infinitely capable in a way that Aurora has never been. Aurora considers Leyla to be insufferably competent. She was that way even as a little girl. Aurora thinks Leyla should be more grateful to her for that. If she had not sent Leyla half a mile down the hill to the grocery store on her own when she was five years old, or "permitted" her to do the family laundry when she was seven, Leyla would never have become so capable. Aurora maintains that she alone is responsible for Leyla's strengths and abilities.

"Fanshily rethponthble?" Those two words cue Aurora's exit from the conversation.

She wrangles a pen and paper from the bedside table. The note-taking is no small effort, allowing for Aurora's luxuriant manicure. The strenuous contortions she employs to grasp things, curving her fingertips, using her knuckles like tongs, is cumbersome. Leyla refers to them disapprovingly as "ghetto nails." Aurora has worn them this way since high school. They grow relentlessly, almost unnaturally, and rarely break, split, or chip. They are a point of pride.

"They're so déclassé," is Leyla's appraisal whenever Aurora reveals a vibrant new shade.

Aurora's long, curling nails are a "bit of pizzaz" that she says give her "a certain *je ne sais quoi.*"

"You don't even know what that means, Mother."

Aurora asks the woman for her number and says she will get back to her once she has "sorted things out."

Aurora regrets answering the phone this morning, but the ringing was so loud she had no choice. Leyla told Aurora to just throw the old phone away and get a new one if she hates the bell so much, but Aurora treasures her banana phone. It's a cherished relic of the house she lost in her divorce. The only real house she ever lived in.

It isn't even a bedside phone. It was the wall phone from the old kitchen. Mustard-yellow, the receiver is a plastic banana with a long, curly cord that's twisted and knotted into a tangled clump. She's been meaning to unravel it for a long time. It's on her to-do list. Aurora is tickled by her banana phone. She loves to pick up when it rings, preferably not so early in the morning, and say, "I'm sorry. I can't hear you. I've got a banana in my ear," in anticipation of laughter.

Leyla is never amused by the banana phone. Whenever she calls, Aurora can feel Leyla's eyes roll right through the phone.

"Let me guess, Mom," Leyla always preempts Aurora's

punchline. "You can't hear me because you've got a banana in your ear."

"What do you know? It's an old Marx Brothers' skit!"

"It wasn't funny when they did it, either." Leyla responds.

"Fetz off. Back in my day—"

"Please don't start with the 'back in my day' spiel, Mother."

Once Aurora wraps up with the nurse, she places the banana back on the receiver, puts the pen down, rolls over, and returns to her preferred state of slumber.

Most people are energized by the adrenaline released when shocked. Aurora's response is the opposite, a kind of reverse drain. Her habitual bedtime nightcap, a full pot of Madaglio d'Oro espresso, has zero impact on her ability to sleep.

"Mother," Leyla says in judgment of Aurora's lifelong coffee and a "cig" before bed, "You are recklessly risking overactive wake-signaling and a reverse adrenal drain!"

"*Ah dio, ija*—Oh god, sweet daughter. That's a bunch of *bavajathas*—nonsense."

"No, it's not nonsense, Mother!"

Aurora wakes up a short while later, inserts her front teeth, and puts a pot of water on the stove to boil. She begins each day with the same routine. A pot of Medaglia d'Oro, two eggs scrambled, one toasted Thomas' English Muffin slathered with margarine, and the *San Francisco Chronicle*. Margarine is getting increasingly challenging to obtain in the wealthy, health-obsessed, liberal enclave of Tiburon where she lives. She's noticed people now refer to her town as an "enclave."

She knows that practically no one gets the newspaper delivered anymore. Leyla has not neglected to inform her that it is "environmentally irresponsible." Aurora loves her morning *Chronicle*. Not so much for the headlines—she gets all the important stuff she needs on TV, all day, every day, from Fox news, which she likes to keep on in the background. Reading the paper is a ritual. It makes her feel smart and well-read. She loves the burnt smell of the English muffin in her old GE toaster oven. The crumb buildup, from decades of neglected maintenance, intensifies the charred smell and smoke each morning. The sequence is complete with the metallic fizz of a saccharin tab (also not easy to find anymore) plopped into her coffee.

Leyla tells her to just read the news online. But Aurora takes comfort in the feel of the dry, chalky paper in her hands and her special way of folding and refolding it each time she moves to a new section with a performative arm's-length snap, and the Costco readers that she rests on the tip of her nose. Anyway, Aurora doesn't know how to do a damn thing on the computer.

Branan gave her the computer as a gift. Branan, who is keeping the peace or spreading democracy in some far-flung, water-poor, oil-rich developing nation half a world away. Aurora is uncertain of the specific geography of her son's tour of duty at any given moment. He is a United States Marine and, at forty-seven, the oldest Staff Sergeant in the history of the Marine Corps. She isn't clear whether his rank is a good thing when she mentions it to people. It's difficult to gauge from their surprised facial expressions.

Branan told her, more than once, that revealing his location is a "national security issue." He gave her the computer so they can exchange emails, which he sends infrequently—mostly on her birthday, Chanukah, and sometimes Mother's Day.

With the help of a patient librarian down at the Tiburon Public Library, Aurora figured out how to open emails, compose, and send them. A helpful neighbor set her up with solitaire on the desktop. Other than that, the computer remains a mystery. She asked Leyla to teach her, they made a few cursory attempts but, as expected, they quickly devolved into frustrating episodes. Leyla accused Aurora of not retaining a "god damn thing." Aurora responded that she learned best by repetition and pressed her daughter to perhaps write out some cue cards for her. Leyla flew off the handle.

"It doesn't work like that, Mom! You have to learn by doing."

Aurora inquired if perhaps one of the boys, Leyla's young sons Josh and Simon, could come over and sit with her and teach her how. They were both a "wiz at all that techie stuff." She rarely saw them without some form of electronic doohicky in their hands.

"Mother, Simon has soccer on Monday, piano on Tuesday, Mandarin on Wednesday, Sensory Motor Workshop on Thursday, on Friday he has social etiquette with his friends at the club, and on the weekends, he has snowboard team. You know this. Furthermore, Josh has Bar Mitzvah blessings class on Monday, theater arts on Tuesday, debate club on—"

"*Ay, pasensya en este mundo*—Oy, patience in this world. Thanks for nothing." Aurora had interrupted. Why can't that girl relax? Aurora wonders. "I never ran you around all over town, and look how you turned out," Aurora said.

"God knows how I turned out the way I turned out. I can't even imagine allowing my children to walk home from school."

"What's wrong with walking home from school?"

"Nothing, I guess, if it's in your own neighborhood. But I was five years old, Aurora, and home was across the highway."

"Oh, pshaw. Things were different then," Aurora replies with a dismissive wave of five long sparkly fingernails.

"No, Mother. Things were not different then."

"Ach, I'm damned if I'm do and damned if I'm don't."

"Damned if *I* do mother"

"You too?"

"*Ah Dio*, Aurora. It was extremely dangerous for a five-year-old to cross the highway then, and it still is now." Aurora senses a heightening of tension when Leyla calls her by her name instead of Mom.

"Don't give me *keshas mi alma*—sticking in the knife and turning it."

"I'm not giving you *keshas*. It's a fact."

"Fine, I'm a terrible person." Aurora's typical response.

Reading the full paper means reading the obituaries as well. Aurora reads them every single morning. Perversely, it is a good day when she sees an old friend's face staring back from the page in some black-and-white glam shot from high school or military service for the men. She hates to miss the memorial of an old friend or acquaintance. Aurora loves a good funeral. There's always a good spread of food and drink and pleasant walks down memory lane with folks who "knew her when." They're the highlight of her social world.

This morning's review of the obits reminds her of the early-morning phone call. She revisits what the nurse said, assuming it *was* a nurse—she isn't entirely sure. The next-of-kin possibility the woman mentioned seems like it might have some potential for profit. Aurora recalls the mention of a will. Then again, it also seems like all this might have some potential for responsibility. As a matter of policy, Aurora avoids responsibility.

These issues are the most memorable amongst the swirl of information and unfamiliar terminology that was dumped upon her this morning. Her instincts tell her that she should keep this to herself, and she decides not to share it with anyone. The woman inquired about a will. Aurora concludes she needs to find out about that.

Could Papa have left a will? She never considered it before. Aurora has no will. Her long- dead mother, Floru, and sister, Reigna, had no wills. There was never anything left to leave anyone. Aurora has no doubt that Leyla and Stephen have a will, with all that Rothstein family wealth. Aurora guesses that her two young grandsons, independently, are already wealthier than she can even imagine.

Aurora has always been in close personal proximity to wealth. Most of her Los Angeles cousins are fabulously wealthy. Branan married a successful woman, and Aurora's friends in Tiburon are all affluent. Robert H. Feldenburg, Aurora's first husband (he was her only husband, but she refers to him as her first), was from a family that was very "well to do."

Unfortunately, during their marriage Robert Henry Feldenburg ran his father's successful business into the ground. Ezra Feldenburg Furs became "and Sons" after R.H.F. returned from Korea and flunked out on a college degree. E.F.F. and Sons swiftly went bankrupt when the young R.H.F. decided he knew better than his father about how to "run things," shipping inventory on credit and handshakes all over the country. His new accounts failed to pay, and Feldenburg Furs owed more than they had in the bank.

The long-enduring, profitable enterprise went "kaput," as Aurora tells it. Aurora and Robert were broke with two young children to raise, and (unbeknownst to Aurora at the time), R.H.'s girlfriend to support. The bankruptcy also rendered her in-laws, Ezra and Fanny Doll Feldenburg, destitute.

Aurora had never unlocked the mystery of how to gain entry to the circle of solvency, no matter how close the connection.

Now she muses about the possibility of a will. That woman on the phone said she was the "next of kin," and Aurora takes it as an official designation. This new classification implies that she is the "sole heir," a title she has longed to embody in her life. Aurora concludes that if the woman said it, it must be the case.

She finishes her second mug of Medaglia d'Oro, calls the hospital phone number, and gets a voicemail. She leaves a message thanking them for "reaching out," saying they needn't look any further, they indeed reached Aurora Hmans Feldenburg this morning, Esther Hmans's stepdaughter (enunciating now with maximum articulation and full dental support), and she will get back to them shortly with the necessary information regarding the "remains."

Aurora begins to hatch a plan to get herself down to Los Angeles and find that will if it exists. She knows Leyla will disapprove of her driving her twenty-year-old Saturn, with 237,000 miles and ten years of deferred maintenance on it, all the way to Los Angeles. Aurora's derelict Saturn, one blind eye, one deaf ear, and advanced age make Leyla appropriately suspect of her mother's fitness for retaining a driver's license.

Little did Leyla know that Aurora has not had a legal license for years. She failed the vision test on her last renewal attempt. Apparently, it's now a "big thing" to have perfect vision for driving.

After her local Department of Motor Vehicles failed her, Aurora tried to pass at the DMV in both neighboring towns of Novato and Petaluma. In the old days, it was easy to do an end-run at another office if the first one was fussy about compliance, but she failed all three tries.

The optometrist who used to write her exclusion letters had retired a long time ago. He was the husband of an old friend from her beloved tennis club.

Aurora had held on to the club membership for as long as possible after R.H. left, but two years in arrears was apparently too many. She was informed by letter that she needed to surrender her tennis-court key. She never played tennis anyway, but all the other divorcees belonged. They negotiated club dues in their divorce settlements. She added it to the long list of ways that R.H.F. had humiliated her.

Anyway, Aurora knows that she can see "just fine." She doesn't understand why they can't just take her word for it.

She decides to call Leyla once she arrives in Los Angeles, and to weather the Leyla storm when it comes. Aurora endures Leyla's disapprovals on a daily basis. It's nothing new.

"Oh well, *un buen plete, trae una buena paz*—A good argument clears the air."

CHAPTER THREE

Kayo el martiyiko y mato al bohoriko.
Catastrophe comes without warning.

★ ★ ★

Leyla stops in the bathroom and does a quick mirror-check before walking into the party. She did one at home on her way out the door and another in the car when she arrived. She is wearing her trusted day-to-night uniform of black mock turtleneck, distressed boyfriend jeans, and Nike Air Max sneakers (selected strategically, as they provide a furtive vertical boost with their thick soles). Wearing heels would look like she was trying too hard, a no-no at Marin parent gatherings.

Emerging from the restroom, she pauses to check texts, then drops her phone back into her bag. At the buffet table, she serves herself some crudité on a small plate. Leyla hates attending these things without Stephen, who possesses the social skills and confidence she lacks, but tonight he's at a "work thing," so she's on her own with her social anxiety. After polishing off the seven raw veggies, it's on to the six-to-eight ounces of Sauvignon Blanc (she accounted for the four extra carbs during lunch) allowed on her diet—liquid courage for the dreaded cocktail-party conversations. Just enough to quell the nerves but avoid inebriation.

Standing in front of the garbage canisters, Leyla agonizes over the array of choices for the disposal of her plate and wineglass. Always a stressful moment and one reason finger food is preferable; dealing with the additional disposal decision that utensils require would put her over the edge.

The plate is paper, so that's recycling—easy. The wine glass is tougher. It's biodegradable, so it's not recycling, but is it compost or landfill? What's the difference? If she gets it wrong and someone sees, she'll be mortified. The waste bins seem to multiply at every school event: garbage, recycling (plastic vs. metal vs. paper), compost, landfill, green trimmings. There are seven bins tonight. The only reason she goes to the buffet table at all is to avoid talking to people. The waste-can dilemma cancels out the benefit of having her mouth full.

Still seeking an excuse to avoid socializing, she pulls out her phone again. No new texts. Moving on to her calendar app, she peruses her schedule for the coming week. Monday: Benny's Bootcamp, microdermabrasion, chiropractor, soccer carpool; Tuesday: Yoga, Botox, bikini laser, lunchroom duty; Wednesday: Pilates, B12 shot, lash tint, Halloween carnival roundtable; Thursday: Piloxing, cryotherapy, fifth-grade snack of the week, Friday: zoom therapy, Bar Mitzvah planner consult.

Every day rolls out to the same rhythm, frontloaded with exhausting, expensive "self-care" and backloaded with daily responsibilities of her quest for supermom status. Leyla crams her life with thousands of dollars' worth of "treatments" in her pursuit of perfection—as many as can be squeezed in before carpool.

The momentum of her commitment to self-improvement has taken on a life of its own. Her mother calls her a "perfectaholic."

The more money Stephen makes, the more she spends on cutting-edge beauty, health, and "wellness" advantages.

She doesn't do it for Stephen—or at least she doesn't think it's for Stephen. The man has never uttered a critical word to her since the day they met. Though he is an affectionate and supportive partner, Leyla has never relaxed into the ease of acceptance and trust that's supposed to come with marriage to one's true love. According to her therapist, Leyla had an under-developed trust-muscle, a scar formed from childhood trauma. Painful memories remain fresh; wounds feel open and raw. It was as if it were yesterday when she was awake in her room the night her dad walked out and overheard Aurora begging R.H.F. to stay.

"Please Robert, you are the only man I have ever loved. Please don't go," Aurora tearfully pleaded.

No response. The front door opened and closed quietly. She never forgot the sound. He didn't slam it or stomp down the steps. He simply left, no hurry, no anger, no goodbye, just walked out. There was nothing worth fighting over. The end of Leyla's life as a child, her security, her daddy being under the same roof, the death of her family as an entity, came quietly.

Sitting up in bed that sad night, Leyla swore she would never love a man more than he loved her. With the way her mother had tipped her hand that night when she'd begged, and what had happened to her life when he'd walked out that door, Leyla had concluded that it was unsafe to want someone more than they want you in return.

Love is power over another's life; the one who withholds love becomes the one with sovereignty. Love can ruin your life if someone takes it away with them, the way her father did. It must be guarded, maintained, controlled.

She stayed committed throughout her life to that original vow of withholding in her romantic relationships. With each new boyfriend, no matter the intensity or authenticity of affection, Leyla withheld just a bit.

When her high-school boyfriend said the first "I love you," Leyla responded with "Thanks." In her early twenties, her long-term paramour professed the same.

Leyla responded with, "I am super fond of you, too."

Stephen is the love of her life—handsome, charming, sweet-natured. They were engaged six months after they met at a Jewish singles meetup. Leyla's best friend dragged her, wanting to meet Jewish men. Leyla had waited at the bar next door, too cool to be caught dead at such an event. Stephen did the same. He found her there, while waiting for his buddy, who was hunting for hotties at the Jewish Community Federation YAD event (Young Adults Division aka Young and Desperate).

They locked eyes and fell happily into love, rushing to the altar full of blissful, youthful certainty. Even so, she remained steadfast to her childhood commitment to hold back. The retention of affection was crucial, always just enough to sustain that essential razor's edge of control. She never felt totally at ease, never trusted without reservation. Over-preparation is another form of perfectionism, and Leyla is prepared, for surviving—or preventing—the potential loss of everything. Love is grand, but also a clear and present threat to safety and stability.

The persistent underlying hum of risk and dread in her life are fodder for her insatiable drive for perfection. Her father's inexorable criticisms of her and her mother imprinted this formula deeply into her consciousness, implying if only you were taller, thinner, blonder, quieter, sweeter . . . I would love you, and I would stay. Therefore, it was her fault that he did not. Her mission became clear. Be flawless, and you won't be left. Anything less is unacceptable and not worthy of love. If you're impeccable, your husband won't leave you for someone else. Leyla operates on the premise that perfection is not only possible, but within reach—with enough research, money, and determination.

She doesn't have a clear picture of what perfection looks like—as if it were a destination on a map, and it would be obvious when she arrived—but her ambition to achieve it is unrelenting. In Leyla's worldview, the graph of life should be an uninterrupted progression toward ultimate impeccability. It's just a matter of working at it, and Leyla loved working.

When Leyla met Stephen, she was a gallerist for a blue-chip art dealer in San Francisco. The esoteric material she spent her days immersed in divorced her from the Feldenburg identity she sought to erase, Aurora and her gift shop aspirations and RHF's shmaltzy, unethical, failed career as a furrier. Neither one had finished college. Leyla was resolute that she would not end up like her mother. She wanted to be educated, refined, self-sufficient.

She loved her job and was ambivalent about having children. Her experience with family rendered her gun-shy, to say the least. She was so happy with Stephen, she just kept saying two more years. Five years into their marriage with the constant drumbeat of Stephen's "Aw, c'mon," she gave in.

Once she got pregnant it became crystal clear that her mission in life to be the opposite of Aurora meant being a good mother, the best mother. For Leyla, that meant being a stay-at-home mom, taking full responsibility. She could not outsource the sacred work to nannies, sitters, and daycare. Leyla fully committed herself to the work of excellent mothering, determined that her children would have everything she never had—opportunity, security, nutrition, working appliances, and a mother with excellent hygiene.

It meant letting go of the artsy, intellectual identity she had carefully crafted for herself as an intellectual gallerist, her days filled with artspeak, but there was no choice. Sacrificing for her children is what a good mother does, something Aurora never did.

Leyla quit her job and redirected her work ethic to mothering. She missed her former identity. She was so proud when she got her first business cards, but her singular goal was now distilled. She had to do a better job than Aurora. That meant turning her attention to mothering and "wifeing." Be perfect. Don't get left.

A manic researcher, devouring information on the latest advances in aesthetic procedures, beauty products, supplements, and superfoods, she approaches her parenting and position in the community in the same manner, scouring the bestseller list for positive parenting philosophies, strategies, and theories for raising well-adjusted, high-achieving children. She serves on any and every board and committee, takes a table at every charity gala and auction.

Her current therapist, Tiffany (Tiffany followed Brittany, on the heels of Lindsey, who supplanted Keely), recently suggested that perhaps Leyla's "issues" with perfectionism should be addressed. Her rolling slate of therapists were all perky, long-haired, middle-parted, white-teethed, thirty-somethings with cheery names ending in chipper *E* sounds. They all held adequate degrees in MFC counseling from well-regarded state schools.

She pursues therapy as part of her health-and-wellness road map to perfection, knowing one should address the interior as well as the exterior. Part of being perfect means being a good patient, "putting in the work," as *E* refers to it. Leyla has the best intentions as she embarks with each new *E*.

She ghosts them all in the end once the work goes a little too deep and a smidge too raw. When the surface of Leyla's soul is scratched, she's done—quits—no note, no thank you, no goodbye. After opening herself to exploring intimate truths, she just stops going. The vulnerability required for true growth and meaningful healing is more than she can or will endure. It demands the surrender of her closely guarded persona of flawlessness, necessitates trust and a relaxation of control. She cannot abide that.

When the depression, anxiety, and insomnia get too much, she finds a new *E* to talk to. The recap is brutal, but less so than staying in the truth with the previous *E* when they/them get too close to the soft chewy center.

Therapy has done little to extinguish Leyla's insatiable desire to fix herself, to fix everything. As a child she could fix her bike, fix her breakfast, and fix the leaky kitchen faucet by the time she was ten years old. No doubt because her mother never fixed anything.

Leyla's childhood home was filled with broken lamps, broken locks, broken blenders, and broken hearts. They changed the channel on the TV with pliers because the knob was broken. Aurora never threw anything away, but she never fixed anything, either. If it broke, it stayed right where it was, like Aurora herself.

It's impossible for Leyla to enter a room without mentally repairing and renovating it, making over people in her mind when she sees them, like a filter, giving them different haircuts, more sensible shoes, less makeup, a few pounds slimmer, maybe a few highlights just around the face, some fringe bangs. It is an affliction.

She never understood why Aurora never repaired anything. It looked so simple in her child's mind. Just fix things; fix your hair; fix the vacuum; fix your face; fix your body; fix dinner. If your husband doesn't want you, fix yourself. If your daddy doesn't want you, find out why and fix it. If she could fix everything, her daddy would come home at night.

After the stressful garbage-bin deliberation, Leyla intends to duck out under the pretense of making a call, another tool in her bag of social-aversion tactics. She mimes the act of answering, holding the phone up to her ear and talking.

"Oh hey, let me just duck into a quiet spot so I can hear you better," she says into her phone. Her commitment to the performance is stellar.

As an introvert, or social isolator, as *E* labeled her, parent socials are excruciating. Her usual strategy is to slink outside, hide until enough time elapses, then leave. She's able to say she attended and doesn't have to lie. As a committed perfectionist, Leyla does not lie.

She prepares for her furtive exit, looking around the room for an opening to slip out.

Shit

Jocylin Mintz—aka poor Jocylin—is on direct approach.

She cannot be seen talking to poor Jocylin, who's walking straight toward her.

Jocylin sees Leyla as an ally. They'd been lumped together to serve as the Chanukah co-captains for this year's winter fair. The annual inclusive holiday event mounted by the parent body—moms—to make the non-Christmasers feel not quite so non-Christmasy.

"Your holidays are so neat," the winter-fair chair proclaimed to Leyla when she bestowed the Chanukah co-captain title upon her and handed over the (very large) holiday fair acceptable food and language binder.

Jocylin now saw Leyla as a friend. Being seen as a friend to Jocylin Mintz is social suicide, putting both Leyla and her kids at risk.

It is a legendary story of AFDS lore. A cautionary tale of a catastrophic social blunder.

Jocylin's son Emile was in the fifth grade, that critical developmental juncture just on the cusp of upper school and its impending arrival of puberty, when emotions run high. Emile was enduring vicious bullying by the notorious LAX thug Spotswood Boffet Jr. (Spotty) who was teasing Emile relentlessly for his lack of athletic prowess. Emile had missed an important goal during the championship game with AFDS rivals AcademyPrep.

Emile had planned a Mario Kart themed birthday sleepover. Wanting to respect her son's emotional safe space, Jocylin left Spotty off the guest list. Kikki Bimington Boffet, his mother, caught wind of the exclusion when Spotty cried about being left out. All the boys had brought their birthday party swag to school the following Monday to show off. It was the Mario Pez that did Jocylin in.

Kikki went into full-court press, wielding her social superpowers to enact revenge. Kikki and her husband, Spotswood Sr., own La Fratello, the hottest restaurant in Marin. It's impossible to get a resy, if you are on Kikki's bad side. They are also a legacy family. Spotswood Sr. was AFDS class of '78

What followed was a legendary circling of the social wagons. Jocyln, Emile, and family were shunned effective immediately, never to be returned to the fold. Left out of every extracurricular social event in perpetuity. It was an irreversible misstep, once made impossible to rescind. Legend had it that Jocylin called the Boffet home relentlessly. She wrote notes, sent gifts, begged for absolution, but it was an unforgivable offense. The Mintzs never ate at La Fratello again.

Damn it, here she comes. With direct eye contact, a hopeful wave, and pleading smile, Jocelyn heads straight for Leyla.

Leyla takes her shot. Phone pressed to her ear, she dashes for the exit and slips out of the performing arts "barn" as the Head of School takes the microphone for the requisite sycophantic oration. The self-congratulatory speech begins, about what they have achieved as a community, all for the children, of course, in pursuit of excellence for their darling future leaders and world changers.

None of it has anything to do with money or status. Yeah, right. They claw and scratch over each other, pull every string, juice any connection to get their little world-changers into All Friends Day School.

Six years of being an All Friends Day School parent is long enough to know the talking points by heart. She won't be missed. The parents who still have toddlers they need to "get in" will stand there rapt and listen to the spiel with Zelle and Venmo at the ready when the "ask" comes. With both of her kids "in," she no longer needs to worry about all that. Those were anxious years.

She creeps away, sneaking into the brand new, forty-million-dollar LEED-certified (Leadership in Energy and Environmental Design) kindergarten "environment." She was co-chair of the capital campaign, putting her hat into the ring for the job back when she needed one last push to get Simon in. Tonight is the patrons' preview of the newly completed early-childhood learning space. She ducks under the large satin bow that will be cut for photo ops later tonight.

Finding a spot in the dark, tranquil space, she curls up in one of the sensory integrative reading pods. There are thirty-six custom molded pods (in plant-based plastic, of course) purchased for four thousand dollars apiece. As campaign chair, she presided over fabric selection and color choice on the design committee trip to Copenhagen the previous spring. The pods were in thirty-six subtly different shades of blue. Leyla delivered the PowerPoint presentation of research data to the board demonstrating how blue promotes memory and enhances creativity. At five-foot-one and 109 pounds, she fits comfortably inside the little husk.

She sits back and begins to relax, only feeling completely

safe when alone. Exhaling to release the social stress and those triggering waste bins, she hears voices.

Damn it, Leyla thinks.

The door to the focus space in the adjacent room opens. She tucks deeper into herself. Leyla's superpower is invisibility. She can will herself unrecognizable, even by people who know her well. Feeling unseen as a child leads to excelling in the ability as an adult.

Leyla loathes running into people, especially her Marin stay-at-home-mom cohort, who engage in the practice of toxic positivity at an unparalleled level. She detests their blood-curdling greetings: "Hieeee, how ARE you!" It's unavoidable when shopping for dinner at Evergreen Market. She reluctantly participates in the ritual, as required by her position in the community and her kids' coveted spot in an elite K-8 private school. She would never do anything to reflect poorly on them or create backlash for their social calendars. If sighted, one must stop and report how very fine one is, initiating the well-honed skill of the humble brag. She's built up her greeting performance muscles and can feign friendliness with the best of them.

One is invariably "great," albeit a bit jet-lagged because one dragged one's family through Italy on the break, and it is exhausting work to "close down" one's summer home on Nantucket for the season. This all must be wrapped up neatly with an even more casually impressive sign-off: "Loved seeing you, got to run. I'm making the charcuterie for a closing party for Stephen's deal team, let's make a date soon." After checking all the boxes—busy, wealthy, family, travel, success, achievement—one may advance to actual grocery shopping.

Endeavoring to evade the ritualized protocol with whomever is approaching, here in the architectural developmental utopia created for kindergarteners, Leyla disappears in place. The acoustics, as expected, are excellent. She recognizes one of the voices.

Hallie Monrowe made the news recently from the sale of her company, HappyDoggyDent. A trailblazer in the cannabis sphere with her breakout product, THC toothpaste for dogs. She cooked it up in her garage and YouTube/TikTok/Instagrammed the results of her recipe tests with videos of herself brushing the teeth of her adorable basset hound, Happy. Her YouTube channel views during shelter-in-place numbered close behind sourdough baking and *Tiger King*.

The Cannabis-infused toothpaste relaxes your dog just enough to allow their teeth to be brushed. It sold off the rails. She just closed the sale to Proctor and Gamble for three hundred and fifty million dollars. Stephen's firm was an early investor.

Hallie and Leyla have not met directly. Hallie's daughter is two years younger than Leyla's younger son, Simon—a generation, developmentally, in grade-school years. Hallie is a single mom. She adopted a little girl from China she named Kallie. She sits on the All Friends Day School finance committee with Stephen.

At the sound of Hallie's shrill, cheerful uptalk, Leyla makes herself smaller.

"I know he's married. But I feel something."

A second voice laughs. Leyla can't identify it. "Here we go again. No good ever comes of this, Hallie. We've been down this road before." It is a female voice.

She smells pot. It sickens her. They snuck into her beautiful new kindergarten building to get high.

Hallie went on to tell her friend about the ski trip, and how she bumped into "him" in Aspen.

Stephen skies in Aspen. His cousin has a place there. Leyla doesn't ski anymore, and she believes it exhibits emotional self-sufficiency to let her husband go have "his own thing" without complaint.

"We had a good time together. He's a good skier, he's handsome, and he's been married for a long time if you know what I mean. I felt a connection. I'm sure of it. It was just a few runs. Next time we'll ski more. Have you met his wife?" Hallie asked.

"Mmm hmm, I'm on the Positive Playground Committee with her."

They were both buzzed now and talking in that slow, throaty way that stoners do. Cannabis repulsed Leyla.

"And?" Hallie asked.

"Let's just say she's intense." Leyla is on the Positive Playground Committee.

It's a very large committee. She hears the unmistakable sucking sound of a toke.

Leaning forward out of her pod ever so slightly to get a look at the second voice, she catches a glimpse of a Black Lives Matter hoodie, a few long strands of beachy-blonde waves, and a blue- and-yellow silicone *Slava Ukraine* bracelet peeking out from the sleeve. Current AFDS parent fashion aesthetic and de rigueur Marin liberal elite virtue-signaling. Could be anyone.

"It doesn't matter what she's like. Hallie, he's married. He has two kids." Leyla hears a long exhale and spastic cough.

"And I have one kid. He gave me his number. We're texting," Hallie says.

"He was being affable. Everyone texts. He has to be nice. His firm invested in your company." Toke, hold, cough.

Leyla sat up. *Affable?*

"Affable?" Hallie responded. "We're meeting for coffee next week at CannaBizCon. I gave him some samples of the new CBN laser whitening gel that we're market testing."

"Laser tooth whitening for dogs? Jesus." her friend responds in a voice strained by the withholding of a toke.

Leyla's heart starts to pound. There are gobs of that stuff in their garage. She's noticed Stephen emptying the trunk of his car with boxes of it. As a senior partner in a private equity firm, people sent tons of samples to Stephen to take home and demo, so it wasn't alarming at the time. But we don't even have a dog.

"Hallie, the last time you gambled on a married man, I could barely get your dumped ass off the floor. I've said it before; I'll say it again. Don't chase married men." Toke, hold, cough.

She finally places the second voice. It's Sherie Price. Sherie is chair of the LGBTQIA+/BPOC parent inclusion and social interaction initiative. In classic AFDS irony, Sherie is a cis-gendered, heterosexual, blonde, blue-eyed, dead ringer for Kellyanne Conway. The *Save Ukraine* sticker that every AFDS community member pastes on their laptop was designed on Canva by Sherie's third grader, Brooklyn. It was one of this year's lower-school student body "funraiser" items, along with hand-painted safety pins, *Trans Rights are Human Rights* t-shirts, and signed first edition copies of *White Fragility*. Sherie is a poster child for uber-wealthy "performative slack-tivism." She's neither friend nor foe, which can be said of almost everyone Leyla knows.

"What else have I got? At my age? In my world? All the decent ones are married," Hallie answers in a long, drawn-out sucking sound.

CannaBizCon, Positive Playground Committee, Aspen, HappyDoggyDent samples, married, WTF? The map of clues seems to lead to her own husband. Leyla stifles herself, but inside she is channeling Grandmother Floru and her flair for wildly combining adjectives.

"Toothpaste brewing, stoner, *shiksa*, slut-skank." Leyla mutters inaudibly.

The last thing I need is some desperately single, mayonnaise-and-cream-cheese-on white-bread-with-chardonnay Stanford grad chasing my husband. Leyla's inner voice now sounds more and more like Floru. God damn son of a bitching bastard. She feels like spitting on the floor right there, but that would alert them to her presence and foul the immaculate new space.

She did not see this coming. Stephen is her Prince Charming, unfailingly dedicated to her through all her anxieties, depressions, mood swings, and fad diets. One of his most endearing qualities is that he never seemed to care about the underwhelming social standing of her nuclear family.

Maybe she *did* see this coming. They had been bogged down lately with raising kids, and the demands of the Rothstein family social calendar tended to get in the way of date night. Stephen is an only child, and the pressure on Leyla from his parents is crushing. She thought their marriage was doing okay. But if she had to be truthful, they'd been on autopilot as of late, and her nightly sleep-hygiene protocol is admittedly unsexy.

But how does one achieve perfection without putting in the work?

Hallie Monrowe is the opposite of Leyla in every way—tall, blond, flat chested, Protestant. Stephen told her that he skied with his cousin on that last trip to Aspen, just the two of them, a guy's trip. Now it would seem there was someone else on the mountain with him, at least for a few runs. Am I being paranoid? She considers, but the details that Hallie is recounting line up a little too well with Stephen's life calendar.

"Hay can go to hall." Her grandmother's heavy accent and ludicrous phraseology come to mind. She twists the evil eye she wears around her neck between her fingers. Stephen commissioned it for her fortieth birthday.

Leyla wants to *etchar ayin ara*—cast an evil eye—but she can never remember exactly how it works. Does it help to keep the evil eye away from your own life, or to send it to others? No matter, she doesn't believe in it anyway. But she does like the jewelry. Leyla's evil-eye pendant is diamond-encrusted with a sapphire forming the iris.

She looks down at her phone and sees Stephen's text from earlier in the evening.

FYI: I'll be in LA next Thurs/Fri for CannaBizCon— heading down solo for quick turnaround Ok by U?

Stephen's firm was investing more in the "green rush" of the legalized Cannabis industry, so the trip makes sense. That Leyla would say yes is presumed. She always says, "Okay, no prob" and means it.

Leyla loves it when he travels, can't get enough of it. She never does anything special, maybe a more aggressive laser session. She can risk looking more inflamed if he's away, and she has an extra few days for the facial bruising to fade.

She likes the treatments and peels, but really, Leyla revels in the alone time. She puts the kids to bed and reads. Social isolation is a self-soothing strategy learned in childhood. When children are forced to solve their own problems, they learn to feel safer when alone.

Leyla is now forced to confront the possibility that Stephen is being pursued by Hallie Monrowe, and perhaps at risk of welcoming that pursuit. It was hard to believe. He is such a devoted father, but she's been blindsided before. Finding out your father's girlfriend has lived down the street for half your life will leave residual trust issues.

Sadly, she learned very young to believe the unbelievable. She rubs her evil eye and wishes her Grandmother Floru were still around to teach her a spell to cast. Leyla may be stunned, but she isn't stupid. She knows thousands of dollars a week in beauty appointments, grueling workouts, and a consistent calorie deficit are no match for Hallie's recent three-hundred-and fifty-million-dollar payday. She makes a mental note to Zillow Hallie when she gets home.

Buck tooth, bony ass, dried up, shit for tits. Leyla decides that she needs to go to LA and see what transpires at this conference.

She responds to Stephen's text, *Of course, no prob,* and opens her TODO list app. She needs to cancel some appointments, a few classes, some committee meetings, and figure out what to do with Josh and Simon. They've never had a nannie or spent one single day in aftercare. She hates to be away from her kids.

The one time she agreed to leave the kids with Stephen's parents for a weekend anniversary trip to New York, she suffered the first full-blown panic attack of her life when the airplane door closed. The resulting gastrointestinal distress from the ongoing separation angst spoiled all the Michelin-starred restaurant reservations Stephen had booked.

True to form, he was understanding, and she never left the kids overnight again. Maybe now that they were older, Bob and Bunny's plentiful staff can keep a watchful eye on them while she goes down to LA to see for herself what's going on between her husband and that cannabitch. Between the Rothstein's chef, driver, maid, and gardener, the kids will be well tended to.

Bob and Bunny are adoring grandparents, dote on Josh and Simon, and treat them like princes. It's one thing Leyla and her in-laws completely agree upon.

She calls Aurora, knowing she will not—cannot—answer. There is zero doubt that right now, Aurora is smacking at the phone in a race to answer before the eighth ring, her nails preventing her fingertips from making contact with the touchscreen. As expected, it goes to voicemail.

CHAPTER FOUR

La ventura es paraken la perkura.
Fortune comes to those who seek it.

★ ★ ★

"I knew it was you. I knew it. I'm a witch!" Aurora exclaims each time she answers the phone and hears Leyla's voice.

"It's always me. You're not a witch."

Aurora invariably retorts with, "*Ija, los korazons avlan*—Hearts speak," said when someone shows up that you were just thinking about.

Aurora insists that she descends from a long line of witches. In fact, her grandmother was the village sorceress in the Juderia neighborhood on the island of Rhodes and was called upon to make *precantatio*—magic—whenever a child was ill, a mother sad, or a father broke. Aurora's own powers of sorcery are mainly utilized to guess who is calling when the phone rings.

For today, Aurora is focused on summoning her magical powers to manifest profitability from her new status as next of kin for her dead stepmother. She is wasting no time executing her action plan to get herself down to Los Angeles. Her witch's intuition tells her she needs to make haste. She wrangles Esther's landlord's phone number from the administrator at Cedars Sinai

Hospital with a teary performance and significant violation of HIPAA laws, then calls the number and leaves a message identifying herself as Esther Hmans's next of kin. Her voice message states that she will arrive "forthcoming to handle all the details," liberally throwing around the officious lingo used by the hospital administrator in that overwhelming early-morning call. When she hangs up, she feels pleased with herself and continues her trip planning.

Aurora rarely leaves her apartment. The price of gas makes car trips precious expenditures, and the treacherously steep incline of the Tiburon hillside, coupled with her eighty-three-year-old equilibrium and ungainly girth, make neighborhood walks perilous.

A recent attempt at a stroll to the store resulted in a black eye and contused rump. She didn't tell Leyla, who would have lectured her for the umpteenth time about not wearing her sparkly mules for walks down the hill. Aurora hates to be seen without sparkle.

She's determined to get to Los Angeles and intends to do so regardless of Leyla's disapproval or judgement, which are a certainty. Leyla never approves of anything.

After the call to the landlord, she phones her cousin Eliezer, who lives in Los Angeles with his mother, Aurora's beloved Auntie Estrella. Most of her Rhodeslis relatives live together with extended family. It is the Rhodeslis way. Aurora has loads of cousins in Los Angeles—most of them wealthy, glamorous, and social. She used to visit them more frequently in her younger days. The modicum of self-awareness she still possesses allows her to comprehend that she doesn't fit in with them anymore.

The last visit to her cousin Fortuna's house in Beverly Hills did not end well. Fortuna was not happy with the oil stains left by the Saturn, and there is still the lingering issue of her visits to

Beverly Hills Nail and Spa, signed to Fortuna's account. It is on Aurora's "to-do list" to pay her back.

She targets Estrella and Eliezer for this spur-of-the-moment trip. Estrella was the wife of a first cousin of the husband of Aurora's father's sister, Rica. In Rhodeslis culture, this meant Rica and Estrella were basically sisters. The value placed on family makes even the most distant relation precious and intimate.

Worldwide, Rhodeslis are always searching for each other. After the deportation from Rhodes to Auschwitz, the subsequent postwar refugee system for survivors and forced immigration based on available visas and family members who left before the war meant that the small, loving, tight-knit world of the Jews of Rhodes scattered across the globe. They still look for one another in an unending state of void. When a community is annihilated, loss and emptiness remain as if one is searching for a missing limb. Rhodes is a small island, and the pre-war Jewish community was a small minority of the population. There are a mere handful of family names all related in one way or another by blood or by marriage. When they accidentally encounter each other, the recognition is instantaneous. They play Rhodeslis Jewish geography.

It always begins with *"Ija de ken sos tu?*—Whose child are you?"

They will ask, dig, pry, and fervidly interrogate each other, spending however long it takes to go through whose aunt's neighbor's daughter's best friend married your uncle's partner's sister's cousin. They don't really know what to do when they find their long-lost *primos* other than hug and cry. Still, they eternally seek the emotional reunions.

It is the curse of the survivors of an entire society destroyed by the Nazis. They didn't just lose family members and loved ones individually; they lost their world. The generational trauma they share is a mystical, meaningful bond.

Rica and Estrella were inseparable when Rica was still alive. Estrella has known Aurora since she was a little girl, spending hours together in Rica's kitchen where the women passed their days cooking, baking, and gossiping. Estrella enthusiastically welcomes any visit from a direct relation of Rica's.

Aurora calls under the guise of informing them that Esther died, and to let them know she is coming to LA to handle the arrangements. She knows full well they will insist she stay with them.

"*Ah dio,*" Aurora cries into the phone to Eliezer. "Esther is dead."

"*Qualu es?*—Who is it?" Aurora can hear Estrella ask in the background. She is certain that Estrella is impatiently pinching Eliezer's bicep for details of who is calling.

"*Este Allegra, ija de Leon, mama*—It's Allegra, Leon's daughter." Eliezer responds to his mother.

Allegra is Aurora's given name, the one her Rhodeslis family still call her by. Allegra Arroyo Hmans is the name on her birth certificate, but she ended up with "Aurora" because of a San Francisco public-school hatchet-job done on her first day of kindergarten. The headmistress in charge of registration at Horace Mann elementary determined Aurora to be a more suitable American name.

"*Qualu dishu?*—What is she saying?" Estrella asks, pinching him again.

"*Leon's sposa sta muerta,*" Eliezer whispers to his mother with an emotional tremble in his voice. Estrella begins to wail.

"*A dio, Allegra, ija de mis prima*—Oh god, Allegra, daughter of my cousin." Estrella shrieks. Sephardic aunties (a term of endearment given to cousins as well as true aunties) possess a remarkable aptitude for excitability. Aurora knows that Estrella is right now pulling an apron over her *fustanika*—her house dress—and reaching through her tears for the flour sack to begin her baking. Her mouth waters as she recalls her auntie's fresh, homemade *borekas*, it had been such a long time. Some people emotionally eat; Sephardic aunties emotionally bake.

Aurora may have gotten the recessive gene for overall productivity, but her ability to get others to do things for her is a lifelong gift of wizardry—a true superpower that grows in strength with age. Leyla is always frustrated by her mother's uncanny knack for enlisting the assistance of others.

There wasn't a boyfriend of Leyla's since junior high who hadn't changed an air filter, swung by the store "on his way over," or cleaned out a gutter or two under the influence of Aurora's charms. Aurora would pick up the phone and intercept their calls before handing it over to Leyla. It drove Leyla wild with irritation and embarrassment in front of her numerous boyfriends.

"Mom!" Leyla would scream and slam her bedroom door with each outrageous request during her teenage years.

"Fine, I'm a terrible person." Aurora invariably declared.

Aurora used to ask Leyla's boyfriends to pick up horrifyingly personal items—Leggs pantyhose at 7-Eleven (control top XL), Psssst! dry shampoo, Vicks VapoRub, More cigarettes by the carton (yes, Aurora asked minors to buy her cigarettes). The boyfriends never seemed to mind.

Aurora and Leyla's suitor of the moment would sit in the kitchen and chat over coffee and a "cig" upon returning from whatever errand he'd completed, while Leyla stomped off to her room, cringing in shame.

Aurora's current spell results in Eliezer not only demanding that she stay with them, but also that he help her clean out Esther's apartment, adamant that she cannot do it alone.

"No *sta shekiandu*—Don't mess around. You might get hurt." Eliezer said.

Aurora acquiesces after just the right amount of polite resistance. Once she hangs up with Eliezer and the hysterical pastry chef Estrella, all that remains is to pack up the car and drive.

She selects three of her least threadbare (they tend to wear poorly in the inner thigh) velour sweatsuits—two rhinestone-trimmed ones she saves for special occasions, and one she considers more sedate (in bright fuchsia) for everyday use—and throws them in her suitcase.

Filling her green hardside cosmetic case takes no time at all. She bought it for her honeymoon in 1958. It still has the "PSA gives you a lift" tag on it. There is only room for essentials. She packs her Costco family-size tub of Ponds cold cream (as it serves triple-duty as facial cleanser, moisturizer, and cuticle cream), her hot rollers, and some Vicks VapoRub.

Grabbing her purse and the keys to the Saturn, she makes her way down the stairs to the carport. Arriving at the bottom of the first flight, remembering her coat, she heads back up the steps and retrieves it.

The only thing that remains of Ezra Feldenburg and Sons Furriers is Aurora's full-length tourmaline mink coat with shawl collar. R.H.F. never "allowed" her to wear fur during their marriage. He always said, "Women who wear furs look like prostitutes," an interesting point of view for a furrier. Aurora lost the house in the divorce and got no alimony, but the judge ordered R.H.F. to split any remaining property from Ezra Feldenburg and Sons, as that was considered a marital asset. They did not finalize the divorce until a full decade after he left because Aurora refused to sign the papers.

R.H.F. married the much younger Vicki without first legalizing his divorce from Aurora. He referred to it as bifurcation;

Aurora referred to it as bigamy. All that was left from the inventory of the bankrupt enterprise was one full-length mink coat and one sable stole. The garments had been in cold storage for over a decade. Aurora selected the mink coat as her half of the community property and still wore it most every day. She thinks it makes a good impression, and the silverish sheen of the tourmaline goes well with the velour of her sweat suits.

On the long drive to Los Angeles, she ruminates on Esther and Papa's finances. She vaguely recalls that Esther worked as a nurse's assistant at one point. Had Esther gotten Social Security or a pension of some kind? Is Aurora entitled to it as next of kin?

Aurora just barely gets by on her Social Security and monthly assistance in the form of checks from Leyla and Branan, receiving nothing but the mink coat and R.H.F.'s cherished collection of swizzle sticks in their divorce. He dumped her in 1976, during the era of community property in California when wives and mothers were generously favored in court. All her divorced friends had been awarded alimony for life. Aurora ended up with nothing, maintaining her perfect record of missing the boat.

Robert H. Feldenburg was a prime example for dispelling the myth that Jews are good with money. The only time he ever demonstrated financial savviness was when he cleaned out their joint bank account and forged Aurora's name for a home-equity loan before splitting for good with Vicki, whom he hid in an apartment up the hill from their home. He pleaded poverty to the judge in divorce court and was freed from the shackles of marriage, alimony, and child support in perpetuity.

"*Hijo sin padre*, hay can go to hall—Bastard, he can go to hell," Floru declared when Aurora had cried and told her mother what the shmuck did. Floru reminded her daughter that she'd warned her about marrying a *Shumechu*—a Jewish person of Ashkenazi descent—and lugubriously spit on the floor whenever Robert H. Feldenburg's name was mentioned. In the Rhodeslis culture a Sephardic/Ashkenazi marriage was considered intermarriage and frowned upon.

"I toll you to fuckus on Rhodeslis!" Floru scolded.

"The word is focus, and please stop spitting on the floor," Leyla had pleaded with her grandmother when she'd overheard Floru lecturing on Aurora's divorce. "Mother, please tell her to stop spitting on the floor," Leyla begged with each expectoration.

After R.H.F. left, Leyla and Aurora procured their groceries at the Rexall Drugstore down the hill, where they had a house charge account. They dined on pharmacy snack food—canned soup, chips, crackers, and-space food sticks—for as long as Abe the pharmacist would float them.

Robert took Branan with him when he left. His son was the only thing that came out of his marriage to Aurora that he'd ever really wanted. When they left, Leyla and Aurora were broke, and the family was divided permanently. Aurora and Leyla sold off items from the house at the weekend flea market in Marin City to get back on their feet.

Now, Aurora's Social Security check is eleven hundred dollars a month. Her rent is fifteen hundred. She depends on Branan and Leyla for the difference, and then some. They each dutifully send their mother a check each month. Neither one of them knows that the other contributes, and both resent their sibling for leaving the other one "holding the bag."

Aurora recognized early on the benefits of having children who were estranged from each other. She does not encourage, nor welcome, the enmity between her two children but doesn't shy away from harvesting the ways it benefits her. With neither of them knowing if, or what, the other is giving each month, she's bound to get more.

While Aurora drives, she fantasizes about Esther having a will and imagines what she will do with her newfound wealth. She fancies herself paying her debts and having no more bi-monthly collection calls from those persistent folks at Comcast. She envisions moving to a new, larger apartment with a real view.

Though she is practically destitute, Aurora lives in Tiburon in Marin County. She is able to live in the affluent town because after her divorce, a friend knew a friend of a friend of the building owner. She scored a rent-controlled apartment at the top of Lyford Drive with its multimillion-dollar vistas. Her unit is on the back side of the building, on the bottom floor, with a view of the carport.

The apartment hasn't been renovated since she moved in forty years ago. It has threadbare brown shag carpeting and peeling wood paneling. There is a smoky back-draft fireplace, which she can't use because the single-pane aluminum sliding glass doors that lead to the small deck no longer open. She used to burn a Duraflame log in the fireplace every so often, but it invariably set off the smoke detectors, and she can't ventilate the apartment because of the stuck sliders. Her lustrous fingernails impact her ability to turn off the smoke alarms, and they are on the ceiling and difficult to reach, anyway.

She promised Leyla and the Tiburon fire department (after the last smoky episode involving a wobbly ladder and a large hammer) that she would not use the fireplace again. The concrete steps that lead to her front door have no handrails or exterior lights. Her bedroom closet leaks when it rains. The tennis court built in the 1970s, so popular in the swinging singles divorcee apartment scene at the time, is now used for overflow parking.

With the windfall she is dreaming of, she can maybe buy a new Saturn, get a maid, and lunch on the deck at Sam's Anchor

Café with its majestic view of Alcatraz Island and the San Francisco skyline. She never gets to eat at Sam's unless it's a special occasion and Leyla springs for it. Maybe she'll buy a whole new wardrobe of her favorite sequined velour sweatsuits from Macy's. Maybe she'll finally be able to return to Fortuna's good graces and repay those mani-pedi charges.

She continues to allow her mind to wander on the long drive, imagining the myriad of luxuries she will be able to afford if she finds even a fraction of what she hopes for. Aurora has made this drive many times over the years, ever since she was a young girl and Papa would come and take her down south to visit his family.

Aurora's papa came and went unpredictably throughout her childhood and teenage years. He'd show up out of the blue in San Francisco where he'd abandoned Aurora, her sister Reigna, and their mother Floru. Papa would simply take Aurora, bringing her down to Los Angeles, where he might or might not have been living, for the summer. He loved to show off his exceptionally beautiful daughter to his many siblings and cousins, taking great pride in her poreless dark skin, cartoonishly deep dimples, and olive-green eyes.

Leonard Hmans married, remarried, emigrated, and immigrated more times throughout Aurora's life than she could bother to keep track of. Her father's unaccountable wanderings did not bother her. She never felt angry or resentful. Aurora did not have an angry bone in her body (a skeleton chock-full of manipulative and stubborn bones, but no angry ones).

"Papa was a rogue," Aurora responded whenever people asked about him. She'd state it matter-of-factly, with the charming lilt her voice used to have (before all the More cigarettes), followed by a shoulder shrug and a pleasant sigh of affectionate resignation. She'd bat her eyes and smile with her signature deep dimples that were at one time quite alluring (before decades of nightly martinis and a lack of interest in, and funds for, dentistry reduced them to harsh hollows).

Papa regularly took Aurora without notice and deposited her just as unannounced at his sister Rica's home with her well-loved children. Auntie Rica lovingly absorbed Aurora into her own brood. Aurora lived with them for the summers. Those experiences were a memorable bounty of sunshiny recollections from a gilded time in Los Angeles. She spent beachy days in Santa Monica and ran after the ice-cream trucks tinkling their tunes down Wilshire Blvd.

When Papa died, Aurora went down to Los Angeles for his funeral. Mama and Reggie were long dead by then, and she was the only one left. Aurora referred to herself as "the only one left."

"How can you be the only one left when you have two children and four grandchildren?" Leyla inquired.

But Aurora likes the way it sounds. She didn't lift a finger for funeral arrangements for Papa. There's that issue of the absent administrative gene, and there was also Esther. Esther was five years younger than Aurora but, as Papa's wife, she took care of the details. Aurora attended the funeral and burial at the cemetery with Papa's extended family members. The Rhodeslis in Los Angeles were quite a crowd in those days—all emigrated from the small island in the Dodecanese, every one of them related in one way or another. It was a fun weekend. She saw lots of friends and relatives. The atmosphere was festive, and there was free, plentiful, delicious Sephardic food and drink.

Rhodeslis women form an efficient, skilled army of cooks and bakers that rally for any occasion. Within hours of a death, birth, or surprise visit from a fourth cousin three times removed, there will appear an astonishing spread of delicacies—warm garlicky spinach *boyus*, flaky potato *borekas*, savory meat-and-cheese-filled *pastilicos*, mountains of crispy, braided *biscocho* cookies, pyramids of aromatic *huevos hamenadas* boiled in onion skins and coffee grounds, countless trays of *bimuelos* dripping with rosewater and honey, and bowls of sweet *sutlach* sprinkled with cinnamon—all whipped up in massive quantities, at light speed, within a magical minute of any momentous or mundane occasion.

At Papa's funeral weekend, Aurora participated enthusiastically in the social whirl of the large family death commemoration. She told stories of old times and shared memories with her beloved *primas*, aunties, and uncles. She cried, shrieked, and hugged everyone repetitively, gorged herself on her aunties' repast, and went home empty-handed.

Aurora is always empty-handed, living her life within striking distance of affluence, but never quite making it because of some catastrophic strikeout or narrow near-miss.

She was never given any reason to expect anything in the way of financial benefit from her father. Esther was the "closer" in Leonard Hmans's long line of wives. She outlived them all, and legally everything Leonard left behind was hers. Aurora assumed "everything" meant a closet full of Papa's high-waisted, pleated wool pants, rayon bowling shirts, his eyeglasses, and some army medals.

Papa obtained U.S. citizenship serving in World War I in the United States Cavalry, stationed on Angel Island in the San Francisco Bay (or not, because every word out of Papa's mouth was possibly a total fabrication). If true, she wouldn't mind getting her hands on those medals. They're probably worth something. A friend down at the flea market at Marin Civic Center sold old military regalia. He would know if they were worth anything if she ever found them.

Papa and Esther lived in the Spanish-speaking neighborhood of Gardena. He never owned a home. Then again, with his secret ways, it was possible he might have a stash somewhere.

It would be just like Papa to have something squirreled away in his mattress, a secret bank account somewhere, or an old safe below the floorboards.

Aurora's imaginings go astray. She visualizes finding a bounty, imagining the will as a scroll, like a pirate's treasure map. She could use a little treasure in her life, a little X marks the spot. She imagines jewels from the old country, a fruit farm in Mexico, some cash in an old shoebox.

At the very least, it would be nice not to see those nasty little "eviction imminent" Post-its plastered all over her door on the twenty-ninth of every month. They leave unsightly little snail trail marks all over the front door and are hard for her to reach to pull down. She knows the landlord puts them up so high on purpose. He knows damn well he'll get the rent eventually, but each month he slaps those snarky little "prepare to vacate" or "potential termination of tenancy" notes. Every month he seems to find a new way to say it with the fancy language and the messy glue on the door.

She has approximately seventy-nine dollars left over each month after rent, the PG&E bill, buying groceries, getting her nails done, and occasionally paying her Comcast bill. She only pays that one when it's absolutely necessary.

Her account balance at present is nowhere near enough to cover the gas to get her down to LA. But Aurora doesn't worry about gas money. She has an old trick for that.

She simply drives until she runs out, and then she calls AAA. They come with emergency gas. Problem solved. Leyla pays the annual fee so her mother will have roadside assistance in case of emergency. The "plus level" membership Aurora requested for "extra safety" allows for a few more gallons at no cost. Her system worked until the AAA Roadside Assistance in Tiburon caught on to her scheme.

She keeps this strategy in her back pocket for rare trips out of town like this one. She never waits until she runs completely dry, but rather makes the call when the "just about empty" light goes on. The AAA drivers don't check the tank.

She only stops for gas once on the way down this time. She saw a Baskin Robbins from the highway at the exit in Tulare about three hours out of LA. The Jamoca Almond Fudge Mud Pie is her favorite. They closed all the Baskin Robbins locations in snobby Marin, so this is a real treat.

She enjoys two slices of mud pie for lunch while waiting for AAA, gets her tank filled, and is back on the road without any trouble.

CHAPTER FIVE

Para nada, un kaldo de avas.
Anything is better than nothing.

★ ★ ★

It's close to seven p.m. when Aurora arrives in Gardena at Papa and Esther's apartment building. She locates the label, *SUPER*, on what appears to be either the building's intercom or door-buzzer system, near the mailboxes under a stairwell at the end of the parking lot. She presses the button beside it, leans in, and puts her mouth close to the speaker.

"Hellooooo . . . this is Aurora! Aurora Hmans Feldenburg," she bellows, using her full name. "I am Esther Hmans's next of kin." she sing-yells into the small, rusted brass speaker while continuing to press the button as it buzzes loudly. Aurora persists, repeating her ring-scream barrage without waiting to hear whether anyone responds or acknowledges her on the other end.

A door slams above. She looks up and sees a short, round, bald man with a dark, black, bushy mustache appear at the top of the first flight of stairs to her right. He waves a stubby, fat hand at her. She waves back, taking this as an invitation to ascend.

Aurora likes for others to see her manicure as a way of

introducing herself and establishing her stature. She uses her most regal wave for him now, a back-handed rotating turn of the hand with motion only from the wrist. Aurora is an avid royal watcher who studied her People magazines closely to perfect her own version of the royal wave.

Aurora begins the climb. The mustached man leads the way. He does not speak to her. She assumes it's the man she spoke to when she called, but it occurs to her that he neither confirmed nor denied this title, and she did not ask him before following him now.

"May I ask your name?" He does not answer. She looks him over, considers the neighborhood, the darkness of his mustache (Gardena is a predominantly Mexican immigrant neighborhood), and asks again in Spanish.

Well, not really Spanish, Aurora's Spanish is Ladino, or Judeo-Spanish. She considers herself to be fluent in both, transitioning from English to Ladino when encountering Spanish-speaking individuals.

Ladino can sound a lot like Spanish, and some words are the same, but pronunciations are different. For example:, *Donde esta* in Spanish is *Ande sta* in Ladino. Spanish O's become Ladino A's. Consonants are missing. *J* sounds like *J* instead of *H*, and *D* is pronounced with a *TH* sound: *Nada* is *natha*. Some words sound the same but have entirely different meanings.

Ladino, aka Judismo, is the language spoken by descendants of Jews exiled from Spain in the 1400s, during the Inquisition. What began as Spanish some six hundred years ago has dramatically altered over generations. Ladino has evolved into a potpourri of Castilian Spanish, Hebrew, Arabic, Greek, Turkish, and French. The balance varies depending upon where the refugee Jews settled after being cast out. In Greece, Ladino is more Greek and Turkish, and in Morocco, more Arabic. Yiddish is the language of Ashkenazi Jews. Ladino is the language of Sephardic Jews.

Ladino is Aurora's first language. When Leyla started school as a little girl, she thought what she spoke to her mother, aunt, and grandmother at home was Spanish. She sauntered in to her first day of Spanish class, in middle school, ready to impress her friends. She proudly greeted her Spanish teacher with, *"Buen dia kuchada." Kuchada* means "lady" in Ladino but sounds like "spoon" in Spanish. Leyla was chastened by the teacher for being disrespectful and embarrassed in front of the class. She stopped speaking Ladino outside of her home permanently.

It took Aurora a generous twenty minutes to ascend to the top of the double flights and arrive at the sixth floor of the building, her full-length mink coat hot, heavy, and scraping on the concrete with each difficult step. She wouldn't dare leave it behind in the car.

The landlord remains unresponsive. He is agile for a man greater in width than height, ascending the flights at a breezy clip without signs of exertion. Aurora's heart rate has not been this elevated in a long time. She is perspiring through the velour of her sweatsuit. Miffed, since she'd told Leyla more than once when they shopped for sweats that she wanted a breathable fabric. She appreciated Leyla underwriting her wardrobe, but in the future, she wants to take more of a lead on the selection. The inner thighs of her pants audibly chafe with each step.

The man pulls a key on a large metal ring from a red leather cross-body bag slung across his torso. The bag is incongruously dressy compared to the rest of his ensemble of white t-shirt and dark indigo Levi's. He unlocks the door. Aurora reaches and snatches the key from his hand as he turns around. She thanks him (*gracias* works in both languages) and brushes past him.

He peers, leans, and tiptoes to see inside, clearly anticipating an invitation to enter. She slams the door in his face. Through the slammed door, he reminds her, in perfect English, that she needs to "clear it out" by the first of the month. Today is the twenty-fourth.

Aurora is unprepared for what she sees once her eyes adjust to the dark entryway. The visual transition from exterior sunlight to interior darkness takes more than a minute due to her one working eye. She also needs some time for her heart rate to return to normal from the exertion of the climb. Once her vision focuses to the low ceiling and dim lighting, she is able to see that her "beloved" deceased stepmother Esther was a bit of a hoarder and apparently a shopaholic.

The small two-bedroom apartment on the top floor of the post-war stucco building is packed to the rafters with full shopping bags. The items they contain have price tags attached. The landlord must have seen it all too, since he'd originally entered the apartment and found the Post-it with Aurora's name.

She wonders what prompted him to enter Esther's apartment. How did he know Esther died? Were they friends? Maybe he knew that she was ill and taken to the hospital. No doubt he called and checked on her and was told she died. Is that when he entered the apartment and found the Post-it? Did he already know about this stockpile and Esther's living conditions? Did he help himself to a few items before Aurora's arrival?

Now that she sees the state of the apartment, she thinks it might explain his lack of conversation with her and his behavior at the top of the stairs. Maybe Mexicans are just unfriendly, she thinks. Leyla's housekeeper, Carmen, never responds either when Aurora speaks Ladino to her. She thinks Carmen is rude and disrespectful. Aurora complains to Leyla about her often.

"She does not acknowledge me and my status as your mother. I don't know why you stand for it."

"Did you ever think she doesn't answer you because you aren't speaking Spanish?" is Leyla's response, which Aurora considers to be ridiculous. Of course, what she is speaking is Spanish.

Aurora takes off her coat and hangs it on the doorknob inside the front door. There is no room anywhere else. She attempts to maneuver through the narrow path of space available between the tall towers of items. It's a challenge.

She was always very, as she describes it, "limber," but she admits that the smidge of added weight she's gained recently makes moving around more of an effort.

Leyla insinuated as much the last time they shopped for sweatsuits at Macy's. She brought a selection back to the dressing room for Aurora to try on. Aurora took out her rhinestone readers to check the tags.

"*Ija*, this is an XXL. I have always been a size four petite off the rack."

"No, Mother, you have never been a size four petite 'off the rack' in my lifetime."

"Well, they just don't cut patterns like they used to," Aurora insisted.

Aurora sees that the short archway bordering the entry is a threshold into a small living room. The state of the apartment does not change as she squeezes herself through the slender trail between the walls of shopping bags.

Inside the bags are more bags. From what she can see, they are women's purses of varying styles, sizes, and materials: shoulder bags, handbags, pocketbooks, clutches, crossbodies. Could this be the reason for the incongruously flamboyant red leather cross-body the landlord was showcasing as he climbed the stairs?

The purses were all inside shopping bags, all with price tags attached. They did not appear to be expensive or fashionable, like the designer handbags her stylish daughter owns.

Aurora could pay her rent for a year with the price of just

one of the "IT" bags Leyla carries. Esther's bags are more of the "pleather" variety. She sees branded shopping bags from Target, Walmart, TJ Maxx. Price tags are visible: $19.99, $18.50, $24.50, $17.95. There is nothing over $30.00.

She intuitively begins a reach-shift-step pattern that enables her to move across the overcrowded space. The motion begins with one foot placed sideways. Then, she stretches her arm out as far as she can reach, leans sideways, and brings her other foot along to join the rest of her body. There is a moment in the process when she is suspended in air. It's a kind of slow-motion sideways leap. Her "healthy" weight provides the necessary gravity to prevent her from getting stuck in the towers of bags.

Employing this geriatric gymnastic strategy, she travels to the opposite side of the room where she encounters another arch that leads to the kitchen. In the throes of a deep side-lean, Aurora glimpses a small white refrigerator. She writhes, squirms, and side-leaps her way into the space. There is a table in the middle of the small, packed room, with one green vinyl place-mat on it. The rest of the tabletop is occupied with more soaring piles of bags full of bags.

The table is an old, square, glossy white laminate with a wrapped metal edge. There is just enough space for one person to sit with a small plate of food or maybe some coffee or tea. Four red vinyl chairs sit around the table, three with bags piled on them. On the wall next to the refrigerator is an old green rotary phone with a number typed on a piece of paper inserted in the center of the dial—Papa's phone number. Beside the phone on the wall is the yellow Post-it with her name written in pencil: Aurora Hmans Feldenburg, 415-555-5555.

Peering through the spires of bags into the two bedrooms that adjoin the living room, she sees more of the same—bags inside bags, stacked, jammed, and crammed on top of every available surface reaching to the ceiling, blocking the lights and windows. The room on the left has a narrow passage that leads to a bed. One side of the queen-size bed remains free of bags. No doubt this is where Esther slept.

It strikes her that the apartment is not dirty as one would expect of a hoarder's house. Aurora is a devoted fan of the cable reality show, *Hoarders*. Some of the episodes show living conditions with shocking levels of filth. Esther's apartment is not like that; it's clean and otherwise tidy. The bag towers, though excessive in quantity, are stacked with evident care. There is no foul smell and very little dust. The kitchen sink is empty and shines. The place is just jam-packed with bags full of bags.

Aurora last visited the apartment many years ago, long before Papa had died. It was clean and modest. During the visit, Esther made *café con leche*, and Aurora walked with Papa to the park. Papa liked to *kaminanda y havlanda*—to walk and talk. He met friends daily at the park to play cards (ironically, they played Gardena in Gardena). This hoard must have accumulated after Papa died.

On the drive down from Marin today, Aurora imagined easily locating a desk or some drawers to rummage through that would contain bank paperwork or a will, but it is difficult to distinguish, never mind access, any furniture other than the refrigerator, kitchen table, and bed. She doesn't see a desk or bureau with drawers. That doesn't mean they aren't here.

She's certain they are obscured by the massive quantity of baggage filling the space. What she can see are price tags. Though the amounts are not individually high, when multiplied by the sheer number, it's clear there is a lot of value here. She feels a spark of hope.

Aurora has worked the once-a-month weekend flea market at the Marin Civic Center for years. She makes crafts and offers them for sale at a small folding table that fits into the trunk of her Saturn. She never really sells much. Her crafts tend toward the sloppy side. She glues glitter and plastic gemstones onto whatever she can get her hands on to "glitz 'em up" and try to sell them.

Her efforts result in a gloppy, gluey mess that she attempts to conceal with more shimmer and sparkle. Her chosen mediums are cheap wallets and reader glasses she buys in bulk at Craig's Discount Warehouse in San Rafael. In the past, she's tried t-shirts (too expensive), belts, and headbands. She knows this activity embarrasses her daughter, but unless Leyla and that stingy Prince Charming she's married to want to pony up more generously, she's going to keep glitzing up bits and bobs to sell at the flea market.

This newfound crop of Esther's bags, all new, with price tags attached, would really level up her table. She might not even need to do any further glitzing of this inventory, though it is her signature style.

She squeezes her way back to the kitchen, takes a seat on the one available red vinyl chair, and pulls out her cell phone. She sees a cascade of bright illuminated boxes on the screen, indicating many missed calls, most from the same number. It is the hospital administrator. She thought she heard it ring while she was driving, but it was just too much trouble to answer it in time. A few of the calls are from Leyla. Aurora hopelessly failed the hands-free phone lesson from Leyla. She didn't even try to understand that one. How on earth can a person talk on the phone without their hands?

Aurora reaches into her purse and retrieves the telephone number for Cedars-Sinai. No matter how many tutorials Leyla has given her on the use of the phone, Aurora retains only the most rudimentary knowledge of its features. She takes out the piece of paper, goes to the wall phone, and dials the hospital number. She pushes the thick, long nail of her index finger into a circular hole, turns the plastic circle of numbers, releases it, and lets it rotate back to its original position.

She loves the way the dialing feels on her nails. She relishes the nostalgia of how her lavish, elegant, pincers were once useful tools rather than hindrances to the current technology she loathes.

The only problem is the darn prompts. Making calls from a rotary phone is challenging when it's time to press options. Press option one for radiology; press option two for the ER, etc.

"*Ay, pasensya*—Oy patience." Aurora is stumped. She hangs up and calls Leyla.

"*Mi alma, Leyluchi*—My sweetheart, little Leyla. Can you do me a favor?"

"Oh god, here we go," Leyla sighs.

"I'll make a call. Can you press the number buttons for me on your phone when I make the call?"

"Huh? What are you talking about? I don't understand. Why can't you do it?"

"I can't. I'm calling from Esther's phone, and it is a dial phone."

"Right, and?" Leyla continues.

"So, I can't press the numbers to get the options to get through the phone system where I am calling."

"So, call from your cell phone," Leyla responds.

"No, this is better."

"Mother, pick up your cell phone and press the numbers."

"It's too much," Aurora said.

"*Ah dio*, Aurora."

Leyla takes her through the steps for the millionth time.

"*Ija, mi korazon*—Darling daughter, my sweetheart. Why can't you do this for me?" Aurora asks.

"Because it's ridiculous, Mom."

"No, it's easy. I'll call on my phone, and you hold your phone to the receiver, you press the buttons from your phone, and I'll hold my phone up so they can hear the tones, and I can get through the prompts."

"No Mother, it's absurd. Use your cell phone."

"*Ijika, mi alma.* This phone is better."

"God damn it, I swear, Aurora, the last time we went through this, I spent three hours on how to use the cell phone. Why do you waste my time when I—"

"*Ija, antes de avlar, pensa lo ke dizes*—Before you speak, think about what you are about to say."

"Why must you always speak to me in proverbs?" Leyla yells.

"Lailiku! *Padre i madre es una vez*—You only get one mother and father," Aurora scolds. The line goes dead. Aurora places the receiver back on the wall. "Why is that girl so angry all the time?" Aurora asks aloud.

She decides the hospital can wait a little longer to hear from her. She will ask Eliezer for help with the phone later. She gets up from the kitchen chair and begins her squish, jam, sideways, slow-motion, leap ballet, back to the front door. She puts her mink coat on and checks to make sure she has the key ring. She opens the front door and peeks around to see if the landlord is nearby. She can't recall exactly which door he came out of when she arrived. She closes the door behind her, walks down the stairs, and gets in her car to head over to Estrella and Eliezer's. They are expecting her, and she is very hungry.

CHAPTER SIX

Boca dulce abre puertas de hiero.
A sweet mouth opens iron doors.

★ ★ ★

Aurora has no trouble remembering the way to Eliezer and Estrella's. As a child, Aurora shuttled back and forth between Esther's house and Auntie Rica's house during the summers when Papa dropped her in Los Angeles. She can't remember where she leaves her reading glasses twelve times a day, but has no problem finding her way around LA.

When she arrives, they're standing in the doorway wearing ardent expressions of adoration and anticipation. Eliezer towers beside his pint-sized mother. Estrella is on the verge of tears. They both lovingly beam at Aurora as she navigates the Saturn to the curb. It takes a twenty-two-point maneuver for her to finesse the car within striking distance of the sidewalk. Aurora knows better than to pull into the driveway. The oil stains her Saturn deposits tend to stress relationships.

Their home in Los Feliz is a small Spanish-style bungalow with bright white stucco and a red tile roof, meticulously manicured with a freshly mowed, spongy, overwatered lawn and close-clipped hedge beneath the front parlor windows. A red concrete path leads to a low, arched, front door.

Estrella howls with joy as Aurora finally emerges from the car. She is immediately hit with the pungent aroma of fresh baked something involving garlic, onions, and cheese.

"Allegra, *allegria*—joyous one." Estrella bawls as she reaches upward for a hug.

The size differential between Estrella and her colossal six-foot-seven-inch son is a curiosity. How that man directly descended from that tiny woman baffles and provokes stares.

Estrella's apron extends down to her ankles. No doubt it is intended to be midlength, but on her diminutive frame it scrapes the ground. It's covered in a bold pattern of large red roses with green foliage background. The ruffled straps climb up over her shoulders, around across the back, then tied at her waist and fashioned into a large bow. The spaces between the buttons on her housedress beneath the apron are closed with large safety pins, something Aurora's mother Floru did to her dresses as well, "to keep out the draft *ija*".

Eliezer is wearing a dark blue suit with a white button-down shirt and narrow, blue silk tie. The effect is dashing but dated. He has a full head of wavy brown hair, long enough that it curls at the ends. He looks like a hip horn player of a retro band, or an oversized, blue-eyed Hank Azaria. It might be intentional hipster chic, or just an old suit.

Eliezer reaches down and hugs Aurora, lifting her off the ground. He smells like he just poured a full bottle of cologne over his head.

"Allegra, *kerida, prima*—darling cousin."

He swings her around and places her down inside the house. Then Estrella and Eliezer both tearfully hug-shove Aurora down the hall into the kitchen where, as expected, she finds a mouth-watering display of Estrella's fresh out of the oven *borekas*, three versions: cheese, potato, and spinach. The small aromatic parcels of hand-stuffed dough are beautifully arranged in a fantastical quantity on large decorative platters.

"*Kome, es bueno. Borekas para todos*—Eat, it's good. Borekas for everyone," Eliezer proclaims.

Aurora places her hand on her heart and breathes in deeply. "Oh auntie, *muy sabrosa*—so delicious."

Estrella baked for her niece, the way Rhodeslis women do for family, no matter the occasion or relation. Aurora's eyes well with tears, partially from joy, but also from the garlic and onions.

Aurora adores the food of her heritage. At every opportunity, she boasts of the super-human cooking skills of the women from the Island of Rhodes, all fabulously talented and tireless cooks and bakers (except for Aurora, who never got around to learning how to make any of the delicious and distinctive dishes). She never even learned her way around a kitchen. Leyla has asked Aurora many times over the years why she doesn't bake like all the other women of her family if she loves it so much. Aurora never really had an answer. It just wasn't in Aurora's nature to try to do something she can get others to do for her.

Eliezer and Estrella continue to embrace Aurora and navigate her to a seat at the table.

"*Ke rico prima*—How swanky cousin!" Eliezer comments as he takes her mink coat and hangs it in the hall closet.

Estrella pours her a scalding cup of sweet *café con leche*, and Aurora begins to ravenously, if immodestly, devour the warm doughy delights. Estrella sits across from her, rests her face on her small clean jeweled hands, and stares at her lovingly.

"*Mashallah, mi alma. Ke haber? Echar Lashon*—What's going on? Let's talk."

"Where do I even begin?" Her mouth full, spittle bits of

boreka fly across the table as Aurora speaks. "It all began with an alarming phone call that came at a ghastly hour. It was such a shock."

"*Mi alma*, your poor heart, to learn of your dear stepmother's passing," Estrella comforts her.

"Well, that, too, but I mean—who phones people at that hour?" Aurora continues. "Anyway, I packed my car and drove straight away to Gardena, and what a state that apartment is in. It will be a lot of work to organize and clean. She had a very large collection of purses."

Aurora noted a small blue truck in the driveway when she arrived and had zero doubt that Eliezer would avail himself to help her in collecting Esther's purse inventory. As if right on cue, Eliezer insists he be allowed to help.

"We can go right now," he says, and slams his enormous hand on the table.

"Oh, thank you Eli, what a nice offer, but I'm still eating," she responds, stuffing another *boreka* into her mouth. Estrella loads a few more onto her plate and refills her coffee cup.

"I thought I would rest tonight and return to Gardena *mañana*. It's been a long day." As usual, the strong coffee relaxes her. She yawns.

"*Perdón, perdón!*" Estrella stands, walks over to Aurora, and gently takes her cheeks in her hands. Every one of Estrella's fingers has a ring on it, including her thumbs. There is a ruby, pearl, sapphire, emerald, and several diamonds. Estrella looks into her eyes and says, "Rest now, *mi alma*."

Eliezer insists she take his room. "I will sleep here on the couch," he adds.

The couch is situated in the bright, immaculate living room adjacent to the kitchen. Aurora eyeballs the small, floral-patterned sofa covered in protective plastic and looks back at Eliezer. It's obvious that he will not fit in repose on that couch. Still, she does not dare risk offense by rejecting his generosity.

Eliezer carries her bag down the hall for her and leads her to his room, placing her bag on the queen-sized bed.

"Thank you, cousin."

"Allegra, *ermozu*, my precious cousin. It is our pleasure. Mama is so happy that you are here with us. It has been so long. She loves to have the house full. Tomorrow, you must tell us all about your beautiful Leyla doll and your darling grandsons. *Mashallah*. Sleep well. What time do you want to go to Gardena?"

"Bright and early," she answers.

"Eight? Nine?" he asks.

"Let's make it eleven."

He gives her one of his bear clench-lift hugs and leaves the room. She closes the door behind him and gets ready for bed.

In the morning, Aurora calls Leyla before heading to the kitchen to find Estrella and Eliezer. She manages Leyla's number with a determined effort involving the pad of her thumb and the knuckle of her index finger.

"Esther died . . . ," Aurora blurts when Leyla picks up.

"Dad died . . . ," Leyla says at the same instant.

They speak simultaneously.

"Esther died . . ."

"Dad died. Stop talking over me!" Leyla says, irritated. "You go first."

"Esther died," Aurora repeats.

"Who's Esther?"

"Papa's wife."

"Which one?" Leyla asks.

"The last one," Aurora responds.

Leyla received an email several years earlier from a genealogist, an over-eager Jewish Studies PhD candidate, doing research for his dissertation. Just another melancholic nostalgia junky in the throes of horrifying rapture over the excavation of his family's Holocaust story. There is an undeniable swoon of forensic trauma which every twentieth and twenty-first century coming-of-age Jew experiences when exhuming their own personal, gruesome, Holocaust narrative.

Every Jew has a Holocaust story, whether it's first person, twice removed, or perhaps a third cousin's, second wife's, grandmother's found letters. Innocently, everyone thinks theirs is the most riveting. Impossible as it is to fully comprehend, there are six million (plus or minus) other horrifying stories underserved by the adjectives available in a MS word thesaurus.

The deportation of the Jews of Rhodes was a Nazi success story—an entire community extinguished in one brutally efficient weekend. The horrors of the war had felt far away from the beautiful sundrenched life on the island they'd shared for generations with Greeks, Turks, and Italians. It had been over five hundred years since their expulsion from Spain.

At the tail end of World War II with the Allies on their way and Hitler on the run, the Jews of Rhodes thought they were in the clear. Inexplicably late in the game, the Nazis organized a major logistical effort to go all the way to this southern island of the Dodecanese in the Aegean Sea because there were Jews there. The Nazis arrived on July 20, 1944.

First, they tricked the men. Any male over the age of sixteen was ordered to come down to the city hall under the guise of registering their "documents." It was a ruse. They were all immediately imprisoned.

Then the order went out for the women to join their husbands, brothers, sons, and fathers or be shot. The Nazis sounded air raid sirens to clear the streets of the locals. They marched the Jews past the homes of their friends and neighbors. Once the women vacated their homes, the Germans, and many of their neighbors, plundered them.

More than sixteen hundred Jews—men, women, children, and elderly—were forced onto decaying cargo ships. The loaded transports then swung by the smaller neighboring island of Kos and picked up ninety-four more people. By July 23 they were on a boat on their way to Auschwitz. They were the last consignment of Jews to be deported from Greece, historically acknowledged to be the last deportation of World War II.

This is Aurora's family's Holocaust story, and by inheritance, Leyla's, too. In one tragic twist of fate, Aurora's Aunt Behora (Behora is the name attached to every Rhodeslis firstborn) was killed when the allies came to defend the Island against the Nazis. There was a British flyover during Shabbat. The family was walking home from synagogue through the Juderia neighborhood. The bombs fell, and Behora was killed.

Leyla and Aurora received calls and emails every so often from Jewish Studies historians and Holocaust scholars seeking to verify the documented atrocities reportedly inflicted upon Aurora's relatives and to learn of her parents' immigration stories. The surviving Rhodeslis community scattered across the globe after the Holocaust and never returned to life in the Juderia on the island. Leyla had tried to shield her mother from these inquiries when they popped up. She worried they might be too painful.

However, in classic Aurora fashion, she welcomed the calls, delighting in the chance to orate on the grand history of her family tree. This Jewish Studies PhD candidate guy knew Leyla's name and her parents', grandparents', and great-grandparents' names, too. Leyla's grandfather Leonard (Leon) was one of the lucky ones. He was already gone before the deportation of his family members. He left the island as a young boy, immigrating to the United States to seek his fortune and send income back to his family.

The student asked Leyla if she had any details or other bits of information about her grandfather Leonard's eight other wives. Shocked and amused by this outlandish claim of eight wives, she laughed it off, assuring him he had reached the wrong Leyla Feldenburg Rothstein. When she got off the phone, she called her mother to have a good laugh about his ridiculous inquiry. Aurora paused after Leyla's recap of the grad student's claim, took a deep breath, and replied, "Well, that we know of."

Leyla was apoplectic. "That you know of? Know of? Eight wives? Aurora? Eight! Why was I never told this?"

"*A dio, ija.* You know what they say, *leshos de vista, leshos de korazon*—out of sight, out of mind."

"Do not repeat this to another soul, Mother." As with everything regarding her mother, Leyla was mortified.

"Who will I tell? *Kuando no pelean dos, kuando ne kere el uno*—It takes two to make an argument," Aurora insists.

Regarding the news today of Esther's demise, Leyla's reaction is more laissez-faire. "So, Esther's dead, huh? Are we sad?" Leyla asks. "Did I ever meet her? Well anyway, Dad died," Leyla replies.

Aurora audibly sucks in her breath. "That god damn son of a bitching *shumechu*. When's the funeral?"

"Mother, you cannot possibly go to his funeral."

But she can't resist a good funeral, let alone Robert Henry Feldenburg's. No way will Aurora pass up the chance to take her place as the Wounded Widow Feldenburg. She could never abstain from the deliciously grim pageantry and chance to mix and mingle among her ex-in-laws.

She truly loves them all, and they return the affection. Robert Henry Feldenburg was a piece of shit, but his family was the salt of the earth, gracious, kind, and endearing.

"*Ija*, I must go. Branan will need my support."

"When is the last time you spoke to Branan, Mom? Don't give me those *ojus*. I can feel your eyes through the phone. I know he never calls."

"Be nice to me, *ija*. I've lost my stepmother."

"Oh, now she's your stepmother? *A dio*, Mother."

"Yes. In fact, I am in Los Angeles right now taking care of the arrangements."

"You are making the arrangements? What arrangements might those be?" Leyla questions. "And please don't tell me that you drove that hideous blue catastrophe-on-wheels by yourself all the way to LA That explains the idiotic touch-tone phone call request from yesterday."

"Leyla, I am the next of kin. Would it kill you to come down to help your mama?"

"Nice try, Aurora. Don't give me *keshas*—Stick the knife in and turn it."

Though she does not understand her, Aurora is proud of Leyla—her impressive, if overwrought, daughter. Aurora likes to throw around Leyla's Rothstein "pedigree" and is constantly angling to get Leyla to show up places to show her off. When Leyla treats her mother to Sam's Anchor Café for her annual birthday lunches, Aurora proudly marches up to the hostess stand and asserts "Rothstein, party of two please," then nods at the hostess while tilting her head toward Leyla. This is met with a dispassionate, "Hey Aurora, the usual double Martini straight up with two olives and a twist?"

Aurora also frequently needs some form of logistical or financial support from Leyla for one kind of scam or another. When young Stephen Rothstein was courting her daughter, Aurora had been certain that there would be some value added for her, a marked improvement in her own circumstances. She's been casting for benefits ever since.

Her most recent passion project was attempting to enlist Leyla's advocacy in taking over a lease on a gift shop on Main Street in Tiburon. Aurora's lifelong dream is to have a shop of her own. Stephen's buddy owns the building. Aurora's business model was: "How 'bout you give me the space for free?"

Leyla has learned over the years to keep a veritable demilitarization zone between Aurora's schemes and the influential reach of the Rothstein family. She fears there might be one embarrassment too many. She has never felt totally secure in her identity as a member of the Rothstein family, though she and Stephen have been happily (or so she thought) married, and she dutifully produced an adorable heir and equally endearing spare.

Leyla never feels secure about anything. Being Aurora's daughter has always been a liability—whether it was enduring the other moms' ire over Aurora's lack of punctuality for her dancing-school carpool day when she was eight (they were lucky when she showed up at all), or the time Aurora invited thirty of her flea market "pals" to Leyla and Stephen's black-tie society wedding at the Stanford Court Hotel on Nob Hill (without even so much as a thank-you note to Bob and Bunny for hosting the lavish affair). Aurora waltzed into the reception with her tourmaline mink coat over a black sequined gown and ill-chosen black "sash" around her waist. Proudly—to Leyla's horror—announcing that she'd made the sash herself with a ream of ribbon she found at a garage sale.

Leyla understands now where this conversation is going. This next-of-kin trip to LA is because Aurora is hot on the trail of another elusive pot of gold.

"How did you find out about your father? Did Branan call you?" Aurora asks.

"No, Cousin Sam posted it on Facebook. Branan would never call me, and I wouldn't talk
    to him if he did. But he won't."

Branan and Leyla had no relationship to speak of. There was no specific falling out or major disagreement. They just didn't speak. When he fled with R.H.F. and Vicki, Leyla was left behind with Aurora. Branan was gone from her life and never returned to it in any meaningful way.

"I know, *ija*," Aurora responds gently. "I bet Branan probably tried to reach me at home. But since I am in LA, I didn't get the email."

Aurora does not comprehend, no matter how many times Leyla explains it, that she can

send and receive emails from her cellphone, and they will reach her wherever she is.

Leyla doesn't bother to step into the opening created by Aurora to take a verbal shot at her brother over his lack of communication. It's an easy target, but she isn't in the mood.

"I'll try to call Acacia later," Aurora responds.

Aurora has more success locating Branan through his wife Acacia than she does by calling him directly. She's nonconfrontational when it comes to relations with her children. She isn't confrontational when it comes to anything. Aurora knows Leyla's relationship with her father was painful and fraught. He had effectively abandoned Leyla when he left Aurora.

Aurora is keenly aware that though they were long estranged, it is not nothing for Leyla to find out about R.H. Feldenburg's death via Facebook. Her father's rejections and lifelong expressions of disapproval forged Leyla's personality. Typical of her hands-off parenting "style," Aurora never protected Leyla from R.H.F.'s harsh criticisms, sneering disdain, and random, unprovoked beatings.

R.H.F. was always at the ready with a, "You're too short," "You walk like a truck driver," or "You ought to be ashamed of yourself." The cruelest of all was, whenever he heard about a new boyfriend, "What does he see in *you?*" He never actually met the boyfriends because he was never around, but when he heard about them he never missed a chance to remind his daughter how undesirable she was. When he met the dashing young Stephen Rothstein upon their engagement, he pronounced that Leyla should "kiss the ground he walks on."

"You ok, *ija*?"

"I'm fine," Leyla snaps.

"*Ija, diremos bien para de todo se aga bien*—Let's say everything is good so that everything will be good," Aurora encourages.

"Right, Mom. Everything is good," Leyla sniffles.

Leyla suspects that Branan's wife, Acacia, finally filed the divorce papers that she's been threatening pretty much since the day they married. Leyla doesn't have the heart to tell Aurora.

Leyla begins to close out the conversation. Terminating a call with Aurora is challenging. The first goodbye unleashes an onslaught of "One more thing." Aurora takes Leyla's, "I've got to go, Mom" as a cue to initiate an entirely fresh topic. It takes a good fifteen minutes and total loss of patience to extricate herself from a call with her mother. It starts with "I've got to go now," and culminates eighteen minutes later, after more reports of "who died," "who's dying," and "so and so is sick." When she starts with "tell me about the kids," and "what's new," Leyla's blood boils. She gets ruthless and hangs up.

Leyla knows that if she stays on the phone today, it will result in an inevitable request for assistance of some kind. Getting involved with Aurora's schemes for monetary enrichment is like accelerating hard on a blind turn, in the same spot where you've crashed once a week for your entire life.

"I'm staying with Eliezer and Estrella Capeluto while I attend to the details."

"Good luck, Mom."

Leyla hangs up on her. Aurora zips up her pink velour sweat jacket and walks out into the kitchen. Eliezer is up and seated at the kitchen table, looking like he's slept on a cloud, not a three-foot settee. Aurora has never been an early riser. She always told Leyla that it was a cultural thing. Anyway, she doesn't think it's so hard for a kid to make their own breakfast before school.

Eliezer is showered, dressed, and well-scented. He's wearing another suit, different than yesterday's. This one is a shiny silver color, but the vintage cut is the same. The two of them drink *café con leche* while Estrella hovers. After heartily consuming the remains of Estrella's baking efforts from the previous day, they drive to Esther's apartment in Gardena.

She doesn't prepare Eliezer for what he sees when they get there. She isn't sure what to say, so, true to form, she says nothing. She simply opens the door (after the twenty-minute, six-flight cardio challenge) and enters the apartment without commentary.

Eliezer displays no reaction. Without discussion or strategy, he goes to work extricating the bags of bags, a tower at a time. He carts them down the double staircases, loads them onto his truck, then does it again, skipping every other step as he trots back up the six flights in his Italian leather loafers—so light on his feet, he barely makes a sound.

He does this on repeat without removing his suit jacket or loosening his tie. Aurora suggests that it would be best "for security reasons" for her to stay in the apartment while he does the loading. She insists that she will "organize" the disarray. Mostly, she passes the time with her NailGlam manicure touch-up kit she keeps in her purse.

It takes two full hours for Eliezer to clear out enough of the bags to make some of the furniture visible. It turns out the living room has a large green linen sofa and a small, wooden coffee table. Obviously, neither of those items are helpful for Aurora, as she is seeking something that contains *things*. She briefly considers whether she can get either piece into her Saturn and back home to her apartment in Tiburon. The coffee table would fit nicely in her small living room, and she's always on the lookout for things to sell at the flea market.

The small second bedroom has only a bed and a small closet. Both the closet and the bedroom are completely full of bags. She hoped they would find more than bags, but so far, it's been an endless cascade of varying versions of the same.

Other than bags, the kitchen has the table, a tall metal stool, and built-in cupboards. The only place so far where there is anything other than purses.

The drawers beneath the counters give her hope once the space in front of them is cleared, but when she looks inside, she finds only pots, pans, utensils, and bowls.

Aurora notices there isn't a junk drawer—that drawer that holds all the little "this and thats" people have nowhere else to put. Even Leyla, whose house is immaculate, has a junk drawer in the kitchen. Of course, Leyla's "junk" drawer is clean, organized, and filled with useful items.

Except for the fact that she had a psychological problem of buying more purses than she (or anyone) ever needed, Esther was a tidy housekeeper. The purse towers are neat, orderly, and organized by size. There is no dust in the apartment, no curious smells or apparent grime, no food left out—not even a crumb that can be seen, and no signs of insects or rodents.

Aurora is losing hope they will find anything else of value. How much money could be left, considering what Esther must have spent acquiring these bags? It's evident they were purchased and not stolen. Aurora finds receipts in every bag she bothers to check, and the purses are all in shopping bags that match the information on the receipts. Esther did not shoplift these purses.

Eliezer does not comment about the strange contents of the small, otherwise unassuming apartment. As the day wears on, he removes thousands of bags. She presumes they will discuss it later.

He gets to the largest bedroom last. It takes him another half hour to remove enough of the cache to reveal a desk. When Aurora sees the top of the old rolltop desk, she perks up. She recognizes it as Papa's. This is the first item that indicates any sign of her father's presence in the apartment. They haven't found any of his clothes. There are no photos of him, or of anyone, for that matter—not Aurora or Reigna, just the deluge of purses.

She slides up the rolltop and finds an empty desk underneath. She's surprised to find that there are no bags inside. She opens the desktop drawer at the top of the desk and sees an old metal letter opener. She doubts that it's real silver, but maybe it's just tarnished. It's bent at the pointed end and dull. There are scratches on the handle, which has a decorative, looping pattern with initials engraved on the handle that read *E.M.H.* She guesses it stands for Esther Mejia Hmans. Aurora takes the letter opener and drops it into her purse, thinking she'll take it down to the flea market and have her jewelry-appraiser friend look it over. Maybe it's worth something. Still no sign of the army medals that Papa frequently boasted about.

There are small cubbies at the back of the desktop; they're empty except for a black stapler, some scotch tape, a pad of yellow Post-it notes, and a black leather cup holding some disposable pens.

Next, she turns her attention to the vertical row of drawers on the right-hand side of the desk, two shallow and one deep drawer. The first contains coupons, neatly cut from newsprint. Aurora rummages through the cache.

They are coupons for food, household cleaning, and paper products. It appears Esther spent most of her money on purses and had little left over for food or other items. Aurora finds nothing else in the drawer.

Moving on to the next drawer, she finds it filled with blank envelopes and an old plastic calculator.

She closes her eyes and opens the final drawer. When she opens them, she finds several large manila envelopes. The metal clasps are worn and bent as if they've been opened and reopened many times.

She pulls one out; it's flat and light in her hands. She opens the clasp. Inside is a single eight-by-ten black-and-white photo of Papa and Esther. They're standing on a sidewalk. It looks like they're staring into the sun, squinting, their chins tipped up in the same direction. Esther is wearing a dark, sleeveless dress, with a white peter pan color, cinched at the waist. She has a small black possibly leather handbag slung over one arm and a small bouquet of flowers in her other hand.

Maybe it's their wedding photo? Aurora thinks. It's hard to tell where they are. It seems like a city street because of the sidewalk, and there are glass doorways behind them with signs hanging in the windows, but they are obstructed.

Aurora never knew any of the details of her father's marriages or weddings—to Esther, or any of the other "wives." She flips the photo over. There is cursive writing in the lower right corner in smudged pencil. It says *Esther and Leon, 1952.*

She takes out the second envelope; it's another photo, the same size as the first. This one is in color with a wide white border. The image is a dark-haired, thick-set man. He's an adult, not particularly old nor young. He has dark skin, and his hair is combed straight back, shiny, and reflective. He's in a field in front of a dirt trail or unpaved road. Behind him is an orange tree. She turns it over. On the back is the same cursive handwriting in pencil. It says *Jose, 1972.*

Aurora is losing hope. She has not found a will or any important papers of any kind. It seems like Esther had nothing but the bags, the furniture they were stacked upon, and maybe a relative named Jose. The discovery of Jose is concerning, as it might present a challenge to Aurora's status as next of kin.

She takes out the last of the three envelopes. It's light, like the other two. She opens it. It's some sort of certificate. It says *Forest Lawn Memorial Park, Hollywood Hills, Los Angeles County, California,* in an official-looking font with a decorative pattern on all four edges. Esther's full name is in large font, on a bold line in the middle of the page. The paper is stiff and translucent, reminiscent of a marriage certificate or diploma.

There are signatures at the bottom of the page. One is Esther's, and the other is a name Aurora does not recognize. Above the signatures is a detailed paragraph of information.

This is a deed to a burial plot. It must be Esther's because Papa is buried at Home of Peace, which is a Jewish Cemetery. Esther was not Jewish and therefore can't be buried there.

There was no will. At least now she knows what to do. She can call the hospital and tell them what to do with "the remains." She'll tell them to take Esther to Forest Lawn and bury her in her plot.

Aurora doesn't feel upset or disappointed, per se. Her hopes have been dashed so many times throughout her life that right now, she doesn't feel anything at all. She is an old pro at disappointment.

Papa didn't give her much when he was alive. She's never been given much of anything from anyone. At this point, she still has her perfect record of missing the boat.

When Aurora's best friend Sue's mother died, they went together to clean out her apartment. Everywhere there were photos of Sue, as a baby, a little girl, when she was a cheerleader in high school, from her days when she was a star at the House of Charm modeling agency. Together they cleaned out the closets and vanity drawers. Sue and Aurora collected her mother's jewelry. There were diamond earrings, a pearl necklace, a charm bracelet, a gold watch, a myriad of bracelets, and bangles. Sue had already been wearing her mother's large diamond solitaire engagement ring during the long decline into dementia. All Aurora had to show from her "stepmother" Esther were two old photos, the purses, and now this deed to a cemetery plot.

Well, it was worth the try and the trip, Aurora thinks. Estrella's *borekas* alone merited the drive, and the purses are a nice, if strange, surprise. She'll turn a tidy profit from selling them.

She (or rather, Eliezer) will finish cleaning out the apartment and tell the hospital to take Esther to Forest Lawn. She'll probably donate the furniture, kitchen stuff, and anything that she can't fit in the Saturn to Goodwill, wrap up her visit with her cousins, then head home with the purses in time for the next Flea Market.

Mas vale poco ke nada—Better a little than nothing.

CHAPTER SEVEN

Una puerta se sera, i sein se avren.
One door closes, a hundred open.

★ ★ ★

Leyla glances up at the rearview mirror. She does a scan of Josh and Simon in the back seat, looks at her own reflection, and practices her smile.

In grade school on photo day, the teachers always pulled her aside to point out that she wasn't smiling. She thought she was smiling; she was certain of it.

"One, two, three, cheese!" they'd cheer.

Leyla did her best, but it did not come naturally. When her father left, she lost her smile. Ever the diligent student, she went home and studied, surveyed her *Seventeen* magazine, and watched her favorite Friday night shows, *The Brady Bunch* and *The Partridge Family.* Those girls really knew how to smile. She rehearsed in the mirror until she had it down. The habit of checking in the mirror stayed with her.

"Okay, guys, let's go," she says, turning on the ignition.

The boys both sit in the back seat, though they are eight and ten years old. The most recent data from the National Highway Traffic Safety Administration states that "ideally," children should be in the back seat until they are twelve. When Josh and Simon protest about it, since their friends "don't have to anymore," she informs them of the most recent recommendations. "Safety first!" Leyla exclaims.

Ever since the AFDS Patrons' Evening, Leyla has obsessed over the image of Hallie Monrowe in pursuit of her husband. She's losing more sleep than normal. Instead of 3:00 a.m., it isn't much past midnight when she wakes. Her nocturnal conjurings of Hallie, Stephen, and Happy the Bassett frolicking together in Aspen are driving her to a state of deranged distraction. She's been forgetting to give the kids their vitamins after dinner and neglecting to pick up Stephen's shirts from the dry cleaners.

Leyla has picked up and dropped off his monogrammed Charvet white dress shirts on Thursday mornings since the day they married, never missing a Thursday unless they're traveling. Stephen still wears dress shirts, a throwback to his early banking days. Most of the world stayed in "goblin mode" after the pandemic, entrenched in work-from-home culture and the now-universal professional attire of athleisure wear. But Stephen Rothstein insists on monogramed Charvet shirts selected in person in New York. He now waives the tie and blazer, but the shirts are nonnegotiable. In addition to forgetting the shirts, she showed up to Pilates on yoga day. At the book-fair buffet-planning meeting, she nodded off during the recipe pitches.

Leyla decides to head to the conference and see what the story is with Hallie and Stephen. There is no other way to put this to rest, but it requires talking herself into leaving the kids. Her frenemies regularly leave their kids for couple's weekends. She rationalizes that it's time to get over her anxiety about leaving her babies.

She tells herself that their grandparents, Bunny, and Bob, adore them; they'll be safe; they'll have fun. She needs to let go and "loosen up a bit," as Stephen frequently reminds her.

Maybe he's right. God knows she's never been known for her looseness. She imagines Hallie is plenty loose. I wonder if Hallie leaves little Kallie when she takes off for "chasing married men" weekends?

Leyla decides to take the leap, leave the kids with their grandparents, and save (or end) her marriage. After multiple rounds of motivational self-talk, deep breathing, and positive affirmations, she musters the courage to call her mother-in-law.

Bunny Rothstein is an uber-fashionable doyenne of Jewish society in San Francisco, chair of the Women's Federation board, president of The Bureau of Jewish Education, head of the Art and Design Committee for the New Jewish Home for the Aged, and honorary lifetime chair emeritus of the Bay Area Hadassah chapter.

Leyla was terrified of her in the early days of their marriage. Bunny Rothstein does not enter a room without every single hair perfectly bleached, blow-dried, and tucked tightly behind the invisibly sutured nook of her ear. She is impeccably coordinated from nose to toes, the epitome of taste and style.

After a few early bumps in the road (such as that one episode when Bunny broke into Leyla and Stephen's newlywed town-house through a back-bedroom window, redecorating every inch of it in one afternoon with the help of her devoted house manager, Sean), she turned out to be a generous mother-in-law and a joyful, fun-loving grandmother.

Bunny apologized for the interior design break-and-enter and now includes Leyla in her annual ladies' summer spa days at The Gilded Gates, the most exclusive invitation of the summer. Most of all, she does not hold Aurora against Leyla and, much to Leyla's chagrin, includes Aurora in all her glamorous hosted fundraisers and family holidays.

Other than an occasional pointed side-eye at Aurora's velour sweatsuits and the ever-present tourmaline mink coat and some snarky comments about the garish nail finishes, she is nonjudgmental. Though when Aurora greeted her with *"Aidi, Kusuegra*—hey Mother-in-Law," at Leyla and Stephen's wedding, Bunny politely yet firmly, responded, "Call me Bunny."

When Leyla phoned about the kids staying over, she explained her plan to "surprise" Stephen in LA, crossing her fingers that Bunny and Stephen would not have reason to communicate before she executed her true intention to spy on him at the conference.

"Yes, of course. What fun!" Bunny responded. Sean swiftly followed up with an email requesting a shopping list of the boys' favorite foods.

Though Leyla did her best to mentally prepare (with extra magnesium in her tea and an additional fifteen minutes in savasana this morning to calm her nervous system), she is trembling as the three of them walk to the entrance of the house. Her neck itches.

Why am I such a wreck? They loved their "Bubbe," as Josh and Simon refer to their grandmother. Bob (or "Bibbe"), their grandfather, secured tickets to the 49er game for Sunday, with seats in the Bank Box on the fifty-yard line. All the pieces have fallen perfectly into place.

Bunny and Bob Rothstein maintain a full household. They have a house manager, maid, driver, and interior designer who is a permanent fixture at their Presidio Heights residence, one of several residences scattered across the country. Their grandparents always dote on Josh and Simon. Leyla has zero doubt they will be treated like princes.

The senior Rothsteins live down the street from the family synagogue in Pacific Heights. They'll be able to walk the kids to Sunday School, and Josh won't miss his B'nei Mitzvah blessings class. Josh started his Bar Mitzvah training earlier this year. He's very excited about it. The whole family is thrilled.

Leyla scratches her neck as they approach the entry. She catches her image in the beveled glass of the large double front doors. She sees red streaks trailing down the side of her throat. She practices her smile again in the reflection and yanks up her mock turtleneck to cover the fresh welts forming on her throat. Her phone buzzes in her purse. It's a text from Stephen:

Hey. Landed. Text you when I get to the hotel. Will be hard to be in touch.

You know conferences if you don't hear from me for a while.

Fucker, Leyla mentally responds.

She presses the doorbell. Sean, the house manager, approaches from the other side of the glass. Leyla looks at the kids with their brand-new, matching hard-side spinner luggage, always red for Josh and blue for Simon. She scrutinizes Simon. He's giving her that look.

It's the same look that he had as a baby when she would put him down in his crib and try to leave the room. He'd look up at her like she was a murderer. Stephen used to joke that Simon cried "like it was open-heart surgery without anesthesia." She saw that same look now. It briefly passed over his eyes, but Leyla saw it. It was unmistakable.

When Simon was a baby, she had an elaborate nightly bedtime ritual. It began with a warm bath, then a bottle, warmed perfectly to body temperature. With him resting on her chest in the rocking chair, she'd read *Good Night Moon*, then she'd sing and rock until he was sleepy. She'd place him in his crib and rub his back gently, waiting until he appeared asleep. Then she'd slowly step away toward the door. The moment Leyla attempted to lift her hand from his back, Simon would bolt upright. His eyes welled with tears, his lower lip quivered, and he would commence howling.

That was it for Leyla. She'd pick him up immediately and

take him in to bed with her and Stephen. Stephen never minded. She just couldn't leave Simon. The distance between their bedrooms, down the hall and through a doorway, might as well have been an entire continent.

Sean pulls open the double doors with both arms, not unlike a gameshow reveal. He stands in the center of the large doorway beaming at them. He's wearing his usual ultrachic uniform of all-black head-to-toe Prada. Eyeglasses, trim-cut gabardine wool suit, close-fitting black t-shirt, and calfskin loafers. Today, he's accessorized his monochromatic ensemble with a red "I love sleepovers at Bubbe's" apron on top of it all.

"Hi, guys! Your grandparents are so excited about having you stay this weekend. We are all ready for you."

He opens his arms. The smells of warm chocolate chip cookies and popcorn waft toward them through the open door. Bubbe always has cookies and popcorn waiting. The boys love visiting, but they've never been left while Leyla is out of town and never for more than one night. She glances at Simon, his doelike, olive- green eyes and trembling lower lip. It takes one second for her to realize, I can't do it. No matter how much mental and emotional prep she's done, she cannot leave them.

Leyla smiles back at Sean, panics, freezes, continues to grin. Sean keeps smiling and waiting for them to enter. They hear the click-clack of Bunny's Ferragamo flats coming down the polished marble staircase in the background. Leyla holds up one finger as if to say, "One minute," turns on her heel, and walks back toward the car—first slowly, then quickly. Josh and Simon follow like ducklings, matching her gait.

She gets into the car and raises her hand at Sean, again holding up the one finger, in a kind of strange static gesture. Sean is waiting at the door with a quizzical look of anticipation.

The kids put their own wheely bags into the back of Leyla's black Mercedes SUV, climb up to their respective sides, and buckle themselves in. Leyla looks in the rearview at their expressions. She gave them no audible instructions. They just know to follow their mom.

"What do you guys think about going to LA with me this weekend?" she asks.

Simon smiles. Josh, two years older, is serene and confident as always. He knew damn well she was never going to leave them. The boys smile at each other and bump fists. They love hanging with Bubbe and Bibbe, but if Mom is traveling, they want to go, too.

Leyla turns on the ignition and backs out of the driveway. She heads toward the airport. Josh put on his Beats headphones and begins his Bar Mitzvah blessings practice.

"*Bar'chu et Adonai ham'vorach.*" He chants.

They've been listening to the repetitive recitations over and over since he first began his B'nei Mitzvah studies six months ago. By now the entire family knows them by heart. Simon and Leyla chant along with him.

Simon looks at his mom adoringly and smiles. She doesn't know what came over her. She better figure out something to say to Bunny, and quickly—and now also needs to figure out how in the hell she's going to stalk her husband, their father, while she has the two of them in tow.

Her phone vibrates. Bunny Rothstein is calling. Leyla hits the side button in a panic. She's not going to be able to dodge that bullet for very long.

Her phone buzzes again. It's Aurora. She puts her on speaker.

"Hi Mom. You are on speaker. We're in the car."

"Hi, *ija. Ande sta*—Where are you?"

"Hi, Grandma!" Simon calls from the back seat.

"*Simonicu! Mi alma, mi korteson, allegria, luz de mi vida*— Simon, my love, my heart, my joy, light of my life." Aurora sings back to him with ardor. This is the Rhodeslis version of "Hi." Their goodbyes are the same.

"I called to check in," Aurora explains. "I'm still at Eliezer and Estrella's. Eliezer is helping me clean out Esther's."

Leyla knows that means that Aurora sits there while Eliezer cleans.

"We're going to Los Angeles with Mom!" Simon blurts. Leyla cringes.

"You are?" Aurora asks, surprised. The cat is now out of the bag. "Lailiku, Los Angeles? Where are you staying? How long will you be here? Why so sudden?"

She does not bother to ask Leyla why the boys are coming with her to Los Angeles. Aurora knows Leyla would never leave them anywhere, other than with her. No matter how irresponsible Aurora is, no matter how much she drives Leyla crazy, the only time Leyla is ever comfortable leaving her kids is with her mother. Although a train wreck as far as being a fully functioning adult, Aurora is a loving and adoring grandmother. Unusual and irrational thoughts are a symptom of chronic anxiety. Leyla is aware that feeling safe when the kids are with Aurora is a manifestation of this condition.

"I just decided to have a weekend away. Just thought we'd head down to Los Angeles," Leyla answers. Leyla can tell that Aurora knows something is wrong. After all, she is a witch, and Leyla never deviates from schedules with the boys.

"*Kualu tienes, ija?*—What's wrong?"

"Nothing," Leyla claws at her throat.

"*Ija, a si biva tus pulgas?*—Who are you trying to kid?"

Leyla suddenly recognizes the obvious solution for her need to stow the kids so she can spy on Stephen. "Stephen is at a business conference. I thought I'd surprise him."

Leyla can't prevent Aurora from sensing that whatever is wrong has something to do with Stephen.

Josh is still chanting his blessings. *"Baruch Chata Adonai."* But Simon also seems to know something is up. He stares at his mother suspiciously.

"Mom, I need you to watch the boys tonight," Leyla says.

"Are you kidding me? Of course! There's nothing in my life that I would rather do! *Ijos di mis Ija*—The sons of my daughter!"

Leyla knows that she doesn't need to ask if it's all right with Estrella and Eliezer. Family is family with Rhodeslis. The kids will be overfed, adored, kissed, hugged, and generally venerated for the entirety of their visit.

"I'll drive straight to you after we land. I'll drop them off and pick them up later. What's the address?" Aurora tells her the address, and Leyla puts it in to her iPhone map. Problem solved. Leyla yells into her phone, "Siri, phone Southwest Airlines."

She needs to get the kids booked onto the flight with her and continues to the airport.

When their flight lands at LAX, Leyla orders an Uber. Once they are in the car, her phone buzzes again. The display says Bunny Rothstein.

Just then a text arrives from Stephen.

What's up? got a weird VM from my mom? I'm sure she's confused. You were going to drop off the kids for the weekend? And then you left abruptly? She's pretty upset. Everything ok? Call me when you've got a sec.

Leyla looks out the window and sees a large highway billboard for HappyDoggyDent—an enormous image of a smiling Hallie Monrowe, her arms wrapped around Happy the Bassett's large, drooping neck. Leyla tugs at her turtleneck for better access to the delicate skin on her neck, now wishing she'd changed before they left for the airport. The J. Crew black cashmere mock turtleneck, one of a dozen she owns, is hot and intensifying the insatiable itch.

They pull up to Eliezer and Estrella's. She asks the Uber driver to wait. The kids get out and run to the front door. She hears Aurora, Eliezer, and Estrella running toward the entrance. The door opens, and the emotional hysteria of saying hello ensues. It's five full minutes before the tears, hugs, and proclamations of love calm down enough to enter the house.

"What's wrong with your neck?" Aurora says when she sees her daughter.

Leyla feels her mother's eyes gathering clues from her appearance. Estrella wipes her tears of joy on her housedress. She takes Josh's hand and says, "*Aide, Hanum*—Let's go, big shot." Estrella tilts her head to the side in the direction of the hallway, then takes Simon's hand with her other hand and leads them straight to the kitchen.

By the time Leyla enters the room with their bags, they're sitting at the kitchen table. Estrella is kissing their heads, decreeing, "*Mashalla, Mashalla*," gazing at them and spitting on them adoringly. Josh and Simon each hold a five-dollar bill, another Rhodeslis tradition of giving children money for no reason at all.

Leyla looks at Simon, maternally taking the temperature of how he's feeling. He barely glances at her. He has powdered sugar outlining his mouth and all over his cheeks, spread out in a smile-shaped pattern exaggerating and sweetening his smile even more. She looks next to Josh; they are both crunching loudly on freshly made *ashuplados*—crisp sugary meringues. Leyla remembered them from when Grandmother Floru made them for her and Branan when they were little. Such a simple recipe—egg whites, sugar, vanilla, and salt, dolloped in spoonfuls onto parchment and baked in a warm (not hot) oven. The house smells like cotton candy as they finish in the oven. No doubt Estrella baked them within the past hour, knowing the kids were on their way.

Leyla's paranoia and anxiety over separating from the kids dissolves with her mother and her Rhodeslis relatives. With Aurora, it's usually replaced by annoyance and frustration, but right now she has no qualms about leaving the boys here, and she can see that the boys harbor zero resistance.

"I've got to run. I'll pick them up after dinner," Leyla says, and abruptly turns toward the door.

"*Ijikita*—darling, wait," Aurora insists. "I want to tell you about Esther's."

"I'll call you later," she responds. She has no time for one of Aurora's protracted, topically meandering good-byes.

She runs out the door and jumps back into the Uber. Once she settles into the back seat, she realizes that she has no plan for how to find Stephen or how to avoid being found by him. She's just going to have to figure it out when she gets there.

CHAPTER EIGHT

Akontese en un punto lo ke no akontese en mil anyos.
What doesn't happen in a thousand years
could happen in one minute.

★ ★ ★

"Let me off here," Leyla tells the Uber driver as they pull up to the Beverly Hilton, site of the conference. They are half a block shy of the entrance to the hotel. It's crowded with people arriving by car and on foot. The marquis in front states *High there! Welcome to CannaBizCon.*

Leyla gets out of the car and walks up the drive past the long line of cars waiting for valets. She makes her way past a crowd of paparazzi toward the lobby. She sees a swarm of people, several large black Suburbans with tinted windows, and a curling cloud of smoke. She sees Snoop Dog emerge from one of the SUVs, arriving with his entourage.

With the attention on the celebrities here to promote their Cannabis products (she saw on the app that Willie Nelson was performing to promote his new brand) and the added distraction from the fact that most everyone is probably high, her confidence is growing that she can avoid Stephen and Hallie seeing her.

She doesn't have a pass to get into the conference, but getting into the hotel past the visible security is not a problem. Her husband has a room—at least he said he does. According to community-property law in California, half of that room is hers.

Leyla walks through the front doors and approaches the check-in desk.

"I'm sorry. I've lost my room key," she says to the guest services "associate" behind the counter.

"What was your room number?" he responds.

"I don't recall. I'm Mrs. Stephen Rothstein."

She is dressed like a harmless yet affluent Marin County private-school "soccer mom." She knows he will not question her further. She wishes that she was not wearing her everyday jeans, black cashmere mock turtleneck, and leather sneakers. They were fine for Marin but far too hot for LA.

She pulls her driver's license from her black quilted Chanel wallet. If the associate does press her, she and Stephen have the same credit card. He uses the Amex platinum for business travel. If she needs to present it, the card will match the one used to secure the room.

Without further discussion, he keys a new card and hands it to her. He wrote the room number on the small envelope that contains the key card, problem solved. She'll need a key to scan into any entrance or exit doors of the hotel and get through security, which is always restrictive at conferences and trade shows. Whether or not she uses it to enter his room—the idea terrifies her when she considers it—she'll need the key to move about the hotel. This front-desk interchange is also concrete evidence that he is here, where he claims to be. She isn't sure if this is a good sign or not.

Next, she needs to figure out how to get into the main hall where the conference is underway.

She examines the schedule on the CannaBizCon app she

downloaded while riding in the Uber. Hallie Monrowe is scheduled to speak about Women in Cannabis at 5:30 p.m. It's a good
starting point. Once she has eyes on Hallie, she'll follow her
to see if she intersects with Stephen. She needs a good spot to
spring into pursuit when the panel concludes.

Everyone entering the main hall has a CannaBizCon pass on
a lanyard around their neck and a green bracelet on their wrist.
The conference isn't open to the public. She sees that security
is individually checking lanyards and scanning bracelets at the
door. Attendees are required to be in the industry—either exhibitors, distributors, retailers, potential investors, or press. The fee
for attendance and participation is steep. Stephen gripes a lot
about how expensive the cannabis trade shows are, something
about onsite consumption and plentiful swag given away by
exhibitors.

She had not thought this through, and it's a problem.
Turning right, she sees a sign for the hotel pool and decides to
follow the signs, sensing it will be a good spot to strategize next
steps. Continuing down the hall through the exit doors, she uses
the new room card to scan through the "Hotel Guests Only"
doors out into the bright sunshine, toward the pool.

The scene has a 60s-glam retro vibe. The centerpiece is a
massive, turquoise-colored swimming pool shimmering in the
LA sunshine. The turtleneck and heavy boyfriend jeans are now
really a problem. Leyla is sweating and itching. Rows of blue
and white cushioned lounge chairs and a border row of striped
cabanas surround the pool. A handful of iconic Beverly Hills
palm trees cluster together in the center of the patio.

She scans the crowd for a familiar face. Her attention rests on
a forty-something, brown-skinned man setting himself up on a
lounge chair near the edge of the pool, close to where she is standing. He's applying sunscreen. There's a dayglo green CannaBizCon
swag bag on the small table beside his chaise. Leyla spots his

conference pass next to the bag and the bracelet on his wrist. He finishes with the sunscreen, wipes his hands on his towel, checks his phone, and slides the bracelet off. Next, he removes his sunglasses, stands up, and walks to the edge of the pool.

He dives in, and Leyla dives for the pass. She grabs the bracelet in one hand, the lanyard in the other, and sprints back toward the lobby. The pass says: *BUDdy LOVE Brands: Finest Flower and Concentrates, Emerald Cup Grand Prize 2019, 2020, 2021.*

Leyla has no idea what any of it means. She doesn't care. She easily slides the bracelet over her small wrist and hangs the lanyard around her neck. With feigned poise, she swiftly moves toward the doors of the ballroom and its blockade of security.

The guards look like posh night-club bouncers, with fashionable, slim-cut black suits. They're all large, male, muscled and serious. There is even a velvet rope. She slows her pace to match the flow of the other entering attendees. People are pouring into the hall.

She pauses and waits for a surge, squishes herself into a group, matching stride alongside a chatty cluster. She holds out her wrist, emulating the people ahead of her. One guard points a handheld scanner at the bracelet. It beeps. He makes no comment, and she easily enters the crowded venue.

From her vantage point just inside the doors, she gauges the extent of the conference. It looks like any other industry expo, with multiple rows of booths all outfitted with slick signage, samples, and product displays. The more lavish booths are in the center of the hall, the less expensive real estate always along the edges. The rows of stalls are separated by wide thoroughfares; attendees are walking, observing, and engaging with each other and the exhibitors.

There are three long lines of booths that extend from one

end of the ballroom to the other. The center rows back up against each other. The edges of the hall are lined with food and beverage concessions, registration, and information stations. At the end is a set of doors under a sign that reads Theater. She presumes this is where Hallie's panel will happen.

As she walks along the exhibition corridor, she takes in the wares of the businesses on display: CannaLabs grow lights, Grass Is Greener seed farm, Blazy Bob's Buds, Cannacures tinctures and teas, KushyKosher cookies, LazyHazy pre-rolls. Everyone is stuffing their swag bags with promotional giveaways.

There appear to be hundreds of companies presenting a myriad of products that range from gardening and growing, to ingestibles and topicals, to stylish paraphernalia for consumption, and of course, the OG plant material itself. Every entry point imaginable for this burgeoning industry is represented.

Leyla is overwhelmed. She realizes her only hope of finding her target, Hallie, in this maze will be in the spotlight at the speaker panel. Everyone will be seated in place, and she can scan for Stephen while shielding herself from recognition.

She heads for the theater, focusing her intentions, resisting distraction from the electrifying sights and sounds she passes. Following a printed foldout map she nabbed from a display, Leyla navigates toward the theater to secure a position for the Women in Cannabis panel set to begin soon.

She continues along the conference corridor, dodging and weaving through the crowd. Leyla is petite. No one ever sees her over the heads of others, enabling her to move among the masses easily and hopefully undetected in the throng if Stephen happens to be around. Moving closer, she scans the room for Stephen and/or Hallie.

Her phone buzzes. She reads the text. It's Stephen checking in.

Hey? Where are you? My mom said you took off. Text me back. About to get on a conference call.

Leyla doesn't have too much more time to avoid explanation before he becomes alarmed by her lack of response.

She passes through the double doors out of the main hall and enters the theater. It is a large commercial-quality auditorium, with three sections of seating across and two deep. There are two wide aisles and a stage at the front under a video screen.

Scrolling on the large screen are company logos, conference sponsors, and pictures of the speakers and panelists.

Next up is the Women in Cannabis panel. The logo on the screen for the panel is a silhouette similar to those seen on big-rig mudflaps. This version is a nude woman's voluptuous form, sitting on a large cannabis leaf, her legs swinging up in the air and her long hair flowing around her shoulders, reminiscent of the postwar sturdy feminine ideal of Betty Grable.

Pretty misogynistic for a contemporary industry, Leyla notes with judgement.

The theater is filling up. Leyla is relieved to blend into the crowd. She scuttles to get into position, surveying for a spot to stand in the back or along the side wall.

The lights flicker, indicating people should take their seats. Then, in the gestalt way you can feel a family member before you see them, she spots Stephen. He is in the front row at the foot of the stairs leading up to the stage.

He is on the aisle, of course. Stephen is claustrophobic. He always needs to be on the aisle. When they buy tickets for Broadway shows on their trips to New York, Leyla must always get an aisle seat for him; when they book their air travel, she calls the disability line to ensure that he has a guaranteed aisle seat.

Hallie Monrowe is standing beside him. Their heads are tipped toward each other. They are talking. On the screen over the stage the picture changes to an enormous image of Happy the Bassett hound, smiling; no doubt he is high as a kite on HappyDoggyDent toothpaste. The lights flicker again.

Leyla appraises Hallie. She's tall, not thin but not fat, strong and athletic-looking, a (self-described) former champion slalom skier. She is what Aurora would call a "bottle blonde." Everyone is tall compared to Leyla. Like her dog, Happy, Hallie has enormous white teeth, like chiclets. With a step, she moves closer to Stephen. Now she is touching him.

They seem like friendly touches, a nudge with her shoulder, her hand cups his elbow. Leyla is incensed. Hallie is laughing at every word. Oh please, Leyla thinks, he's not that funny. It's nonstop touching, over and over. Now that she's locked on his location and has eyes on him, Leyla responds to his text.

Hey, all's well. Simon has the sniffles. Thought it best to raincheck the sleepover. Sorry your mom's bugging you. How's the conference?

She sends it, watches him turn his wrist and look at his Apple watch. He puts his hand back down. He does not respond.

"Fucker," Leyla mutters under her breath.

A personal-assistant showrunner type, replete with clipboard and headphones, approaches them and clips a mic on Hallie's shirt. Hallie turns to face Stephen. She reaches up and brushes his shoulder as if clearing it of dandruff or perhaps a stray hair. It is a tender and familiar gesture, something a wife or mother would do—someone who had presumed permission to the real estate of someone's person. Leyla imagines digging her nails into Hallie's large, rough, masculine paw as she pries it away from her husband's shoulder. She shakes off the vision.

From where she stands and what she's seen so far, it's impossible to determine if the contact is friendly or intimate. Nothing she has witnessed or overheard would be admissible in a court of law, should she decide to act upon her criminal inclinations and require due cause for her defense. Then Hallie leans in close and whispers into his ear. He smiles and nods. She tosses her head back and laughs (performatively, in Leyla's opinion). Hallie turns and bounces up the stairs to the stage. Stephen takes his seat.

Leyla remains glued to her spot on the side aisle. Her neck itches insatiably. The pull of her ponytail feels like someone is yanking her hair from above and behind, and whoever it is just tightened the elastic

The lights go down, and the moderator begins the introductions. Five women, including Hallie, sit in a forward-facing row of chairs on the stage. They look like something out of a comic book, a straight guy's idea of multiculti. There is a blond (Hallie), a brunette, a redhead, a hot Asian, and a supermodel-looking black woman.

A young man walks onto the stage. He has the requisite zipped-up black hoodie, grey crewneck t-shirt, black jeans, and On Cloud sneakers—your basic Cannabis/Tech Bro Hybrid. Leyla scoffs, thinking, Women in Cannabis were clearly put there by Men in Money, an old story.

"Thank you all for coming to our Women in Cannabis panel. I am thrilled to present five of the most successful, bold, *trailblazing* women in the industry." He emphasizes "blazing." The crowd whoops and hollers. Oh please, you mean five of the hottest women in the industry.

"It is my honor to introduce our first speaker. A former champion slalom skier, junior Olympics sailor, Miss Teen Newport 1995, single mother, the author of the self-published memoir *Cha-ching: My Journey to Adopt a Chinese Daughter*, and, of course, the founder of the wildly successful HappyDoggyDent THC toothpaste for dogs, please welcome Hallie Monrowe."

As the applause quiets, Hallie rises from her seat and steps slowly into the spotlight at center stage.

"Thank you. As a successful woman in the cannabis sphere and an honored member of this esteemed group of women, I'm going to talk to you about something I know a lot about—overcoming challenges." She pauses, looks down for a moment, then raises her face to the light and smiles. Good lord, high-school public-speaking 101, Leyla rolls her eyes. "My daddy warned me when I was a very little girl. He sat me down and said, 'Hallie Bear, pretty and rich is not an easy path to walk in life.' He was right, and I have had to swim in these rough seas all my life. Being born rich and beautiful comes with distinct struggles. It makes it challenging to connect with others, particularly other women, and also challenging for people to take you seriously."

Is this bitch for real? Leyla looks around to see if anyone is taking this seriously.

"So today, please, for the purpose of this presentation, I ask that you put aside what you see and just try to overcome your preconceived notions of jealousy and resentment, while I share my story. I, like other members of this panel . . ." Hallie turns and looks directly at the beautiful black woman over her left shoulder, who looks back at her in horror. Hallie nods at her earnestly and continues, ". . . have had to wrangle with bias. My life has been one long curse of privilege. The day I won my first regatta, I was twelve years old and, I must admit, a true phenom. Daddy bought me a classic J24, a loving reward for my accomplishment from my dear father. The other girls at the yacht club were jealous. They were cold and harsh to me at the brunch buffet after the award ceremony. But I invited them out on the water in my new sailboat. I learned that day to share. I learned that inviting people into my world was a way to bridge the distance that being me creates."

Hallie's voice was rising and intensifying. She was reaching a crescendo.

"That was the beginning. What I have endured has emboldened me to live a life of service and connection. I refuse to allow the barriers of advantage to dissuade me from my calling, a calling to help," Hallie pauses, then continues. "With my beloved Basset, Happy, I was able to find a way to implement, and monetize, my aspirations at the highest level. I realized that I had unleashed the power to solve what was a painful and stressful scenario in otherwise loving relationships. Perhaps the most important relationship in one's life. I am talking about the relationship between a dog and their person. Brushing your dog's teeth can be a stressful, even tearful time—so traumatic, in fact, that some pet owners forgo it completely, leading to tragic outcomes of oral-hygiene neglect. With HappyDoggyDent, I built a bridge where owners can care for their beloved pets without the stress, strife, and conflict that canine dental care creates. Not one more puppy ever needs to live in a world of tooth decay and halitosis."

Leyla couldn't listen anymore. Four more panelists like this and I'll have to hang myself.

She let her mind wander, thinking about the last time she was at this hotel, in this ballroom, at an event honoring Stephen's dad, Bob Rothstein, the annual gala of The Jewish Hall of Fame awards for philanthropy.

Leyla and Stephen were recently engaged to be married at the time. She was so excited to attend, back in the day of black-tie, rubber-chicken, fundraiser galas. She charged a new dress that she could not afford. Stephen doted on her. He was so proud of her then, showing her off to his parents, their friends, and community. It was a glorious night. She feels nostalgic and sentimental now, remembering the electrified optimism of falling in love with her Jewish Prince Charming all those years ago.

They call it falling for a reason. It really is a reckless, unguarded tumble, like tripping on the street. You don't see it coming, and you can't properly prepare, so you fall. If you're lucky, you land unhurt and continue your forward momentum, gracefully maintaining your stride. If not, you break a heel on your favorite stilettos and limp off to work damaged, mis-aligned, and knowing the rest of your day will be shit.

Stephen danced with her that night. He never dances with her anymore, always griping about that old ski injury that keeps his knee from cooperating.

Apparently, it doesn't hurt too much to take a few runs with Hallie in Aspen. Leyla pivots from sentimental to infuriated.

She never would have imagined that twenty years from that night, she'd be standing here, gouging at her neck, tugging at her ponytail, stalking him to determine if he is predator or prey.

Leyla misses her ex-BFF in moments like this. It's been tough to live without her ride-or-die bestie, now her "exie," that one person you can call anytime, from anywhere, just to say, "You are not going to fucking believe this." She just can't bring herself to call her anymore now that she is a virulent Trumper and unapologetic antisemite.

Leyla briefly considers calling Aurora for support. But of course that's a ridiculous idea. Whenever she calls her mother, the conversations end up with her blood boiling in aggravation. Leyla wishes Aurora could text. She just wants to send a quick message and not endure the inevitable slog through the mud of a phone call with Aurora.

The lights go up. Leyla is brought back into time and place by the sound of applause. Hallie trots down the steps of the stage straight toward Stephen. Leyla springs into pursuit, deter-mined not to lose sight of them as the crowd converges. She starts to walk down the aisle toward the front of the theater.

"BUDdy LOVE brands! I've been trying to get a meeting with you forever! Can I have a few minutes of your time?" A tall, handsome, excited man is suddenly standing in front of her, blocking her path and her view.

Shit. Leyla is caught off guard. She remembers the lanyard. She glances down at his pass. It says *Buzzy Baruch, Founder, Managing Editor, BuzzWorld.*

"I'd love to interview you for *BuzzWorld*. Your company is getting a lot of buzz . . . heh heh . . . and I'd be happy to give you more." He looks fiftyish. He has a small blue sapphire earring in his right earlobe, light blue-green eyes, short, dark, thick, wavy hair with a shock of white at the temple. His salt-and-pepper beard is trimmed close. He's wearing a white collared shirt, blue blazer, faded Levi 501s, and New Balance running shoes. He reminds her of an old boyfriend she was crazy about.

Leyla realizes she knows the name of the company, but not the name of the person on her lanyard. She wants to look down and glance. She doesn't dare.

"Uh," Leyla says, still stunned. She doesn't want to call attention to herself by being rude and brushing him off. She also cannot look away from his mesmerizing eyes.

He puts out his hand to shake hers, and she takes it. Over his shoulder she sees Hallie and Stephen stroll away together. She must decide quickly whether to remain in pursuit of her husband and Hallie, or rudely ditch this stunningly attractive man.

"Shall we go back to your booth and chat there?" He suggests cheerfully. "I hear you're doing great numbers with your recent product launch of BUDdy's Brownies and Bars. I'd love to get a look at the new releases. It'd be great to get a photo of you for *Buzz World* at your booth with your full product line. We can even talk about doing a cover. I am surprised they didn't ask you to be a part of this panel. But I know you are speaking at the Edibles presentation."

Leyla panics at the suggestion of a photo and a chat. She has no sense of industry lingo. It would be impossible to fake it.

Leyla hates cannabis, marijuana, or pot (as they called it when she was in high school). She thinks it weak and sloppy. She does not partake when she sees it go around at parties she and Stephen attend. Leyla always lets the "puff, puff, pass" pass her by. Already prone to depression and anxiety, she's read that it can trigger those tendencies, and she can ill afford anything that risks an increase in appetite.

"Uh." Leyla is speechless and realizes she needs a better response.

She cannot go to that booth. She has no idea where it even is. Being seen with this lanyard by the male swimmer she nabbed it from is a material risk.

Leyla is hungry. A little forced fasting every so often doesn't bother her, as it is a bonus calorie deficit, and she's been trying to lose that quarter of a pound she gained on their trip to Italy last summer, but she's starving now and feels dehydrated. Calculating the odds of his pursuing her if she bolts, it is apparent that she's stuck.

"Let's go to the café. We can chat there," she blurts. There is always a café. It feels like a sure thing, and she's now impressed with herself for thinking on her feet.

As they walk, she hopes to spot some directional signs. Her new plan is to walk with him, grab a snack, some water, get a "call" or something, and lose him more elegantly, then reboot her strategy to find Stephen and Hallie.

"We loved the sample bags you sent over to *BuzzWorld*," Buzzy says enthusiastically.

"Uh." Damn it, Leyla; say something. She scolds herself as they walk.

She scans for signage and slows down her pace, jockeying for position behind him, so he can lead the way. She spots a sign as he turns a corner. It is a large coffee-counter setup in a velvet roped area marked VIP. Buzzy saunters in. Leyla follows.

The café is outfitted like a stand-alone brick-and-mortar business and not a pop-up kiosk at a trade show. There are several turquoise-green overstuffed couches of nubby boucle fabric and low white melamine coffee tables in varying organic shapes. Tossed about randomly are orange velour bean-bag chairs and LED-lit glowing purple-and-blue cylindrical stools in differing heights. It's a midcentury-modern fever dream.

The cafe is crowded, like everything else at the massive conference. Everyone seems to know Buzz.

"Dude," a barista calls out, and offers a fist bump.

"Buzz Bomb," someone hollers from behind the counter.

"Buzzy B. My man!" Another apron-wearing twenty-something chimes in.

More people yell chipper greetings with smiles and high-fives as he passes through. Leyla continues to slyly hunt for Hallie and Stephen. She no longer feels hopeful about spotting them again.

Buzz walks to the counter. He turns and calls over his shoulder to Leyla, "Can I get you a coffee?"

"Just water, thanks," she answers. Leyla never drinks caffeine after 2:00 p.m. because of her insomnia.

There is an assortment of free samples at the end of the coffee counter on raised cake stands. Her stomach is gnawing. She tries to find a label for one that says low-carb or gluten-free, but the counter is high, and the treats are on platters even higher. At five-foot-one, Leyla is at a disadvantage for surveying countertop signage.

The Starbucks she takes the kids to on the way to school always gives out samples at the counter, and it's easy to find a low-cal version of treats they like. She spots a small, handwritten, paper tent sign that says *Grain Free Blueberry Wake n' Bakes.*

Being petite, or "vertically challenged," as Stephen

affectionately teases, prevents Leyla from getting a clear view. She wants to avoid anything involving chocolate, butterscotch, or frosting. Blueberry Wake n' Bakes sound healthy, reasonably low-cal, and breakfasty.

Leyla grabs two of the small precut pieces and pops them into her mouth. How many calories can they possibly be? The pieces are the size of a large sugar cube. They taste good, not too sweet, with an aromatic aftertaste as if they were flavored with blueberry essential oil. Reaching up for a couple more, she looks over and catches Buzzy Baruch looking at her as she chews and swallows them. Embarrassed, she hates to be seen eating, it triggers her (a throwback to a brief bout of bulimia in her early teen years). Hoping there aren't any leftover bits of blueberry in her teeth, she runs her tongue across her front teeth.

"Bold." He's nodding and smiling at her as he walks back with her water and his coffee. Leyla is mortified. "Nice to see a CEO partake in their own product. But I suppose if you have a lot of experience, you can handle 40 milligrams or so at a business conference. Maybe that's why you're so successful," he beams. He has a beautiful smile. "Aren't you speaking on a panel later?"

Confused, Leyla turns and looks back at the tray and from her position now sees another smaller sign she missed on her first pass: *10MG bites. Compliments of BUDdy LOVE Bakes.*

"I must admit, I thought based on your name that you would look different," he says, still smiling.

She finally looks down at her Lanyard and finds the name. It reads: *Anupal Gujarati, CEO, BUDdy LOVE Flower and Concentrates.* She claws at her neck. Her sweater is hot and feels like it's choking her. The tight ponytail is making her eyebrows hurt. She presses one palm against her brow bone, audibly whimpers, and pulls on the turtleneck with her other hand.

"You should maybe put a little topical CBD on your neck

there," he mentions with a disarming wrinkle of his nose, pointing his finger at her neck. His eyes are a strange, but beautiful, combination of cerulean and jade.

"Shall we?" He holds out his phone, opens the voice memo app, and taps the record icon. "So, Anupal. Do people call you Ann? Let's just jump in. How about a few words on your trailblazing approach to vertical integration and how you concentrated your high-potency THC for your first foray into the edibles market. Any reservations about the psychiatric dangers of such high-intensity THC strains in your new, fruity, wake and bakes, since they seem targeted at a younger market? Apparently microdosing isn't your thing. Heh heh."

"Uh." Leyla isn't sure if she said it out loud or not.

CHAPTER NINE

Segun el tiempo, se abolta la vela.
According to the weather, shift your sail.

★ ★ ★

Leyla slowly lowers herself down onto one of the turquoise boucle couches. It's surprisingly springy. When her bottom hits the cushion, she bounces back up, a manifestation of her sense of being thrown off-balance.

Buzz Baruch sits down across from her, smiling expectantly. The distressing reality of her situation has reached a tipping point. Leyla is in way over her head. The list of complications is long.

First, the issue of misrepresenting herself as a man named Anupal Gujarati, by virtue of wearing a business conference ID obtained dishonestly (or rather, stolen).

Second, she's about to be interviewed by a well-known, well-liked, seasoned industry journalist whose aim is to publish her words as those of Anupal Gujurati.

Third, her total lack of knowledge regarding the industry as a whole and zero direct personal experience of cannabis.

Well, at least my comments will be attributed to someone else, she reassures herself.

That would be okay, so long as he does not publish a picture of her, which will reveal the depth of her deception. If that isn't bad enough, she (or Anupal, it would seem) is expected to speak on a panel within the next hour, so there goes the identity cover.

Finally, and perhaps worst of all, Leyla is not in control, and her entire essence is about being completely, totally in control. Not only is marijuana unfamiliar terrain, but total surrender to organically unfolding circumstances is even more foreign.

Leyla has attended her share of mindfulness retreats. It's one of Bunny Rothstein's favorite mother-in-law/daughter-in-law recreations. Leyla consistently fails at the "live in the moment" workshops.

With no experience of getting high, she has apparently just ingested, judging from the look on Buzz Baruch's (gorgeous) face, a hefty dose of THC. She can't spit it out, take it back, or change her mind. Leyla is twenty-five years sober from her last bout of bulimia, so vomiting is out of the question. It's inside her stomach and on its way to doing whatever the hell it does when one eats it.

Leyla does what she always does when faced with an overwhelming personal challenge—internally shatter while maintaining supreme outward composure. She looks into Buzz Baruch's twinkly eyes, smiles, buries her thumbs tightly in her fists, and clenches her molars—a lifelong habit that leaves her with a chronically aching jaw.

She scans her body and brain for signs of intoxication but doesn't know what to look for. Will her heart begin to race? Will she hallucinate, rip off her clothes, run around in circles screaming, and lose her ability to form complete sentences? How will she find Stephen? Even worse, what if Stephen finds her? What about the kids?

Leyla knows all the horror stories from the Parents Against Drugs workshops at the Preparing for High School sessions at

AFDS. She started attending them as soon as Josh received his acceptance letter for kindergarten. She learned about the correlating depression, anxiety, phobias, and developmental delays of early cannabis usage.

She already has the first three symptoms, and she doesn't even smoke pot. What if she gets the munchies and completely blows her regimented commitment to daily calorie deficit?

Buzz's smooth, deep, paternal voice breaks her reverie of terror when she hears him say that it's good that she's finally stopped scratching at her neck.

Leyla realizes her neck doesn't itch anymore. She reaches up and touches her throat. The skin on her neck feels smooth, soft, and cool to the touch. She runs her hand up her head and notices her ponytail no longer feels tight. In fact, when she puts her hand in her hair, it feels soft and silky. She wonders why it needs to be in a ponytail at all.

She wraps her finger into the tight elastic band and slowly pulls it out of her long brown mane. It's straight because she spends hours straightening it. She coconut oils it, Brazilian blow-dries, irons, sprays, and twists it into its tight elastic band every single day without fail. She never wears it down—never just lets it be in its natural state of lustrous, copious curls, an insecurity hangover from her father's expressed contempt for her "Jewish girl hair." But now, after yanking out the elastic band, she gives in to the carnal urge to tousle it. Buzz speaks again. He says that she looks "really different" with her hair down.

He slides his phone across the table until it's directly in front of her. She looks at the phone and then at him. Her heart is not racing. She doesn't feel high. She isn't sure what that would feel like. She feels relaxed and at ease. She wants to kick off her shoes, so she does. She wants to just sit there and look at Buzz. He's so nice to look at. She leans toward him and audibly inhales through her nose, wanting to know what he smells like. Does he smell as good as he looks?

"Shall we begin?" Buzz asks.

Here goes nothing. "Yes, let's," Leyla replies confidently.

"Tell me, what inspired you to take BUDdy LOVE brands from the farm to the dispensary?" Buzz looks at her intently.

Is it possible to feel someone's eyes, rather than see them?

She pauses and unclenches her jaw. She's cornered. She came to the conference to find Stephen and discover if he is having an affair, and somehow she entered a side door into this complicated predicament. She can't see a way out. Though it doesn't feel all that bad to be sitting here with the "Buzz Bomb."

Maybe those edibles were duds? She doesn't feel crazy, anxious, or afraid. She could just get up and walk away, but she feels compelled to stay. Without another thought, she inhales deeply through her nose and answers.

"Well, Buzz. I'll tell ya. It was a no-brainer. I just knew there would be a market for something that was intensely THC-forward, yet curative. I wanted to fill a need and address the stresses of the sandwich generation whose emotional angsts and physical demands are distinctly unique."

She thinks of her mother-in-law Bunny, the social grammarian, who takes a red pen to improperly punctuated thank-you notes. She would have been all over that sentence. "Unique is unique, dear," Bunny would have scolded.

Leyla is energized and clear-headed. It's a different feeling than her beloved morning single shot of Nespresso Hazelizo with two droppers of butterscotch Stevia and a dash of cinnamon to balance blood sugar. This is a different kind of awake—a more serene, self-assured awareness. She feels *really* good.

She continues unchecked, "I have always been committed to the hybrid approach, you know? I sought to find a balance between the intensely potent *indica* strain that just leaves you on the couch, and the more energizing *sativa* subspecies, if you will. I mean, as a stay-at-home mom, I know from personal experience that it is just not possible to lie around on the couch."

"Stay-at-home mom?" Buzz responds. "Wow. I mean, cool, to be a CEO of a hundred-million-dollar multistate operation and still identify as a stay-at-home mom. I guess you've committed to working virtually?"

"Huh? Oh . . . yeah, right . . . it's all about how we identify." Leyla replies, realizing she's stumbled out of character. "It's all about challenging the norms, Buzz, you know? Defying expectations. I wanted to create a bridge between the restorative benefits of an *indica* full-body high and the surging euphoric creativity of the classic *sativa* head-high."

Leyla is rubbing her hands up and down her quads. She has unconsciously rearranged herself into a lotus position.

She has no idea where the industry-speak is coming from. She's winging it, throwing around phraseology from articles she's read. She looks up. There are people standing around her. They're smiling. A lanky young woman plops down on the bean bag next to her and curls her long, lithe legs beneath her.

"Word," the woman says, while snapping her fingers on one hand and nodding at Leyla.

Buzz looks down at his notes and continues, "I read your remarks from last summer's Malibu conference on psychoactive medicinal strategies. You spoke about your adherence to pure, high potency distillate, with single-strain, live-resin, terpene extract. Can you speak more about that?"

"Um . . . uh . . ." Leyla clears her throat, reaches up, and pulls on her earlobes. "Well, Buzz, cannabis is a plant, right? And uh, organic in its, um, essence, like we are. We are organic in our essence . . . and, uh, cannabis contains many different . . . components . . . like we do."

"Yes," Buzz responded, "THC, CBD, CBN."

"Right . . . right . . . THC gets you high, and uh . . . CBD is a nonpsychoactive compound that has many potential health benefits."

Leyla finds that she has a photographic memory of the label of her CBD tincture bottle that she keeps at her bedside as part of her sleep-hygiene protocol.

She continues, "You can consume cannabis in different ways. You can smoke it, vape it, eat it, or use the oil for transdermal delivery. The effects of cannabis can vary depending upon the strain, method of consumption, and person consuming it." It is becoming apparent that she knows quite a bit. "Cannabis has been used for centuries for its medicinal properties. It was even legal in the United States until 1937. Today, a broad array of demographic groups is exploring cannabis for its potential health benefits, for pain relief, anxiety support, and seizure prevention." She's now straight-up parroting the investor pitch on Stephen's firm's website, surprising herself at how much she retained during the cursory read through when he asked her to take a look.

Buzz nods encouragingly.

"Buzz," Leyla says, "when I really examined the ways that our individual endocannabinoid systems work, I realized there is no one right approach. I am sensitive to metabolic flexibility, Buzz. That lock-and-key system." She joins her hands together at her fingers in a kind of prayer-clench for emphasis. "Every one of the eight billion human souls on our beautiful, inter-connected, global organism called Earth is different and has different needs. We are one, Buzz. We are different, but we are all the same. Do you know what I mean, Buzz?" Leyla hugs her-self lovingly, her arms wrapped around her torso. She caresses her shoulders.

"I do, Ana, I do. May I call you Ana?" He asks.

"Huh? Oh, sure." Leyla is startled and wonders why he would

want to call her Ana. She remembers the lanyard, but she's on a roll and continues her treatise. "I mean, Buzz, why do we have to choose? We are fluid, right? I mean; we are all fluid one way or another. Why can't our cannabis experience be fluid, too, Buzz? So, I thought, why not make it all? Flower, tinctures, edibles, oils, topicals. It's all about fluidity, Buzz. You know? That's what I say to my kids." She's shaking her head back and forth now.

Leyla is fever pitched. She feels beautiful, intelligent, alive, fierce. She reaches down, grabs her turtleneck, and buries her nose in it, deeply inhaling the smell of her own perfume.

"Be an artist; be a doctor; be an athlete; be a boy; be a girl; be yourself. You know what I mean, Buzz? I mean, we are all in pain, right? We are born in pain. We are born *of* pain. In our hearts, in our heads, in our relationships, we are all in pain. We are afraid. I want to help people get out of pain, Buzz." Leyla's eyes well with tears.

She looks around and sees there are more people sitting around her. All the orange velour bean-bag chairs, strewn about the CannabizCon VIP coffee lounge, are now full of people staring at her. They overflow the furniture, sitting on the floor, on top of the tables, and at her feet. There is an older couple snuggling on one bag. There's a guy with a man bun and nose ring sitting cross-legged on a yoga mat he pulled out of his backpack. He keeps saying "dope" repeatedly. They are all nodding and leaning in.

Leyla continues, "I want to get rid of the stigma, you know, Buzz. Make it conventional, make it accessible, and make it yummy." She's rocking her body back and forth toward Buzz, his phone, and his mesmerizing eyes.

The woman next to her reaches out her hand and Leyla takes it. The feeling of the hand in hers is like a bolt of pure dynamic love. She feels a wave of energy surge from her hand to her heart. She can't feel her feet. She thinks she might be levitating. She starts to laugh exuberantly, and everyone else does, too. She is completely free of her usual anxiety and stone-cold restraint.

They hear an announcement about the edible panel convening shortly on the main stage. Leyla looks at her watch. She's hungry.

"I really wish you didn't have to go to the talk. This is amazing stuff," Buzz says, smiling at her. She looks around, and there are easily thirty people congregated around them in the lounge.

"Why would I have to go?" Leyla responds, feeling like she never wants this moment to end.

"They're announcing your panel," Buzz says.

"Panel? Oh yeah, my panel, right. Well truthfully, I prefer a more intimate back-and-forth of shared passion and raw discourse. So, uh . . ." There's no way she's going to speak on that stage. She thinks of Josh and Simon with Aurora, and she sees the counter of baked goods at the café. She's so hungry.

"Maybe your marketing director could cover for you on the panel?" Buzz suggests.

"Right, cover for me," she responds

"Maybe just text him?" Buzz says.

"Right. Text him." It's like he is a spirit guide, directing her to safe choices and bringing

out her best self. She takes out her phone, as if to text the marketing director, but texts Stephen instead:

We are with Aurora. Esther died. TTYL

She doesn't care right now about whether Stephen wants to ski with Hallie Monrowe with her fake blue contact lenses and bullshit, beachy-blonde hair extensions. She isn't worried about anything right now. Her heart is overflowing with love and equanimity, but her stomach is growling loudly.

"Can I give you a lift to the after-party?" It's the young woman with flowing strawberry-blond hair who is lovingly holding Leyla's hand. Leyla looks at the girl's name tag: *Ayelet Havenport, Head of Sales, Dossie's Dabs.*

"After-party?" Leyla thinks about Josh and Simon. "I have to go pick up my kids."

"Great. I'll give you a ride." Ayelet leads the way, and the group moves like one singular organism out of the café, through the main hall, and out the door to the front of the hotel.

"I'll just call my driver," Ayelet says. The driver pulls up in a shiny white Mercedes G-Wagon SUV special-edition limousine. They all pile in.

"Let's skip the party and go get some food," Man Bun guy proclaims. "Tell us more, Anupal. You're so incredibly knowledgeable and inspiring."

"I love the food of your culture, Anupal. Where can we get some?" Ayelet asks.

"Actually, I know exactly where we can get some amazing food of my culture," Leyla answers.

Leyla turns to the driver and gives him the address of Eliezer and Estrella's in Los Feliz. Man Bun lights up a blunt, and they begin to pass and puff. Leyla, true to form, lets it pass her by. But somehow she doesn't mind the smell anymore and doesn't feel that these lovely, interesting, and curious people are lazy slobs, as she would have in the past.

As they pull out of the driveway, out of the corner of her eye she sees Stephen and Hallie. They're standing outside the front entrance in the Uber line, together but within a larger group. It's hard to tell. She can't really make out the dynamic of the situation.

The G-Wagon is pulling away with her in it, and she just isn't that interested in figuring out what is going on with her husband and Hallie Monrowe. Anyone who wants Hallie Monrowe can't want Leyla. It's an apples-and-oranges story, and as her grandmother would have said, "*El selo pudre los guesos*— Jealousy rots the bones."

What's the point? she concludes. She feels so good right now she just doesn't care. She is feeling what it's like to feel and then remembers that she is high, probably very high, though she is not sure because she has no experience with variations of highness. She laughs out loud at the convoluted considerings she is manifesting. Her nerve endings seem sharp, hypersensitized, and refined, but soft and pliable at the same time. Her mind moves toward imagining what nerve endings might look like.

Oy, she thinks.

She turns her contemplation toward her enchanting new friends here in this fantastical mode of transport. Her eyes alight on Buzz. He is beaming at her. They lock eyes and hold each other's gaze. That's all—just hold each other with their eyes. It is an innocent moment; she doesn't necessarily feel desire. But she does feel warmth and an appealing affection. It is a power- ful affirmation—a somehow nostalgic, while simultaneously immediate, experience of being alive—a fully realized human identity outside of her little world of Rothsteins, Feldenburgs, and the lethal community of Marin moms that have been suf- focating her lately. For a moment she is outside herself looking in. No doubt it's just the cerebral dissociation that occurs after a walloping dose of THC, but she is rocked in a wonderful elec- tric way and feels saturated with the light from his eyes.

Someone Bluetooths their playlist to the G-Wagon sound system, and they head down Beverly Glen Boulevard in a white cloud of earthy terpenes and the bass beats of Snoop Dog and Dr. Dre, who dropped a beat in honor of CannabizCon.

When they pull up to the house, it's 7:30 p.m. Leyla leads the way up the front path, her band of sweet, smiley, *sativa*- saturated disciples in tow. She rings the doorbell. Eliezer opens the door. When he sees her, he reaches down and gives her one of his signature swooping hug-lifts.

"*Prima, Lailiku, kukla mu, kerida*—cousin, little Leyla, little doll, sweetheart!"

When he puts her back down, he gets tangled a bit in her lanyard name tag. She looks down at the name tag and then back up at him. Then she looks over her shoulder at her posse as they begin to enter, single-file, past her. With pleading eyes, Leyla tippy-toes up to Eliezer's ear and whispers, "Call me Ana."

Eliezer looks at the open, friendly faces filing past him and smiles and winks at Leyla with an almost undetectable nod.

He beams, "*Lo ke sale de me mano vaya a me hermano*—Everything will stay in the family." He smiles warmly and shakes hands with each one of her band of friends as Leyla introduces him. He slaps a few on the back as they pass.

Once they all enter the house and are led to the kitchen by the welcoming Eliezer, Leyla dashes into the living room to find Josh and Simon. They are sitting side by side on the settee, legs sticking straight out, happily playing with their Nintendo Switches. They look up at her, anticipating disapproval. But it does not upset her the way it usually does when she scolds about too much screen time and harshly polices their digital minutes. They hesitate, cautious of their mother's uncharacteristic behavior, curious expressions on their faces. Then they smile. She leans in, hugs, and kisses them each on both cheeks, turns, and goes back toward the kitchen. Their eyes return to their screens.

The combined aromas of garlic, onions, and warm dough baking in the oven is blissful. Estrella is standing at the sink. She has flour in her hair and all over her *fustanika*—her little housedress. She is squeezing a fistful of warm, wet spinach. The green water drains from between the rings on her fingers and into the sink. She leans her cheek out toward Leyla for a kiss. Leyla happily plants one on her cool, soft face. Estrella smells like rose petals and flour.

Eliezer walks up behind Leyla. He put his giant hands on his mother's shoulders and whispers, "*Onde pishas, no mostres*— Don't divulge everything to everyone, Mom." Estrella looks at Leyla, sees her lanyard, and regards the new friends entering the kitchen.

Estrella scrunches up her eyes, purses her lips and says, "*Vites al asno, ni preto ni blanko*—See nothing, hear nothing." Then she shrugs and announces, "*Sieta te . . . aqui, aqui!*" She waves at the table and chairs, motioning for everyone to take a seat.

Estrella rinses and dries her hands, shoves one into a quilted oven mitt, and pulls a tray of hot *borekas* out of the oven. The happy, high troop of friends follows orders, sits down around the table, and overflows onto the floor.

Estrella goes to the fridge and begins to remove a large quantity of colorful Tupperware containers. Out come more *borekas*, *boyus*, and *bulemas*—handheld baked pastries filled with cheese, potato, and spinach; *keftas*—lamb meatballs with cumin, paprika, onions, and fresh herbs; *tomat a la turka*—casserole of vegetables with delicately seasoned meat and rice; *makaron reynado de karne*—macaroni and meat bake; *biskotchos*—crisp ring-shaped cookies with sesame seeds; *pan esponjado*—orange sponge cake; and *curabiye*—rich nut cookies with almonds and walnuts, rolled in powdered sugar. The quantity of food is astounding for a woman who lives with only her son. It was like she knew they were coming.

"*Aidi. Mi alma. Kome*—Go ahead sweetheart, eat. *Kome kon gana*—Bon appetit."

Wondering where her mother is, Leyla asks, "*Ande sta mi*

mama?—Where is my mother?" Leyla fell back into Ladino without thinking.

"Allegra *sta dormiendo*—Allegra is asleep," Estrella says. "*El suenyo karea suenyo*—Sleep makes more sleep." Estrella raises her shoulders, throws up her little hands, and turns back to her flour sack. It makes sense to Leyla. Her mother always needed to sleep, a lot.

The gang in the kitchen hears them speaking in Ladino.

"Is that a Southeast Asian dialect, Anupal?" Man Bun asks with his mouth full. "Funny, it sounds a lot like Spanish."

Leyla vaguely nods up and down and side-to-side simultaneously, then stuffs a warm *boreka* into her mouth. It tastes better than anything she has ever eaten in her entire life. It's like she is tasting it with her whole body.

They are all so happy and their mouths are so full, they don't bother to question her further. They proceed to consume massive quantities of Estrella's magical buffet, chewing and laughing with abandon.

Estrella is radiant, standing in her kitchen watching these strangers relish her creations.

"*Gracias*, Auntie. *Una meza de alegria de bendichas manos*—A table of joy from blessed hands." Leyla hugs Estrella.

Once they lick clean the bowls of sweet *sutlach*—rice pudding with orange flower water and cinnamon—it's time to go.

Estrella stands at the door and reaches up to hug each one.

"*Nuchada Buena*—Good night," she says as she waves them off with kisses thrown from her hands.

Buzz stops after his Estrella hug and turns to Leyla.

"Will you be at the conference tomorrow?" He says it with slow, deliberate sincerity and a piercing stare. "I'd really like to continue this with you."

Leyla looks wistfully into his aquamarine eyes one more time. She looks back at Josh and Simon on the couch.

After a long pause she says, "No," and puts out her hand. Buzz reaches for it and holds it firmly between both of his large, warm hands while looking directly into her eyes. Leyla does not flinch nor evade his gaze; she looks right back at him. Estrella is craning her neck between them, looking back and forth from Leyla to Buzz, and back again. Buzz releases her hand, turns, and walks down the path to the waiting G wagon.

Leyla walks into the living room and curls up between Josh and Simon in the puppy pile the three of them naturally fall into together. She checks her phone. There are ten texts from Stephen. She opens the first one.

Who is Esther? And where the HELL are U? My mother is very upset!

Leyla is lucid enough to note that his first concern is for his mother. She puts the phone back in her bag, too sleepy to answer.

CHAPTER TEN

Muchoguar rikezas, muchoguar ansias.
Increase riches, increase worries.

★ ★ ★

Leyla wakes up on the couch between Josh and Simon, who is clenching a fistful of her now wildly curly hair. Someone covered the three of them with a blanket. It's the softest blanket she's ever felt, pink polar fleece—thick but lightweight with a satin trim. It smells like roses. Her watch says 6:00 a.m.

Holy Shit! She realizes she slept through the night. She really, truly, deeply slept all the way through the night. Her body feels energized and electric, like the taste of the air right after a lightning strike.

Her insomnia lately has been so brutal, so achingly chronic, she'd normalized the feeling of starting each day physically and emotionally wretched. She isn't sure if this moment is real. She briefly considers she might be dreaming, but if it's a dream she'd be asleep, and she never sleeps. Therefore, she concludes, it must be real, but it feels too good to be true, a miraculous development.

Is this a side-effect of yesterday's accidental ingestion? She wonders, How long do edibles last in one's system? Maybe it isn't the Wake n' Bakes, but rather the positive outcome of Estrella's magical old-world feast of unrestricted dairy, meat, and carbs. As a firm rule, Leyla never eats within three hours of bedtime. Last night was a delectable, luxuriant, change from her stringent routine.

Who cares, she thinks, why dwell on it? She feels amazing, as if her brain has been placed in a washing machine on heavy-duty-with-extra-rinse-cycle and come out clean and fresh. The world looks and feels different, better, lighter, clearer, prettier, happier—sparkly, even.

How was it possible that on Estrella and Eliezer's diminutive plastic-covered chintz settee, in a tangled pile of her unwashed children, she had slept like a baby?

If forced to choose, she suspects yesterday's afternoon snack of BUDdy LOVE's samples are the source of her somnolence. She feels as if someone switched out her body in the middle of the night, took away the achy, stiff, anxious, dreadful, version of Leyla and replaced it. So, this is what sleeping feels like.

She did not brush her teeth or wash her face before collapsing into slumber, nor did she wash her children's faces or brush their teeth either—another Leyla daily nonnegotiable. They fell asleep with their Nintendo Switches in their sticky, grubby, hands. All of it violated the prevailing bedtime regimen.

She did not read a full chapter of a literary "classic" to the boys, also de rigueur at home. Leyla has a gift for accents. Each character from their nightly bedtime reading is performed with accurate inflection and emotion, every chapter a full theatrical performance. Story-time is firm on the schedule nightly at 8:15 p.m.

Leyla knows well that the advanced development of precocious vocabulary is a direct result of being read to and had tracked the data of reading to young children all the way to measurable differences in college-acceptance rates.

Last night she broke every bedtime rule.

The kids are curled around her and each other. Still deep asleep, Simon holds fast to Leyla's hair, just like he did when he was a baby and, just like then, she does not mind at all. Not wanting to disturb them, she gently uncurls his hand and takes her hair back. Then she wriggles herself out from between them, kisses them each, and covers them again with the blanket.

"*Durme kon los anjelitos*—Sleep with the angels," she whispers and sneaks away.

The house is still dark. She walks out of the living room toward the hallway and hears the familiar roar of Aurora snoring, a sound that is not human, more mechanical in nature. It's remarkable that Aurora can sleep through the sounds her own body makes when asleep. Aurora's snoring is not a symptom of old age. She's always snored that way, a result of a botched childhood tonsillectomy.

Leyla did not respond to Stephen's text from last night. Her original plan was to pick up the kids and take them back to the Hilton to spend the night.

But it's just as well she didn't stay at the hotel. She needed the time to process the events of the past twenty-four hours. Yesterday's escapade was not the caper she envisioned when she commenced this adventure. She imagined a scenario where she'd use her intelligence, keen detective skills, and sharp sense of suspicion to catch her cheating husband with that *shiksa* cannahag Hallie, or not—if he is not involved in a tryst. She's still not convinced, merely wary at this point. In one contrived, dramatic imagining, she uses the cleverly obtained room key to find them together, busts down the door, slaps Hallie hard across the face, while Stephen desperately begs her forgiveness, tearfully pledging his undying devotion.

The dramatic twist to the story is her own unexpected transformative experience that had nothing to do with Stephen.

Yesterday's happening was revelatory. For once, she can't wait for her next session with *E*.

She walks to the front hall to get her purse and check her phone. It has practically no charge. She needs to touch base with Stephen and Bunny. They are no doubt concerned, if not alarmed, by now. She finds her cord, plugs it into the wall outlet, and leaves it on the floor. She needs coffee to cope with the Bunny Rothstein "mea culpa" call.

She makes her way past the ball-bearing machine-shop sound emanating from her sleeping mother and goes to the kitchen where a light is on. Estrella is there wearing a fresh, clean, flower-patterned *fustanika*; again, each space between the buttons on her shift is closed with an enormous safety pin. Her grandmother, Floru, used to do the same thing, "to keep out the draft, *mi alma*." Leyla had always thought, why don't they just buy dresses with a zipper?

Estrella has her apron on over her pinned-up *fustanika*. She is simmering a fresh pot of *sutlach*. The kitchen smells just like homemade rice pudding—warm milk and cinnamon. When Estrella sees Leyla, she beams with delight and shoves her cheek out for a good-morning kiss.

"Good morning, auntie." Leyla kisses her cheek, savoring the scent of damp roses, orange flower water, and cinnamon.

"*Lailiku, mi alma sieta te, kome*—Sit down and eat, darling." Leyla sits down at the table. Estrella places a cup of thick, grainy Turkish coffee in front of her. "*Kave para ti*—coffee for you, *mi alma*."

She returns to the fridge and excavates the container of *borekas*, plates them, and places them in front of Leyla. Estrella then returns to the stove to monitor the rice pudding. Leyla stares down the *boreka*. It is unimaginable that there are still *borekas* left over after last night's all-you-can-eat buffet of Sephardic delicacies. She will never forget the way food tasted last night.

She looks at the petite savory handheld pie on the plate—pure carbs.

These *borekas* are the potato version, so they really are pure carbs. Leyla never eats within the first four hours of waking, holding firm to a 16/8 cycle of intermittent fasting. Considering how amazing she feels, having slept on a couch in her clothes with yesterday's mascara still caked to her lashes, she decides it's worth experimenting further with this strategy of no strategy at all.

She picks up the *boreka* and puts half of it into her mouth, then takes a sip of the coffee (more like a bite of coffee). The Turkish brew is grainy, chewy, and strong. She feels it staining her beautiful bonded veneers, but today she doesn't care.

Eliezer walks into the room and kisses Leyla on the head as he passes on his way to his mother. Leyla tries to recall if she's ever met these two before yesterday. It is all so familiar yet foreign. Eliezer sits across from Leyla at the table.

"*Lailiku*—Your children! *Ke ermozo. Mashalla. Mashalla. pu pu pu.*" He waves his two fingers across his face to mime spitting on them. "They are so handsome. So smart. So gorgeous, *pu pu, Mashalla!*"

Leyla knows this is the way. Whether children are (or are not) handsome, smart, and gorgeous (of course hers are), children are venerated and cherished by Rhodeslis.

Estrella pours his coffee and plates a *boreka* for him. She adds a platter of *huevos hamenados*—hard-boiled eggs cooked with onions skins and coffee grounds—in the center of the table. She pours a cup of coffee for herself, sits down, and places a cube of sugar in her mouth before taking a sip.

Estrella lifts her coffee cup as if to toast and says, "*Cafes de alegria ke bevamos siempre*—May we always drink coffee in happiness." Estrella commences staring adoringly at her son. The three of them sit together, chewing and sipping.

Aurora appears in the doorway in her silver sequined sweatsuit.

"Allegr*a! Allegria!*" Estrella shouts and jumps up to fill a cup for her.

"Where are the boys?" Aurora asks, manicured hand held dramatically to her chest in alarm, as if they've been suddenly kidnapped.

"Asleep on the couch," Leyla answers.

"Oh. Thank God!" Aurora responds.

She sits down at the table. Estrella places a cup of coffee in front of her and pushes the bowl of sugar cubes across the table toward her.

Aurora immediately begins to stuff her face with *borekas*, reaching with her free hand for the *huevos*.

"*El kamino del korason pasa por el estomago,*"Estrella says, while nodding at Aurora. "—The way to the heart passes through the stomach."

"What's the story with the Esther situation?" Leyla asks.

"We are all done. Eliezer helped me yesterday. We cleaned out the apartment. When you are done eating, I will show you what we found." She speaks and chews. *Boreka* and *huevo* spittle bits fly across the table.

"Was there a lot?" Leyla asks.

"You might say that." Aurora looks at Eliezer for a reaction.

"Anything interesting?" Leyla is hardly interested.

"I found no will, if that's what you mean."

"No will, huh? That's a shocker." Leyla says.

"I didn't find Papa's medals, either. Just some, uh, purses . . ." She looks at Eliezer again and continues. ". . . and a piece of paper for her cemetery plot."

Eliezer sits up, displaying a sudden dramatic shift in energy and interest.

Then they all hear the rumbling, tumbling sounds of her

boys' running full speed down the hall. Josh and Simon propel into the kitchen at top speed, falling over and into each other through the doorway.

Estrella leaps up for plates. Eliezer pulls chairs from the dining room and places them at the table. Estrella puts the fresh rice pudding on the table for the boys. She pours each of them a mug one quarter full of Turkish coffee, adds a handful of sugar cubes to each mug, and fills the remainder with milk. Leyla looks on in horror. They both drink, then smile—their teeth coated with coffee grounds. In the spirit of the morning, Leyla lets it go. They attack the fresh rice pudding.

"A cemetery plot?" Eliezer bellows. "You didn't tell me!" He sits himself back down at the table, aggressively pulling his chair between his legs, moving closer to Aurora.

"What's to tell?" Aurora shrugs. "There was a piece of paper in the desk in an envelope. It said Forest Lawn Cemetery and Esther's name."

"Forest Lawn?" He throws a giant hand up and slaps it down hard on the table. "That is a fancy place." he thunders in his deep baritone. His sudden robust enthusiasm seems odd to Leyla.

"Yes. Forest Lawn." Aurora recoils as he leans in closer. "Esther wasn't Jewish, so it's probably because she can't be buried with Papa at Home of Peace. I'll call that nurse today and tell her to put Esther in the cemetery plot and be done with it. Then I guess I'll figure out a way to get the bags home." She gives Leyla a hard stare.

"Bags?" Leyla questions.

"The purses," Aurora responds.

"Call the nurse?" Eliezer asks.

"How many purses did she have?" Leyla asks, assuming this was just her mother's penchant for drama and exaggeration.

"Yes. I have to call the nurse back. She asked me what to do with the remains. Now I can tell her," Aurora responds to

Eliezer. Turning toward Leyla, Aurora says, "There are a lot of purses."

"*Ah Dio*, Mother," Leyla says.

"You can't just tell them to put her in a grave. *Ah Dio*, Allegra," Eliezer barks.

"What? Why not?" Aurora answers.

"There is more to it than that. You must prepare the body, you must buy a casket, you have to deliver her to the mortuary, you need a special car that you must arrange. You have to pay for the burial!" He is waving his hands and raising his booming voice.

"A special car?" Estrella asks.

"It costs a lot of money. I know. When my papa died, it cost us a fortune, and it was not so fancy a place." He looks at his mother. Estrella begins to weep, holding the corner of her apron to her eyes.

"Don't cry, Mama." He reaches out his giant hand for hers and holds it.

Aurora is confused, but Leyla knows that her mother has never had to take care of the details of anyone's funeral or burial before.

When her grandmother Floru died, Leyla took care of the details, just as she did for Auntie Reggie.

"Those cemetery plots cost a lot of money," Eliezer continues. "It's like owning real estate. People pay them off like mortgages. Sometimes people don't even bury their loved ones in them. They just sell them."

"Sell them?" Estrella says.

"Sure. You can see on Craigslist. People sell them for a lot of money!"

"*Ke hamor murio?*—Who died here/what's going on here?" Estrella puts her hand up to her mouth. "But what about the dead people?" She asks.

"What's the difference? They're dead." Eliezer says.

"*Es verwenza*—What a shame," Estrella says, now putting her hand to her forehead.

Aurora begins to cough, then choke. Estrella jumps up, socks her on the back, and spits on her (to prevent the evil eye from entering when she coughs.)

Leyla recoils as she always does when the spit starts to fly.

"*Speda, speda*—wait, wait." Aurora coughs once more and clears her throat.

"How much money, these burial plots, how much money do they sell for?" Aurora asks Eliezer.

"A lot of money. For a posh place like Forest Lawn? Maybe fifty thousand dollars," Eliezer answers.

Aurora goes back to choking, more violently this time. Estrella returns to her backslapping and spitting.

"That's it. I'm out. I need to shower and change," Leyla says, disgusted with the curative assault and accompanying expectoration at the breakfast table.

"Don't rush off, *mi alma*. It's not good for the digestion," Estrella says.

Leyla hugs Estrella gently before leaving the room. Aurora gives her the *ojus*. "Hey *hanum*—fancy lady, what about me?" She stops choking just enough to get the comment out. Leyla gives her a kiss on the cheek too.

"C'mon, guys," she says to the boys. "Time to get cleaned up. Let's go." She shifts back into mom mode.

Off they go to shower and change. Aurora goes back to choking as they leave the kitchen.

They head to the back to the bedroom where Aurora slept. Leyla directs them to shower and brush their teeth while she lays out a fresh change of clothes for each boy.

She retrieves her phone and purse from the hallway. The phone is fully charged. Cringing, she enters the password, anticipating a rant from Stephen. There are no texts from her husband.

Leyla is taken aback but surmises that he must have been busy last night—thinking back to the original reason for this trip and flashbacking on the image of Stephen and Hallie from the roof of the G-Wagon as they pulled away from the conference. Leyla heads to the bedroom to shower and dress. When Aurora enters, she is blowing out her hair and corralling it back into its ponytail.

"So, *ija,* where is Stephen?" Aurora asks, her eyes narrowing.

"I'm not sure," Leyla responds. "But I am going to find out. I need to leave the kids with you again this morning."

"Of course, *mi alma.* They are my precious darlings. *Pu mashalla.* But before you go, I need to show you something," Aurora says.

"Okay but make it quick." Leyla answers.

Leyla didn't have a plan yet. She didn't even know where Stephen was but decided to fire the opening salvo. She grabbed her phone and texted:

Hey. We are in Los Feliz with my mom and cousins. Call when you can.

It felt noncommittal as an opener.

"Come with me," Aurora says, and starts to walk down the hall.

"I'll be back in five, guys, be ready," Leyla calls back to the boys.

She follows her mother down the hall and through the kitchen. Estrella is doing the breakfast dishes, and she has a large chunk of raw potato fastened to her forehead with a dish-towel. Leyla pauses and looks at her inquisitively. Aurora gives Leyla a look as if to say, What, have you never seen someone strap a potato to their head?

"*Tengo shakayica, mi alma*—I have a headache," Estrella whines and points at the potato.

They continue through the kitchen, exiting from the opposite side and through another short hallway leading to the garage. Aurora opens the door and turns on the light.

Leyla peers into the garage and sees the bags of bags. She turns back to her mother.

"What is this?"

"It's all from Esther's apartment. They're purses," Aurora responds.

"I see that they're purses. But what are they for? Why so many? Did she have a store or something? Was she just nuts?"

"I think so," Aurora answers, nodding slowly and staring at the bags.

"What are you going to do with them?" Leyla asks.

"Going to take them home somehow and sell them at the Flea Market."

"Good idea. Should be a good haul."

Leyla turned around to leave.

Aurora is surprised by Leyla's positive response. She expected the usual snarky judgement her daughter conferred whenever Aurora talked about her flea-market table. This is where Leyla usually begins to lecture her. Leyla figured that the only reason she showed her the purses was to try to enlist her help in transporting them back up to Marin.

"You won't even need to add any extra bling. Just sell them as is," Leyla says as she walks away.

"*Ija*, what's going on with you? What's with Stephen? Why are you down here with the boys?"

"I think he might be having an affair," Leyla answers with her back turned. She can make this reveal if she doesn't have to look her mother in the eye. It was the first time she said it aloud. All she really knew so far was what she overheard with Hallie and Sheri, and of course, what she observed during the laughing, talking, shoulder-touching at the panel. It was merely a feeling, and now she gave voice to it.

"*Kualu dishu?*—What did you say?" Aurora asks.

"You heard me." Leyla says.

"*Hijo sin padre*—He is a bastard," Aurora hisses while shaking her head. Her tone has a tinge of resignation, a sort of foregone conclusion that all men are shit.

"Don't jump to conclusions, Mom. I said, 'I think.' I don't know yet. I don't even know what I do know. But I have a bad feeling, and I need to find out. Don't start spitting on the floor just yet."

"Okay. I will wait for you to tell me when I can start spitting on the floor. I've been there, *ija*. I know," Aurora says with arrogance.

They both went silent, remembering Robert Feldenburg, his lies, the humiliation. They were hard years after R.H.F. left with Vicki and Branan. Just the two of them together, they clawed out of the emotional and psychological debris he left in his path.

Aurora has told Leyla the origin story of her marriage many times. It was often repeated in the manner of a cautionary tale rather than a storybook romance. Robert H. Feldenburg had proposed to Aurora on their first date. He'd met her when she was sunbathing on the Marina Green in San Francisco. She was "laying out," awash in baby oil, when he spotted her. He walked up to her and asked her out. He took her to Trader Vic's and proposed over a Pu Pu Platter and Tiki bowl.

She had been an extraordinary beauty, Aurora frequently reminded Leyla. Sephardic Jews were considered exotic in those days in San Francisco. Aurora was a Spanish-speaking (Ladino), dark-skinned, editorial model with a twenty-inch waistline. She did print work for the City of Paris and I. Magnin department stores. Robert H. Feldenberg was a furrier, a glamorous trade in those days. It seemed to most everyone to be a perfect match.

He'd never encountered anyone like her. She wasn't from any of the known and more acceptable families his parents, Ezra and Fanny Doll, mixed and mingled with at the Concordia Club or Temple Emanuel, bastions of reformed Ashkenazi upper-class society. She went to Mission High School, not Lowell, where all the nice Jewish girls went. She had no college to speak of, merely dabbling at city college for a few classes here and there. Ezra and Fanny Doll Feldenburg were holdouts. They were not pleased with the sudden engagement.

Aurora was unquestionably stunning, that "Funny, you don't look Jewish" type, but she was not from their "community." Aurora's mother, with her chain-smoking (Floru Hmans could suck down an entire cigarette in one single draw), curse-throwing, Ellis-Island fashion sense, and Reggie, Aurora's sister, with her childlike simplicity, were not what they had in mind for their precious youngest son.

But, Floru spoke six languages, five fluently—Italian, French, Greek, Spanish, Ladino—and one poorly, English—seamlessly transitioning from one language to another as needed. She'd size up a person upon meeting them and decide what language was appropriate, whether they spoke it or not. She always spoke French to Ezra Feldenburg, her first choice for the most refined members of society.

Be that as it may be, Ezra Feldenburg did not scrabble his way from Budapest through the streets of New York and Jewish Harlem to build a successful wholesale fur business so his son could marry down. They were concerned that Aurora was from the Mission, a neighborhood of mostly Mexican immigrants and blue-collar workers. They were also concerned about Aurora's fondness for martinis and cigarettes.

R.H.F.'s elegant mother, Fanny Doll, did not approve of

the "ghastly" long nails. Ultimately, they acquiesced. Aurora's beauty and warmth had won them over. At the end of the day, she was Jewish. She knew that they saw her as one step up from a *shiksa*, but at least he hadn't brought home a *shiksa*. So, they accepted her.

"I know you've 'been there,' Mom. But I'm not 'there.' I'm not you, and Stephen isn't my father. At least, I don't think we're there. As of this morning, we're not there. Oh, God, I don't know *what* I think right now."

"Far be it from me to be the bearer of bad news. I'm just saying, I know men. I've warned you before. They only want one thing."

"Aurora, please don't start."

"I'm not starting, but you know, the clock is ticking. You are not as young as . . ."

"As what? As young as what?" Leyla snapped.

"Sweetheart, don't be stupid like I was. Thinking he is faithful to you, that he isn't looking for *it* elsewhere."

"Jesus, Aurora, when I was younger, it was the way I walked, or my height, my hair, my posture. Now it's my age? Why are you so good at seeing the ways that men can't want me and will leave me?"

"I'm just trying to prepare you for the inevitable."

"The inevitable?" Leyla is about to blow, but she takes a deep breath instead. She thinks of the kids, Estrella, Eliezer, their welcoming home, and last night's joyous feast, and decides not to cause a scene.

"Okay Mom, thanks for the wisdom. Anyway, I need to leave the kids here today."

"Got it," Aurora responds.

Leyla orders an Uber and walks back through the house. She checks her phone. Stephen hasn't answered her text. With each check of her phone, no new text from him, and Aurora's lecture on the ways of men, her angst intensifies. She goes to the back bedroom to say good-bye to the boys.

"You guys are hanging with Grandma again today. Okay?" She watches Simon for a reaction. He's smiling.

"Grandma, can we go to the movies?" Josh asks.

"Of course, *mi alma.*" Aurora answers from behind Leyla. "Anything you want."

"Transformers?" he pushes.

"Of course," Aurora says.

"Auntie Estrella told me they have an ice-cream truck in her neighborhood." Simon adds.

"She taught me how to say, 'You're treating me to an ice cream!—*Me vas a tratar un ayiscrin'.*"

"Of course, *mi kortisone de me vid*a—my heart of my life, I will give you all the money you need when the ice-cream truck comes," Aurora says.

As she says this, she holds out her open hand to Leyla and wiggles her pointy, purple, shellacked digits. Leyla takes two twenty dollar bills out of her wallet, rolls her eyes, and places them in her mother's open hand. Aurora continues to wiggle. Leyla adds two more twenties.

"We'll have a swinging time," Aurora says to the kids.

"Did you ever visit your grandma in LA when you were a kid?" Simon asks.

"Well. My grandma was at Auschwitz. So, she wasn't much of a swinger," Aurora answers with a straight face.

"Mother!" Leyla is irate.

"What? It's true, why should I lie?" Aurora says.

"*A dio*, Aurora."

Josh puts his headphones on and begins his chanting. "*Baruch chata adonai notain ha toraaaaahh.*"

"I've got to go. I'll call you later." Leyla says and heads toward the door.

"Leyluchi, remember, *no hagas locorias amargas*—Don't do crazy things that'll make you regret the outcomes." Aurora calls after her.

If she only knew, Leyla thinks, recalling the unexpected and incredible events of yesterday. It's behind her, but she knows that somehow things are never going to be the same, regardless of what she finds out about Stephen and Hallie. She can't deny that her spirit guide, Buzz Baruch, and his beaming smile are popping into her head this morning.

She searched her soul. The raw truth was, on an objective level by any measure, he was stunningly attractive, but she didn't have any desire for Buzz. It was more the experience of being desired that seemed to awaken something in her. It had been so long since she had that feeling of electricity, that pure knowing that you are an object of desire by a person who is desirable. It was empowering, and it stirred something in her, reminded her of something that had been out of reach, quieted in her during these years of chasing this unattainable super-mom/daughter-in-law/woman status. No doubt the Wake n' Bakes opened the gates of awareness, so that she was able to see and feel that again. It felt very good.

CHAPTER ELEVEN

El mal entontese, i el bien agudese.
Lack of money makes a person ignorant,
while wealth makes everyone smart.

★ ★ ★

Aurora and the kids wave Leyla off in her Uber. Aurora walks back into the house. Josh and Simon stay outside on the curb to wait for the ice-cream truck. Estrella drags out her aluminum folding lounge chair.

Estrella was born in Rhodes. She survived the deportation and Auschwitz. She was one of only a handful of survivors remaining who lived in and remembered the Juderia neighborhood on the island, where the women sat at the windows of their homes each day after they finished their baking, cooking, and housework.

They talked and sang to each other across the courtyards from one house to the other. Estrella continues the practice, but with a contemporary spin. Each day when her baking and cleaning are done, she pulls out her twenty-year-old, five-dollar aluminum lawn chair and listens for the ice-cream truck.

No one in Los Feliz sits on their front lawns to talk and sing to each other. She doesn't even know her neighbors at all.

In the old days, her cousins, friends, and sisters-in-law were, if not next door, near enough to be in each other's kitchens daily. Those days are gone. People got old, moved away to be closer to their children, or died. Still, Estrella unfailingly pulls her chair out almost every day. Sometimes an Amazon driver or a UPS person will wave to her.

★ ★ ★

Josh and Simon are holding today's five-dollar bills from Eliezer in anticipation of the ice-cream truck. Josh has his headphones on, practicing his portion. Estrella and Simon are singing along to the blessings. The chorus of, "*Shehecheyanu, v'kiyemanu, v'higgy'anu,*" can be heard throughout the neighborhood.

Aurora leaves them on the front lawn and goes back to the garage to look at the handbags and strategize. She opens the door leading into the garage. The light is on.

Eliezer is standing in the center of the garage. He's holding a clipboard and a pen.

"*Gracias para todos, primo*—Thank you for everything, cousin. I'm so grateful for your help. I apologize for all this clutter in your garage. I'm sure Leyla will help me drive it all home as soon as she's done with her . . . errands." Aurora says it with conviction, while knowing full well there is no way in hell Leyla will agree to drive this haul up north. "I just don't see how I can possibly fit them all into my little Saturn," Aurora laments as she eyes the empty flatbed of Eliezer's truck parked between them in the garage.

"Of course, I will help you. You shouldn't drive all this home by yourself. It's too much."

"Oh, my dear Eliezer, thank you. You've done so much already, and now offering to drive it all to Marin by yourself. How can I ever repay you?" She places her sparkly purple spears on her heart in a gesture meant to be both regal and appreciative.

"Allegra, *kerida*, no. We can, I mean . . . *you* can sell them here. Why would you drive them home with you? It's too dangerous. You might get robbed when you stop for gas if someone sees all these purses in the car."

"Oh, Eliezer, your concern is touching, but I am not worried," she answers.

It hadn't occurred to Aurora to sell the bags here in Los Angeles. She always intended to sell them. Though she does not remember mentioning that to Eliezer. Unloading them here is the obvious solution, but there is the irresistible temptation of being able to show up at her flea- market table with the impressive inventory. It would be the first time that she had anything anywhere near this substantial, and she wants that moment. She wants to show off to her friends that she is a somebody. She is someone's next of kin. Someone has left her something. More than the money, this means something to Aurora. On the other hand, having someone take care of all the details holds a magnetic attraction.

"We can list it on Craigslist or Nextdoor," he says.

"Next door? Next door where? Who lives next door? Which neighbor? How do we sell it next door?" Aurora is confused.

"No. Sell it *on* Nextdoor," Eliezer says, emphasizing *on*.

"*On* next door? *Kualu dishu?*—What are you saying? How do you sell *on* next door? I don't even know your neighbors. Are they nice?" she asks.

"It's an app," he responds.

"It's a what?" Aurora asks.

"It's an app!" Eliezer is raising his voice in the same way Leyla does when she gets impatient giving instructions.

These young people are so quick-tempered.

"What's an app?" Aurora asks again.

"*Ay pasensya*, Allegra. You can sell them online on the internet. You take pictures and post them. People buy what you post, and you send them what they buy. Nextdoor is the name of the app!" He's yelling now and smacking the back of one hand with the palm of the other.

Aurora puts her hand up in a stop gesture. She was becoming as irritated with him as he was with her. She wonders if Estrella has any more potato left over for her head. "I think it's just better all-around to bring the purses home with me," Aurora deflects.

"Suit yourself. But this is much easier for you," he snaps.

"Thank you anyway, Eliezer," she replies haughtily. She does not want him upset with her. "For everything, all your help, with the kids. Being here with family, it's like old times." she adds, nodding sweetly.

"*Sí, verdad*—You got that right. Just like old times," he says.

Something in the way that Eliezer says it troubles Aurora. She isn't sure how he means that. So, she just smiles at him, working her dimples and batting her lashes.

"Tell me about this Craig person. You said that he has a list? Does he sell cemetery plots on his list? I don't think I could sell a cemetery plot at the flea market," Aurora says. She wants Eliezer to stay away from her purses, but she could use the help with the cemetery plot.

"*Ah dio*, Allegra. Come with me." He is exasperated. Eliezer squeezes himself out of the middle of the garage where he's wedged between his truck and the towers of purses. He puts down his clipboard and walks through the inside door that leads to the kitchen. Aurora follows him. He reaches in behind her and turns out the light.

"*Siete te*—Sit here." Eliezer pulls out a chair for her at the kitchen table. He sits down next to her. His iPad is on the table. He reaches for it and pushes it in front of her.

Aurora squints her eyes very tight and purses her lips. This is the look that she gets when someone tries to teach her something new involving technology.

Eliezer opens the iPad case and signs in. He goes to Craigslist and shows Aurora the *For Sale* tab.

"You see? So many things for sale here, cribs, barbecues, garden hoses." He scrolls through. She nods affirmatively, shifts her eye sideways at him and then back to the small screen as if it makes perfect sense, and she understands completely.

Then she asks, "How does it work?"

"What do you mean, how does it work? You see something you like, and you buy it from the person who is selling it." Eliezer is incredulous.

"But how do you get it? I mean, you said, 'you post it' before. Do you go to the post office, or is it one of those little Post-it notes?" Aurora cannot comprehend what she considers to be the mysterious magic of the internet. Whenever Leyla emails her pictures of the boys, Aurora calls from her landline and asks, "How do I get them off the computer?" as if there is a secret door where she can reach in and pull the pictures out. This triggers a long confusing explanation from Leyla, which does not help at all.

Eliezer continues, "You message them in the app, and you say, 'I want it. I will pay for it.' Or maybe you make an offer for less than they are asking. Then you pay with PayPal, and you can go pick up what you bought if they're close by, or they can ship it to you," he explains.

"Oh. Okay. Craig is your pal. Okay. Now I understand. Well, why didn't you just say so? How do you know this Craig person? If you know him so well, then maybe just call him and ask him about selling the cemetery plot," Aurora says, rolling her eyes and shaking her head as if this is the obvious solution rather than all the internet *bavajathas*—nonsense.

"*Aidi mazal despierto*—Oh, c'mon, dummy." Eliezer mutters under his breath. He continues, attempting to stay calm, "Allegra, Craigslist is a website. Nextdoor is an app. They are both places for you to sell and buy things and communicate with people. It's like the Want Ads in the newspaper." He hammers his fist on the table.

"If it's like the Want Ads, then why don't we just go to the want ads? The want ads work perfectly well. Why do they need to complicate things with all this techie stuff?" She's fluttering her manicure at the iPad in an agitated and dismissive gesture.

Eliezer might as well have been speaking to her in Martian. What he is saying is impossible for Aurora to comprehend—PayPal, Craigslist, Nextdoor, Apps—it's all too much.

She squints her eyes smaller and purses her lips tighter, as if those actions will make her smarter and help her understand better.

"Go ahead, search," Eliezer says, gesturing with his hands. She is flummoxed, having no idea what to do with an iPad. At home, she still follows the handwritten index card from the Tiburon librarian taped to her kitchen table with the steps to open her email on the computer Branan sent to her five years ago.

Eliezer looks at Aurora and waits, then he looks at her fingernails. It's obvious, between her ignorance and her nails, she's never going to navigate anywhere on the iPad.

"*Alimpia la ver*—Get out of the way." He reaches across her, elbowing her ever so slightly as he types "cemetery plot for sale" in the search box and navigates to a page with multiple listings for various brokers and also ads looking to secure cemetery plots to sell.

"See? Look how many. Look how much they sell for," he says, pointing at the screen for emphasis.

Aurora can see number signs through her squint. The asking prices range anywhere from ten thousand to sixty-five thousand dollars. She goes bug-eyed, squint-eyed, and back to bug-eyed again.

Forget the bags, she thinks. I'm rich!

She says, "Oh, well, okay! Let's sell it."

"Well, let's just see what it is worth. Go get the deed so I can see it. We can look at where the plot is located on the map and find out what yours would sell for."

Aurora gets up and goes back to the bedroom to get the deed, moving as fast as her bulk allows.

Eliezer is an attorney, or *was* an attorney, like his father before him. Aurora is reminded of this when she sees his degrees framed on the wall of the bedroom.

No wonder he is so smart, she thinks. He graduated from UCLA with both his bachelor's and law degrees.

Aurora remembers how proud Estrella had been when he passed the Bar exam. There was a big party for him at the house. The entire Rhodesli community of Los Angeles was invited. Estrella and her platoon of aunties cooked and baked for days for the celebration.

But there was some story that's in the back of her mind now. Aurora can't quite remember, some "funny business" about him getting into trouble. The details escape her. The family does not talk about it. She vaguely remembers Estrella crying at Rica's kitchen table. Whatever happened, it was the other guy's fault. Eliezer no longer practices law. Estrella is no less proud of him and still introduces him as "My son, the attorney."

Aurora returns to the kitchen with the deed.

"Here we are. Now, let's put this on your friend Craig's list!"

"*Ay, pasensya en este mundo*—Oy, patience in this world." Eliezer rubs his forehead with his thumb and middle finger, shakes his head from side to side, then types the details of the plot and location information in the search box.

"Do you want me to get you a potato for your head?" she asks with sincerity.

"No, thank you," he answers.

"What kind of law did you practice, Eliezer?" Aurora asks, trying to look over his shoulder. He is typing very fast.

"A little of this and a little of that," he answers without looking up.

"Mmm," Aurora responds. "Well, what does Craig say?"

"There are a lot of brokers. You are in luck. There is high demand. Just look." She peeks over, squeezes up her eyes, and reads the first ad:

WE ARE PLOT BROKERAGE. WE ARE SELLING GOOD FOREST LAWN PROPERTIES, THEY GO FAST. PEOPLE ARE WAITING TO PAY YOU FAST CASH! Plot Brokerage works with cemeteries to authenticate ownership. We create confidence in the market. Buyers, Sellers, and Cemeteries can be confidence in working with Plot Brokers knowing we process and verify all property and ownership with confidence. We have over 90 years of experience. We will guide you through the process. Customer Service is very best with us.

"It looks like a good lot at Forest Lawn sells for anywhere from thirty-five to fifty-five thousand dollars," he says after surveying the page.

"Sell it. Sell it!" she yells. "They're going fast. Call Craig right now!" She claps her hands together.

"It's not a cash register or an ATM. You don't just list it and get the money out. First, you contact the broker, and they go through the steps."

"Okay, what are the steps?" Aurora asks.

"Well, you must find a good broker."

"I like this one. They say they are very confidence."

"*Speda, prima*—wait cousin. So, then you show them the deed. You give them the proper identification. You must demonstrate that you are the rightful owner, the legal owner—as you say, the legal next of kin. Then they either buy it outright from you, or they sell it, and you pay them a fee."

"Okay. Let's do that," Aurora says excitedly.

"Are you the rightful owner?" He asks warily.

"Yes of course," she responds, recoiling her jaw and bringing her hand dramatically to her chest, as if offended by the suggestion that she might be otherwise.

"The woman from the hospital said so on the phone. I am next of kin," Aurora insists.

"Allegra, you need more than that. You can't just tell them the woman said so on the phone. You need to show how you are related. You must show that she left this to you, that you are her legal stepdaughter, and you are therefore the beneficiary."

"The what?" she asks.

"The beneficiary? You must show proof. Do you have some proof, some legal identification?"

Aurora thinks about not finding a will from Papa or Esther and then remembers that her driver's license is expired and will not be useful as "legal identification." She can't tell Eliezer. He might tell Leyla, who would have a snit.

How is she going to demonstrate that she is the sole heir? She thinks of that color photo in the envelope showing the man in front of the fruit tree. He could be Esther's brother, uncle, cousin, or maybe her son? What if he shows up, suddenly comes out of the woodwork?

In the distance they hear the tinkling tune of the ice-cream truck. Aurora feels a prickle of excitement, just like when she was a child and the ice-cream truck was on its way.

The music gets closer. She gets up and goes to the window to check on the kids at the curb. The three of them are standing there. Josh and Simon are holding their five-dollar bills with Estrella, in eager anticipation as the truck pulls up.

Aurora decides to go out and join them. She'll think about her ID and the cemetery plot later.

"Where are you going?" Eliezer barks. Aurora wanders out of the room without responding. Eliezer goes to the refrigerator and takes out a potato while mumbling under his breath, "Just like old times. *Ay pasensya.*"

CHAPTER TWELVE

Ninguno saven lo ki hay en la oya,
si no la kuchara ki lo menea.
No one knows better what is in the pot,
than the spoon that stirs it.

★ ★ ★

Leyla texts Stephen again when she gets in the Uber.
Hey, checking in, call when you can.

She's breaking an unofficial rule by asking him to call. By some long-forgotten agreement, or habit, they do not speak by phone when he travels. He usually just texts with messages of how busy he is and why he can't communicate: *Sorry, busy, txt you later, you know how conferences are,* or *Call you from the airport on the way home,* and the old faithful, *Back-to-back conference calls. Call you later or text me.*

But he never calls. It started once the kids arrived. It bothered her at first. They quarreled a few times about it.

"A husband and father is supposed to call from the road," was Leyla's point of view.

R.H.F's absence on "business trips" when she was a child, which eventually was revealed to be an entirely separate life and the ultimate demise of her nuclear family, made her sensitive to this dispute.

Now, Leyla wonders if it's her fault. Blaming oneself for everything is another symptom of childhood neglect, according to *E*. Leyla is a loner. She likes being alone, maybe too much? Is she too self-sufficient? She prides herself on her independence. She thought it made her more attractive. She's proud that she can never be accused of being needy.

She never grills Stephen about where he is or what he's doing. She realizes now she's been stupid. She trusted him, trusted that he loved her, and that she loved him, that they belonged to each other. What a fool I've been.

Leyla knows women who constantly police their husbands. That's not her thing, never even occurred to her. She never thought to question their trust, loyalty, or faithfulness, which now seems ridiculous considering her background. Perhaps what she thought of as her independent streak was interpreted as neglect. Maybe he felt ignored.

Fuck him. He could have said something. He could have just asked her to come skiing. They used to ski together, though admittedly Leyla didn't love it—the cold, the layers, the equipment, the constant schlep in lift lines. Once they got busy with the kids, she let it go. She figured he had his cousin in Aspen to ski with, and of course, she cherished the downtime. Still, it would have been nice to be asked. But if she is honest with herself, would she have gone? Even now she isn't sure if she really cares or is just angry with a bad case of bruised ego.

Leyla tells the Uber driver that she wants to be let off a block away from the hotel, same as yesterday. Like the day before, she has no well-thought-out plan. It's a strange experience for someone whose days are usually scheduled and executed down to the minute.

The Rothstein family calendar is organized, supervised, and

masterminded by Leyla with military efficiency. She plans summer in early January, the minute they return from their annual Hawaii "festive" break. School breaks and holidays are booked by June. Nutcracker tickets are confirmed in mid-August the day of their release, row AA, center aisle, the Friday after Thanksgiving. She put Josh's name on the waitlist for All Friends Day school on the day of his bris and booked the St. Regis for his Bar Mitzvah reception on the day of his first blessings class.

The past few days of winging it are out of character. From the moment she turned and walked away from Bunny's front door, she's been moving through time and space like an escaped prisoner, fueled by raw emotion and intuition.

She only knows that she wants it resolved, today. She wants proof one way or another. Either Hallie Monrowe and her husband are a thing, or they are not. Leyla needs to prepare for the sadness, anger, and humiliation in the way she prepares for everything. There is a sense of foreshadowing, as though she always knew this was coming. Hadn't Aurora warned her, preparing her all these years for the inevitable rejection by her husband and his ultimate departure for something better; wasn't it always a foregone conclusion?

Her trepidation today feels less acute. Perhaps a bliss hangover from the residual THC she is still metabolizing. She is less anxious about the outcome. She just wants to know. Looking out the window, daydreaming various scenarios as she rides in the back of the car, she realizes it makes her more sad than angry that he would choose some bullshit, *shiksa*, chiclet-smile, bottle-blond, over her. She doesn't know where these angry lists of adjectives are coming from, but they continue to populate her inner monologue.

She has to admit to an element of terrifying thrill when she considers leaving him. The idea of moving about in the world under her own direction and name, not the wife-of, or daughter-in-law-of, is lusty and freeing. This is, of course, impossible. She loves Stephen, her boys—the small precious family she created that is her very own. Still, there are those nagging flashbacks of Buzz Baruch's blue-green *ojus*.

Imagining herself single, the old butterflies come back. The same terrifying excitement she experienced when she ran off to New York to escape Aurora. She was eighteen years old, with seventy-five dollars in her pocket. It was stupid, reckless, dangerous—but she knows she still has it in her if she is required to dig deep and resurrect her most defiant independence.

The one thing she cannot do without, not for one second, is being the mother of Josh and Simon. This is the only part of her identity that is nonnegotiable. She cannot fathom an existence where she is not Josh and Simon's mom when she enters the room.

Watching the world go by from the back of the car, it's been so long since she's been in LA, and she was never really that familiar with it. The Uber pulls onto Rodeo Drive. Leyla checks the map on her phone and sees that Rodeo leads into Santa Monica Boulevard, which than leads to Wilshire and straight to the Beverly Hilton.

She remembers back to when she was younger, how streets like Rodeo Drive thrilled her—the obscene wealth, glamour, fashion, and jewelry. Stephen loves to buy Leyla jewelry. He's always been lavish and romantic. For Hanukah, her birthday, their anniversary, and Valentine's Day, he never fails to present her with a beautiful box containing an exquisite, expensive piece of jewelry.

Cartier is his favorite. She smiles now at how much it means to her. The jewelry gifting makes her feel young, beautiful, desirable, intoxicated. From the very beginning of their courtship, she felt enchantingly owned.

The world is different now. It's all about equality, #MeToo, cancel culture, and toxic masculinity. Young women have different goals and values. But for Leyla, the expensive gifts make her feel feminine, cherished, and loved. She knows it may appear shallow or trite, but they are pure symbols of love and security for her.

She relishes the feeling of walking along the street in any given city where they travel—New York, Paris, London. Stephen will walk her to the door as if to surprise her, as if she doesn't expect it and want it. He opens the door, holds it for her, and allows her to walk in first, Mrs. Stephen Rothstein.

She recalls the way she practiced her signature as soon as they were engaged, deciding how to curl the capital R, making loops with her pen on the page. She couldn't wait to drop Feldenburg—drop-kick the curse of that name.

The jewelers they visit pull items out of the display cases for her to examine. She and Stephen *ooh* and *ah*.

"Oh no, I couldn't, it's too much," she always says, feigning humility.

"No, choose one. I want to," Stephen insists.

He was her Prince Charming. Fuck Peter-Pan complex. She wanted to be saved. If he was a predator, she was his willing prey.

As they got older, the gifts were markers for milestones. A Panthere watch for their tenth anniversary, an infinity ring on the birth of Simon.

The last addition to her collection, a rose-gold-and-diamond Love bracelet came on Mother's Day. Her collection tells the story of their life together. It's a materialistic, old-school, patriarchic dynamic, but given Leyla's origin story of dinner charged on debt at the pharmacy, the ritual was enthralling.

Looking out the window at the lavish shops they pass on Rodeo Drive, daydreaming her history of romantic jewelry gifts from Stephen, she sees the unmistakable deep-red awning and large golden C of the Cartier store coming toward her from the next block.

She stops smiling, remembering why she's here in the first place. The image of her Jewish Prince Charming, whooshing and swooshing in Aspen with Hallie Monrowe, CannaShiksa 2.0, returns to her thoughts.

Then the Uber passes in front of the store, and she sees them. There is no mistaking the thick pate of salt-and-pepper hair, accented with carbon-grey Oliver People frames. Stephen has a distinctive swirling cowlick on the back of his head, a spiral growth pattern like his father, as do both Josh and Simon.

Standing next to him is a head of blonde hair, fashioned in unoriginal beachy waves, long, frayed, dried-out hair extensions with a hard middle part. It's Hallie. She's leaning her body into him, shoulder brushing shoulder.

Leyla feels a sickening surge of pure unbridled adrenaline releasing into her body. There it is, unequivocal, the evidence she has been looking for, but not hoping for. Her heart is shattering. Stephen and Hallie are inside the Beverly Hills Cartier store, together. They are head-to-head looking intently down at something on top of a display case. She swallows hard, then takes a deep Ujjayi breath to keep from throwing up.

"Ss . . . ss . . . stop . . . Stop . . . STOP!" She whispers it at first, then repeats the word until she screams. The driver pulls to the curb.

Leyla grabs at the door handle, pressing the button on the lever, inadvertently locking and unlocking it multiple times. She tumbles out of the car and runs toward the store. The driver is yelling at her, "You must cancel the ride!" She turns back and fumbles with the phone to do as he says; it falls to the ground, smashing the screen. Her hands are shaking violently.

She looks around to see if anyone is staring, afraid that she will be outed by the screaming Uber driver. She has just enough sense remaining after the shock of sighting them to realize she must consider strategy. If she bursts into the store without a plan, she will be on the defensive, not them.

She's trembling. What is there to learn now? He's in *their* favorite jewelry store playing Prince Charming, but to someone else. She spotted them yesterday at the conference, and now here they were. This is third-grade math. Stephen plus Hallie plus one night equals Cartier.

There's no way she can enter that store undetected. She might be able to avoid recognition by Hallie, but not by her own husband.

She wants to get close enough to take a picture, so he can't lie and deny when she confronts him. She wonders if the smashed screen will affect the quality of the photo; will it be admissible in court? She doesn't even have an attorney. Will I need an attorney? Leyla is reeling. She needs to hear what they're saying. Her head is swimming, entertaining a thousand different approaches. She needs to get closer, so she darts into the closest door, the store directly adjacent to Cartier.

She didn't pay attention to the signage. It's the Tory Burch store. Not really my style. She moves through it like an assassin, mission-driven in forward motion on pure rage and adrenaline. At the accessories display, she grabs a pair of large, round, black plastic sunglasses, then pulls a shiny, Day-Glo-yellow, full-length puffer coat from a display rack. There's no extra-small, only mediums—gargantuan on Leyla. On the way to the register, she grabs a yellow crocheted bucket hat to match the puffer.

Why am I trying to match? Catching a glance at an image of herself in the mirror, she looks ridiculous. Leyla spends her days in a curated uniform of understatement, black mock turtleneck (long-sleeved for fall/winter, short-sleeved for spring/summer), distressed boyfriend jeans (Rag & Bone), Nike Air Jordans, LV Neverfull, and a high, tight ponytail.

She yanks the elastic band out from her hair and gives it a shake. The heat of LA and the untimely hot flash she is experiencing have turned it into a mop of curls again, her "Jewish girl" waves rebelling against her smoothing products and exploding in wild ringlets from the poorly chosen crochet bucket hat. Though the added obfuscation is helpful and vital.

An array of brightly colored silk scarves is spread on a table, arranged with clunky costume jewelry. She snatches an orange-and-black silk scarf, patterned with the TB logo, and wraps it around her neck. Leyla approaches a salesperson and hands them her credit card. The woman taps the card on the terminal and scans the tags, not bothering to look up. Without being asked, she pulls a pair of scissors from the drawer and efficiently snips all tags from Leyla's bizarre ensemble.

Leyla supposes she can't be the first woman on Rodeo Drive to need an emergency disguise. This is Beverly Hills, after all, rife with people out shopping while recovering from facial "procedures," stalking paramours for evidence of infidelity, or paparazzi lying in wait to surprise a Kardashian or two. She asks for a shopping bag and puts her purse inside, so Stephen won't recognize it. The shaking has not subsided.

She stuffs her hands deep into her pockets. Stephen would recognize her hands. He'd see her wedding band and enormous emerald-cut solitaire.

★ ★ ★

Stephen and Leyla fell in love and got engaged in a romantic rush. There was no ring or elaborately planned knee-on-the-ground proposal. He swept her away for a romantic weekend in Maui, the first time Leyla had ever been to Hawaii. They were sitting on the beach watching the sunset.

"Say something romantic to me," Leyla demanded.

"Will you be my wife?" was his response.

"Will you be my husband?" she countered. She didn't care about a ring. She didn't even think of it at the time.

When they returned from the trip, Leyla heard through the grapevine that her father was on perhaps his fourth or fifth financial rock bottom. His third marriage, to Katrine Devolay, was falling apart. Stepmother number one, Icky Vicki, had dumped him hard after cleaning him out of the proceeds of the sale of Aurora's beloved house. He was deep in debt and out of assets to sell or strip.

R.H.F.'s beloved mother, Fanny Doll, came through and gave him her exquisite diamond solitaire to sell and save his ass, even though it was he who had destroyed his father's business and screwed them out of a comfortable retirement in the process. His parents had to depend on the charity of a friend who owned an apartment building in Cow Hollow, and they moved from their grand, bay-view penthouse on Russian Hill into a modest two-bedroom in the Marina, continuing to hold their heads high. Then nearing the end of their years, with truly nothing left, Fanny Doll had given her son the ring off her finger. Fanny's ring was a flawless three-full-carat emerald cut in a platinum setting with two large baguettes.

When Leyla mentioned the sad story to Stephen, he marched right down to Sydney Mobell's, where R.H.F. had anonymously put the ring up for sale. Syd was a local jeweler known to help Jews in trouble by discreetly selling their family heirlooms. Stephen called ahead and told them to pull the ring from the case. He bought the magnificent heirloom for Leyla, sight unseen, without haggling. Neither one of them had any idea about the size or quality. Leyla had never seen the stone; Fanny Doll rarely wore it because she could no longer afford to insure it.

Leyla thought it the most romantic thing ever. He was truly her knight in shining armor. He saved the family heirloom, and she relished the irony of R.H.F. being bailed out and outed by her dashing husband-to-be. Stephen did all of this without questioning any of the tawdriness of the whole dirty Feldenburg family spectacle.

★ ★ ★

Now, sufficiently, albeit outrageously, disguised, Leyla walks out of the store and turns toward the entrance next door. Stephen and Hallie are standing against the counter. The salesperson has a small velvet tray on top of the glass case. Leyla tucks her face deeper into the scarf and yanks up the collar of the puffer coat. She turns around and pushes her back into the door to avoid taking her hands out of her pockets as she enters the regal domain of the Beverly Hills Cartier store.

Hallie is leaning in very close to Stephen. Leyla can't see her face, but she can see Stephen's face in the reflection in the mirror behind the salesperson. He has that self-satisfied look he gets when jewelry shopping, enjoying himself, in charge. The salesperson is fawning over him. No one knows better than Leyla that right now Stephen feels powerful, successful, masculine, desirable. His ego is on a feeding frenzy.

Hallie's phone goes off. Leyla hears her excuse herself to take the call. Hallie turns in the direction of Leyla, who panics, pivots, and pretends to admire watches in the wall case. A salesperson approaches.

"May I help you?"

Leyla shakes her head, her face buried deep within the oversized puffer collar, obscured by the scarf and hat.

"Do let me know if I can be of assistance," he says, and smiles.

Hallie is standing a few feet away. She takes out her phone and answers.

"Hey. Yeah. Still in LA," she says into the phone. "No. Yeah.

FINE, I'M A TERRIBLE PERSON | 163

I spoke at the panel yesterday, it was fine. I'm with Stephen
Rothstein, at Cartier if you can believe it. No, don't get all
excited. He said he wanted to 'show me something' at breakfast.
Nope, it was a total bust. He's here selecting the most gorgeous
pieces for his fucking *wife*. It's all he talks about. Jesus, what
a waste of time. Did I ever get it wrong. He wanted my opinion on jewelry for his wife! What a piece of work. I practically
threw myself at him. We went to dinner. We drank wine. He
wanted to know what was in the pipeline for HDD. I thought,
cool he's pretending to be professional. Then he couldn't stop
talking about how much he loved Happy. I thought he was just
being charming, you know, interested in me—not my business.
I totally thought, this is happening. Then we went back to the
hotel. I mean; I tried. I was braless, for fuck's sake. I showered
and shaved! I barely ate any of my dinner so my stomach would
be flat. I was ready. We walked to the elevators. I asked if he
wanted to come up. He looked at me like I was speaking a foreign language, shook my hand, and said goodnight.

"Then he texted me and asked if I wanted to grab breakfast
this morning, said he wanted my advice about something. I
thought, okay, maybe I had the vibe wrong last night. Maybe
he's taking it slow and needs a firmer hand to guide him out of
his fidelity and into my bed. We had coffee. Then he asked me
if I would take a walk with him. We walked to Rodeo, and he
walks into Cartier! He asks if I would help him decide between
some bracelets for his wife. This is ridiculous. What does he
take me for? I'm outta here. The guy loves his wife. Boy, I can
pick 'em. I know, I know. Don't say it.

"Anyway, so, some important things. The chef will be deliv-
ering Happy's food for the week. Make sure you check the
delivery before you sign. It must be the organic, custom-blended,
vegetarian, plant-based protein, hypoallergenic, nonGMO. The
last time you signed you did not check, and it was not the

vegetarian blend, and Happy had to eat grocery-store food for two days while we waited for them to blend a fresh batch. Please pay closer attention to important things like this. I need to be able to trust that you are taking care of these critical things when I am on the road.

"Anything else before I go? Kallie? Oh, yeah, how's she doing? Great. Cool. No, not now. Tell her Mommy can't talk right now, she's working. What show? South Park? It's a cartoon? Parental advisory? Yeah, whatever, she can watch whatever she wants. Yes, I know how old my own daughter is, and I do not appreciate your tone. I'll text you when I land."

She puts the phone in her bag and walks to the counter where Stephen is hemming and hawing. "Hm . . . mmm," Hallie says. "Yeah, I'm sure she'll love it. Listen, I've got to get going." Hallie says impatiently.

Leyla leaves the store. She tears off the hat and sunglasses as she emerges into the bright LA sunshine and continues to walk while peeling off the coat. There's a homeless guy spread out in front of the Rodeo collection stores; she hands them all to him except the scarf, thinking it adds a little pizzaz to her black mock turtleneck.

She pulls out her phone and texts Stephen:

Hi U, don't worry about us, just text me when you can.

CHAPTER THIRTEEN

Asperar y no venir, son kosas ki hazen morir.
You can die waiting for nothing to happen.

★ ★ ★

Aurora, Estrella, and the kids are sitting in front of the house eating ice cream when Leyla pulls up. It's every kid's best day when they get to have their pick of the ice-cream truck, and Simon and Josh are relishing the experience. There are no ice-cream trucks in Marin. The steep driveways of the Rothstein's exclusive Kent Woodlands neighborhood, with its dazzling views and seven-figure median home prices, are not amenable to ice-cream-truck culture.

Leyla never allows midday ice cream, anyway. A good report card or high test score might be a rare exception. Even then, she never permits cheap, commercial options like those on an ice-cream truck, with offerings named for violent nonfood items like Bomb Blastsicles or Cannonball Crunches, chock full of chemical additives and multisyllabic fillers.

When she gets out of the car. Josh and Simon run toward her at full speed and wrap themselves around her. Standing there together on the front lawn, she soaks up the clump of love the three of them form.

"We bought you a Creamsicle. I saved it for you," Simon says, and pulls a bright orange, cellophane wrapped pack of melted mush from his back pocket and hands it to her. "I remembered how you said you always wanted one as a kid," he says, looking up at her with his father's olive-green eyes.

Leyla starts to cry. She takes it from him, tears the wrapper and slurps the creamy, warm combination of artificial orange flavor and air-filled lab-made nondairy fat. It's sublime.

"Thank you very much," she says, after wiping her chin with the back of her hand.

They sit down on the front step to finish their ice creams. Estrella dozes on her lawn chair.

"I thought you guys were going to the movies?" Leyla asks.

"We waited a long time for the ice-cream truck," Simon answers. Josh has his headphones on now.

"*Siete te.*" Aurora says and pats the stoop beside her. Leyla trades places with Josh next to Aurora. Simon moves to sit on her lap; then Josh moves to sit on Simon.

"Can I do my blessings for you? I learned a new one, and I want to show you first before anyone else," Josh says from Simon's lap.

"Sure, sweetheart."

"*Barchu et Adonai chamevooooooooraaaach.*" He chants.

"Awesome, Joshy!" Leyla applauds. Josh beams over his shoulder at Simon after his mother's acknowledgement.

"Mom, can we play with our Nintendo Switches? While you *siete te* with Grandma?" Simon asks.

"Yes," Leyla answers.

They run inside. Unprompted, Estrella wakes from her slumber, hoists herself up, folds her lawn chair, and follows the boys inside.

"Why you back so soon? Everything okay? What's with the scarf?" Aurora eyes Leyla with an arched brow. She is suspicious of her daughter's caloric indifference with the Creamsicle and the snazzy and colorful silk scarf.

"Everything's fine." Leyla answers.

"*A dio, el amor es dolor de kulo ke no desha durmir a dinguno*—Love is a pain in the ass that doesn't let anyone sleep. You know, my mother—your grandmother—warned me about *Shumechus mi alma*. I didn't listen."

"I know, Mom. I remember the spitting. I was the one who always cleaned the floor."

"Look, *ija*, Stephen has some good qualities. But you have to wonder what a guy like that sees in you."

The comment lands like a blow to her chest. Leyla turns and looks directly at her mother.

"Here we go."

"Well, I'm just saying. You're no Barbie Doll. Men like Stephen have choices, sweetheart. He is a very handsome man."

"You've said that before, Mom. I guess I never really heard it. You think he is too good for me. What's with the Barbie Doll reference? You sound like my father."

"I'm just saying, a guy like that and a girl like you—well, let's face it, you aren't young anymore, and we certainly don't have anything to offer money-wise. You shouldn't be surprised if he seeks greener pastures."

"Greener pastures? We? What the hell does all that mean, Mom?"

"You have to work to keep a guy like that, *mi alma*."

"Keep a guy? We're married?" Leyla responds.

"I mean, well, you know what I mean."

"No, I don't, Mom. What do you mean?"

"I am just saying I've been there. Girls like you and me—well, you are not tall, you are not young, you have no money of your own. God knows I was where you are now."

"You're saying that is why dad left you? Because you were

like me? Or I am like you? And what's with the 'money of my own' comment? Stephen doesn't control me that way. It's *our* money."

"Oh, Lailuchi, don't be naïve. It would not be easy for any woman to hold onto a guy like Stephen Rothstein. He's got a pedigree and family money—big family money. *Avrete los ojus antes ke te los avran otros*—Open your eyes before others open them for you," She says while pointing her finger at Leyla.

"Why are you saying this to me? Why do you always talk this way to me? Why do you want me to believe I am not good enough for my own husband, Aurora?"

"Oh no, *ijika, mi alma*, sweetheart, I would never say that. It's just . . ."

"It's just what?"

"Men are men, sweetheart, and they only want one thing, and you have to be realistic."

"What makes you think my husband wouldn't want that one thing from me or with me?"

"Oh, Leyla, don't be disgusting."

"Why is that disgusting? Why do you always think sex is disgusting and something 'men want'?"

"You know I think the world of you, my darling, *ermozu*. I tell everyone; my daughter is exceptional. *Pu pu mashallah.* I am just saying be prepared because I know *men*. They're cheaters, and I love you, and I want the best for you. You know, sweetheart, you can tell a lot about a man by the way he treats his mother-in-law."

"*Ah dio*, Aurora," Leyla chuckles.

Aurora had verbally undermined Leyla's love affairs since her first boyfriend, freshman year in high school. She has deftly slung lovingly supportive insults at Leyla since she hit puberty. There was always a "don't trust men," "they are bad," "they don't really love you," "they only want sex, and sex is dirty" ethos to the wisdom she doled out.

R.H. Feldenburg was consistent in his disdain and ridicule throughout Leyla's childhood, always ready to point out what she lacked in his estimation—somehow, Leyla failed to see that Aurora did the same thing, just with a different spin.

Aurora emotionally positioned herself on Leyla's side when it came to R.H.F.'s insults and slights. She took an "us against him" tactic. It made Leyla feel safe as a child. Aurora was all she had; their alliance felt like a fortress against the threat of navigating the world without any family at all. It was in Leyla's best interest to deny the obvious truth of her mother's narcissism. Aurora sought advantage by deflating Leyla's sense of self.

It was in Aurora's best interest to make her daughter feel ugly, unlucky, and unlovable, reenforcing and solidifying the bond as the mother-daughter duo of rejected outsiders. "You and me against the world, kiddo," she used to say.

Leyla feels stunned and awake. Aurora hasn't changed, but Leyla has. There is a shift.

"*Ija*, I need a little help," Aurora begins.

Leyla shudders. Aurora never needs "a little help." The help Aurora needs is convoluted, ridiculous, elaborate but never just a little. Each absurd scheme she proposes, in Aurora's fantasy world, will somehow result in money.

There were the gold-dipped roses, a shipping container full, she'd asked Leyla to "help" her buy from China. The plan was to flip them quickly at the flea market for Valentine's Day. They arrived as a giant clump of rotting, gilded, garden debris, melted and reformed by the heating and cooling of the container stuck at the customs port for three months.

Then, there were the rainbow satin visors she ordered from a "source" in Tijuana. They would stylishly shield sunlight and

UV rays. Aurora planned to bejewel them. Too bad they didn't handle perspiration well and leaked fabric dye down the face of the wearer.

Aurora's schemes never result in anything but aggravation and expense for Leyla. She'd lost thousands of dollars and hours of her life to Aurora's endlessly imaginative ploys for enrichment. She was trying to learn how to say no, working hard with E to set boundaries, but she failed time and again. Her mother somehow always worked her black magic, roping Leyla into her farcical plots for profit.

Leyla knows Aurora's pitches are ridiculous. She embarks upon each caper with her eyes open and appropriate skepticism. She isn't stupid, but she does hold a tiny modicum of hope that one might result in a windfall, just once. If Aurora ever hits a home run and makes a little on the side, it would relieve a stressor between Leyla and Stephen.

* * *

They've had more than a few arguments regarding Aurora's monthly check. Stephen never questions or expresses any concern over Leyla's spending, ever. The sky is the limit for her and the kids, but he makes it clear that he is not thrilled to be shelling out a monthly payment for his mother-in-law, whom he considers to be toxic.

"She doesn't care about you. She takes advantage of you. She never protected or provided for you. You were her cook and housekeeper when you were a kid, she flirted inappropriately with your boyfriends, made them run her errands and play Mr. Fix-It, and now she expects your rich husband to pay her rent. She is divisive. She uses you and brings you down. Why can't you see that? She compliments you while insulting you, she undermines your confidence and security, and draws you in to her schemes. She's always trying to get whatever she can from you—from everyone, for that matter. She is a sociopath. A classic narcissist," Stephen lectured her the last time they argued.

"Since when did you become a licensed psychologist? Now you're an expert in mother-daughter codependency? I wasn't aware that you were qualified to diagnose personality disorders," Leyla responded.

"Leyla, I love you. You and I would not be arguing right now if it were not for your mother. Think about that for a minute."

Arguments like this made Leyla defensive and ashamed. He was right, but it was too painful to admit it to herself, let alone her husband. It was never easy to be Aurora's daughter. It was becoming apparent that Aurora was impacting Leyla's marriage in a destructive way, and yet here she is again, listening to Aurora's latest ruse.

"So, what's your pitch this time, Mom?"

Aurora begins. She tells Leyla about the first early-morning phone call and the nurse's claim that she is the next of kin. She describes the condition of Esther's apartment, all the purses and her plan to sell them. She tells Leyla how Eliezer is going to help her with his friend Craig and maybe a neighbor next-door.

She reveals the lack of any written will, the unearthing of the deed for the cemetery plot, and finally, Eliezer's instructive lesson on liquidating it and the valuations they found on the internet.

"Wow. That's a lot in just a few days. Even for you."

"Leyluchi, *mi alma*, you are so smart and so capable. *Merci munchos*—thank you so much for helping your poor mama."

"Just so I'm clear, you want to figure out how to sell your dead stepmother's burial plot?"

"*Ija, mi korazon*—daughter my heart. She left it to me."

"She left it to you. She left *you* her burial plot. Uh, just a shot in the dark here, but wouldn't she want to be buried in it?"

"Well, she probably did, but there is no money left for all of that. Evidently, this happens to people. They run out of money at the end."

"No doubt she spent it on all those handbags."

"I am the next of kin. I don't see why I can't do what I want with what has been left to me."

Leyla is tempted to launch into a lecture on ethics but stifles herself. Aurora is eternally broke. Leonard, Aurora's old goat of a father with the eight (or so) wives, never did much for her. Robert H. Feldenburg, her first and only husband, stripped her clean of the meager assets they shared in their brief and miserable marriage. Who is she to begrudge her mother a little found bonus bounty? This is how her train of thought tends to derail every time.

"Probably should start with Forest Lawn. Let's give them a call and inquire about next steps," Leyla says.

"Oh, my darling. *Ermozu*, my brilliant, beautiful daughter. *Mashallah*."

The more Aurora presents herself as helpless and hapless, the more capable Leyla becomes, another one of Aurora's parenting strategies.

Everything that seems difficult and complicated for Aurora is simple by Leyla's definition and easily within her abilities. It always seems like a quick and painless task—a call, an email, a check, an errand, a Google search. Leyla approaches Aurora's problems with a "what's the big deal" attitude, but somehow things always go sideways.

"Let's just go out to the cemetery, present the deed to the plot, and ask for the proper paperwork to transfer title. We put it up for sale, and you cash out," Leyla drills it down to an effortless errand. She maps the cemetery on her phone. It isn't too far away. "No better time than the present. Let's go now."

"My darling girl. You are a genius. I tell everyone—my

daughter is incredible, brilliant, and beautiful. Mashallah, I knew I could count on you. *Aidi vre!*—Let's go, you!" Aurora says excitedly.

"Go get the deed. I'll call an Uber. The kids are happy here with Estrella and their video games."

CHAPTER FOURTEEN

Puedes deskujer tus amigos ma no tus parientes.
You can choose your friends, but not your relations.

★ ★ ★

On the way to Forest Lawn, Leyla googles "how to sell a cemetery plot." Amused, she thinks, Nothing like a little mother-daughter time. A lot of information comes up. It doesn't look all that uncommon for heirs to disregard the last wishes of their loved ones to cash in paid-in-full eternal resting places. As it turns out, cemetery plots are a lucrative real-estate sector, a good old-fashioned cash grab. What do ya know? It's not as obscure a project as she had assumed.

Leyla has never witnessed a burial. When her grandparents on the Feldenburg side passed away, she was not "invited" to their funerals. They had plots at Home of Peace in Colma, where well-to-do Jews in San Francisco are laid to rest.

R.H.F. was married to Katrine, wife number three, during the era when Ezra and Fannie Feldenburg passed away. Leyla made Katrine feel "uncomfortable." Leyla's father was happy to comply with his wife's wishes to keep his daughter at a distance. Leyla was excluded from their funerals as well as most other Feldenburg family occasions.

It was painful when Leyla saw photos of Thanksgiving and Passover holidays framed on the shelves of her grandparent's apartment during her infrequent solo visits before they each died. The pictures depicted large happy family gatherings with faces of aunts, uncles, and cousins whom she recognized—her own brother Branan smiling, his arm draped over his father's shoulder at the corner of the table. (R.H. had two other brothers with wives and children.) The pictures showed long tables and bountiful spreads, the frame so full of people they needed to squish in to fit everyone in the shot. Smiling faces, shoulders, elbows all scrunched together, holding up their glasses, toasting to the day's happy occasion. It was everything Leyla longed for. She wanted family. A sea of familiar Feldenburg faces all together, except for Leyla's.

She had family; she just wasn't a part of it.

When Floru, Aurora's mother, died, fourteen-year-old Leyla took care of all the details. As always, Aurora had no money. Leyla came up with the idea of cremation and scattering the ashes at sea. She saw an ad for The Neptune Society in a magazine in the waiting room of the hospital where Floru lay dying of emphysema. It was a good solution. It was the cheapest option, and she thought that maybe by scattering Floru's remains in the San Francisco Bay, her grandmother would somehow ride the currents back to the Aegean and her beautiful homeland, the island of Rhodes. It was romantic and dramatic, in that way teenage girls tend to be. Aurora bought in to the plan immediately. So long as someone else took care of the details, Aurora didn't care how it went down, but it wasn't really a funeral, a true burial in a cemetery.

The Neptune society was supposed to handle the "scattering at sea" part, but Aurora only had enough for the bare-minimum cremation package. Leyla had a boyfriend whose uncle had a boat and agreed to take them out on the bay. They were supposed to have permits and proper paperwork but pretended ignorance and hoped to avoid the harbor master.

Leyla tossed a bunch of roses she picked up at Safeway into the water, and the boyfriend dumped the ashes from the plastic bag that The Neptune Society had handed them after they handed over the check. It was quick and cheap, but not totally without grace. They had no relatives to help them grieve, sit shiva, tear clothes, and cover mirrors. No one dropped off casseroles and coffee cake.

She reads on her phone that the person at the cemetery who handles "property" (plots) is called the sexton.

"We have to find the sexton," she tells Aurora as they pull into Forest Lawn.

"The what?" Aurora asks.

"Never mind."

They enter the front door of the Forest Lawn Cemetery and Mortuary reception where the driver drops them. There is a metal signpost in the lobby that lists the services for the day, white magnetized letters stuck on a black horizontal grid. There is a dearth of o's. *Sue Fishik ff's mem rial service is scheduled for M nday at twelve n n.*

The walls and furnishings of the interior are dark, swathed in various gradations of brown. The room is cold. Aurora gives Leyla a smug and vindicated nod, pulling her collar up around her chin, knowing she exhibited good judgment in delaying them by going back for her mink coat when they left the house.

A tall, mature woman approaches. She is wearing a dark-burgundy wool, skirted suit with a mauve silk blouse. It has a large, loose bow at the neck. Her dyed hair is a dull brown, and she wears it in a helmet style that is both timeless and outdated. The overall effect of her personal presentation is serene joylessness. Leyla thinks she looks precisely appropriate.

"How may I be of assistance?" the woman asks.

"We're looking for the sexton's office," Leyla responds.

"Of course, right this way." The woman gestures elegantly, unfolding her arm in a swooping motion. Leyla and Aurora turn and see a dark hallway. They walk in the direction of the woman's hand, Aurora following behind her daughter, and come to another metal sign that says: *ffice.*

I wonder what happened to all the *o*'s?

Aurora stays behind Leyla, allowing her daughter to continue in the lead. They enter the office.

There is a young woman sitting behind a high countertop of dark-brown faux-wood paneling, bundled up against the subarctic thermostat setting.

She wears a beige turtleneck with matching beige knit scarf. Her long blondish-beige hair is worn loose in large waves that fall around her shoulders, parted in the middle. She looks up and smiles with a closed mouth.

"Hello, how can I help?"

"We are here to inquire about a family burial plot," Leyla answers.

"To purchase?"

"No. We own the plot," Leyla responds.

"I see. Is this your personal plot? Or are you here representing a family member?"

"It belongs to my mother. But she is still alive. Obviously she is still alive, I mean here we are. Here she is. So, it's hers, but it's not for her. If you know what I mean," Leyla's words and mouth are getting away from her. She clears her throat and begins again. "We are interested in liquidating a recently inherited asset." Leyla gestures toward Aurora. She realizes she is imitating the first woman's languid directional gesture. She puts her hand down.

"I see," the woman says. "Allow me to direct you to our property department. They are charged with transfer inquiries."

"Are they available today?" Leyla asks.

"We are always available. The needs for our services require that we not be restricted to conventional business hours. Life goes on, or rather does not go on, if you will," she says solemnly.

"Of course," Leyla nods, mirroring the woman's solemnity.

"If you would be so kind as to provide me with the deed, title, and legal identification? Once I complete the verification and validation of your paperwork, you can move ahead and speak with our property department."

Leyla looks at Aurora, raises her eyebrows in encouragement, and nods. Aurora remains immobile, staring with a blank face at the woman behind the desk.

"The documentation?" the beige woman repeats herself.

Leyla raises her voice, as if she were giving directions to her children. "Mom, give the woman the deed."

Aurora pulls the envelope out of her purse and hands it over the counter to the woman with a manicured flourish. The beige woman excavates the deed from the envelope, using only her fingertips, and examines it. She appears to find it in order.

"I'll just a make a copy." She turns and puts the document on the copy machine behind her. "This is a deed and certificate of endowment care. Now I'll need to make a copy of your identification?"

"Endowment care?" Leyla inquires.

"Yes. Endowment care means that the original owner invested extra funds for the ongoing maintenance and beautification of the site. A trust fund, if you will, for the continued conservation and preservation of their eternal resting place, in perpetuity," the beige woman answers.

"Oh," Aurora exclaims. She raises her eyebrows, nods at Leyla and reaches over the counter to hand the woman her expired driver's license.

The beige woman takes the license, once again fingertips only.

"Oh, I see here that the name on the deed is Mrs. Esther Hmans? This driver's license belongs to Mrs. Aurora H. Feldenburg.

"Yes of course. The H is for Hmans. My maiden name is Hmans. The H is silent. Esther was my stepmother. She died last week," Aurora responds.

"Oh. I see. Well, I'm very sorry for your loss. I sincerely apologize for the misunderstanding. Allow me to direct you to burials."

"I do not want to bury her in it. I want to sell it," Aurora says.

"Well, Mrs. Feldenburg, or rather Mrs. H. Feldenburg, this deed is in the name of Mrs. Esther Hmans and, unless you are going to inter the deceased in her fully endowed eternal resting place, I need to see where this property was willed or deeded to you. As she is, or was, the property owner of record and I simply cannot—"

Aurora cut her off, "I am the next of kin."

"Yes, of course. I understand completely. You simply need to provide the legal last will and testament, trust certification, or other valid estate documentation that shows you as the rightful beneficiary. Then there are a few simple steps we need to take, in order to convey title, and then you may do as you wish. Keep it for your own future needs. Transfer ownership to a loved one perhaps or, as you say, sell it." The beige woman looked up from the documents she was holding in her hands and directed her gaze at Aurora.

"Yes. I know. There is my ID," Aurora said, thrusting her open hand toward the woman.

"Unfortunately, Mrs. Feldenburg, anyone other than Mrs. Hmans herself—who I might add, would also have to present her valid, legal, and current identification if she were alive and wished to transfer her property, God rest her soul— must prove they are the rightfully designated, legally empowered heir. Is there a will perhaps that establishes that this was legally deeded to you?"

"The H stands for Hmans," Aurora responds.

"Mom, I thought you said Esther left this to you?"

"The woman said I was the next of kin when she called," Aurora responds; she is glaring at the beige woman.

"You might be next of kin, but that's not legally binding proof of an inheritance of property, Mom," Leyla sighed. She is regretting once again assuming a baseline of sanity from her mother and not vetting evidence and legality before they embarked on this quest, chalking it up to the THC/dopamine infused rose-colored glasses she was wearing this morning. More than likely, it was Aurora's ability to weave her magical siren spells that got people to do things for her. Why did I agree to this? Why-oh-why do I always slide into this nonsense with my mother?

"The H stands for Hmans," Aurora repeats. This time with an added soupçon of vocal aggression.

"Pardon me," the beige woman says and hands the ID back over the counter to Aurora. "I'm so sorry, perhaps you're not aware, but your license is expired, quite some time ago in fact," she adds with a crinkle of her nose as if there were suddenly an unpleasant aroma in the room.

"Thank you for pointing that out." Aurora grimaces at the beige woman. She reaches over the counter to retrieve her license. Leyla bypasses Aurora's arm and snaps it out of the woman's hand before Aurora can get to it. She sees the expiration date.

Aurora looks at Leyla, then turns to the women behind the counter, and gives her the "look." The same look she used when

Leyla was a little girl, and they went to the dry cleaners. The manager would inform Aurora she couldn't have her clothes until she paid her past-due bill. Aurora would thin out her lips and roll them together like someone who has just finished applying lipstick. Then narrow her eyes and say: "I've lived in this community for over twenty years," as if the tenure of her residency somehow forgave the financial responsibility to pay for dry cleaning.

This, or some other version of this scenario, was a constant in Leyla's young life—whether at the drycleaners, Abe's pharmacy, or the dentist. Aurora maintained that her "position" or "tenure" in the community should "command" respect, and that respect allowed for minor "delinquencies" every now and again. Aurora considered any attempt at legitimate bill collection a flagrant display of disrespect and responded to the offense accordingly.

Aurora opens her mouth now to give the women in beige a version of "the lecture." Leyla preempts her mother's spiel, puts her hand up in the universal gesture of "that's enough," and says, "Thank you."

She reaches and grabs a handful of the shoulder of Aurora's mink coat in her fist and drags her mother out of the room. Leyla marches Aurora down the hall. They pass one of the small chapels where a service is underway. A small gathering of mourners is seated in front of a large wooden casket with large, ornate brass handles. Heaping, large mounds of flowers on top of and surrounding the coffin fill the room with a nauseatingly sweet, overwhelming scent. Aurora begins to sneeze.

Leyla is livid. She orders an Uber. Once they are in the car she lets loose on her mother, "You said you had proof!"

"I do have proof."

"You do not have proof. There is no will. Your name is not on the deed. Your name isn't anywhere."

"My name is on my license."

"Your name is Feldenburg, and your license is expired."

"The H is for Hmans."

"I swear to God, Aurora, if you say that one more time . . ."

Aurora continues her farcical sneezing. She leans forward and asks the Uber driver for a tissue.

"How could you drag me out here? How could you? You knew there was no proof. You knew your license is expired. Why on earth would you put me in this position?"

"Leyla, where does all this anger come from? Why are you always so angry? Maybe you should talk to that shrink about your anger issues. Maybe all those crazy supplements aren't working?"

"Are you kidding me? My crazy supplements? It's my supplements that are crazy? Did you ever think that for maybe, for just one minute, Aurora, you could think about something other than yourself? Maybe just for one moment you could think about what it feels like to be dragged into these ridiculous—"

"Oh, look, there's Home of Peace. That's where Papa is. Can we go?"

Leyla was dumbfounded. She turned and looked out the window and saw a sign on the freeway exit for Home of Peace Cemetery. She knows her mother has relatives buried there, including her father, Leon, and a cousin or two, so it does make sense that it would grab her attention.

It was a typical display of Aurora's convenient ADD and conflict-aversion tactics; the woman has the attention span of a swallow combined with a fine-tuned ability to avoid any acknowledgement of discord with her daughter. Aurora's capacity for obfuscation and redirection is unmatched.

Leyla realized she should know better than to expect anything that resembled reason or any evidence of accountability from her mother.

CHAPTER FIFTEEN

Mas poko saves major es.
The less you know, the better.

★ ★ ★

They turn off the freeway to the entrance of Home of Peace. Leyla was inclined to deny her mother this bonus stop when she requested the detour. Tired and worn out from the fiasco at Forest Lawn, her mother's daft boldness never ceases to amaze her. "The H is for Hmans." Good god, does she really think that will suffice as evidence of property ownership?

It's difficult to determine whether Aurora is a complete idiot or a brilliantly bold manipulator. Leyla has always assumed it was a little of both.

She knows better than to facilitate the pursuit of the spindly threads of Aurora's screwball attempts toward solvency. Yet here she is. Here she was. She is sick of Aurora, but also sick of herself.

When Leyla was a teen, Aurora's financial antics got weirder, creepier—like the macramé phone receiver cozies that the blind, diabetic friend down the street made for gifts. Aurora had a plan to tie-dye and sell them. She sent Leyla to the store to buy the dye with her Girl Scout cookie money.

Leyla had asked her mother, "Why don't you just get a job like other people?" She'd always thought Aurora would make a great hand model.

Every now and then, Aurora would find some legitimate employment. Leyla could never figure out how Aurora could convince anyone to hire her. But Aurora would work a little magic, get hired, and invariably screw it up in record time.

The most recent entry into the annals of Aurora's employment resume was doing end-cap coffee demos at Costco. They recruited at the library during senior internet-learning sessions. Leyla was thrilled when Aurora called to tell her she'd been hired. All she had to do was demonstrate brewing coffee in a Keurig-pod type machine but, as always, she did more than she was asked.

Aurora felt the demo needed a little "pizzaz" and showed up in her mink coat and patent-leather tap shoes. She refused to wear the hair net, and of course her nails got in the way of managing the coffee machine, all those tiny little sample cups to fill and balance on trays. Her manager asked her to please cut her nails and informed her that tap dancing was not allowed under California's workman's comp regulatory guidelines. She responded with, "Back in my day, young man . . . ," and was terminated effective immediately.

"Mom, all you had to do was drop in the pod and pass out cups of coffee."

"Now *Leyliku*, back in my day—"

"No. This is your day, now. You are still alive. There is no other day but today."

"*Ija*, now you sound like one of those hippie shrinks. Ahem, back in my day we really knew how to sell. A little song and dance always do the trick."

"You weren't selling, Mom. You did not need a trick. You

were just supposed to demonstrate the machine and give out samples."

Leyla's objections to Aurora's schemes and plans invariably triggered well-manicured wave-offs followed by the obligatory, "Fine, I am a terrible person."

Today's attempt was as tragically comical as any of the others. Once again, Leyla conceded to Aurora's request, and here they are, pulling into the Home of Peace Cemetery instead of dumping her mother's "lazy, sequined, sweat-suited ass" (Stephen's term of endearment for his mother-in-law), picking up her boys, and reuniting with her husband.

Perhaps she suffers from the same "what if" syndrome that Aurora does. What if this one was the one? So much for setting boundaries. Leyla sees how ridiculous this idea is. She is disappointed in herself.

Why can't she ever just say no? She's always inclined to deny everything to Aurora. Every absurd, contemptible request, every simple or brash imposition, her initial gut reaction is to recoil, rebel, resist. From her earliest memories, every fiber of her being burns to scream *NO!*

Even though she is working on this with *E*, she still says yes more often than she says no. The *E* before last told Leyla she suffers from "fear of abandonment," a result of being raised by an incompetent, alcoholic, childlike parent. This "parentification" (reverse-parenting role dynamic where the child supports the parent, rather than vice versa) explains Leyla's chronic willingness to indulge Aurora in ways that defy logic. She wonders how many *E*s she needs to go through before it all sinks in.

Today, after fifteen years of weekly *E* sessions at two hundred and fifty dollars a pop, she concedes against her better judgement to visit two cemeteries in one day.

The driver pulls the car up to the curb in front of a low

stucco wall covered with a dense growth of blooming bougainvillea. Leyla is enthralled by the bougainvillea growing everywhere in LA. She admires beautiful shocks of the pink, papery, blossoms creeping up walls and fences everywhere. She's always wanted to plant it at their house in Kentfield, but bougainvillea doesn't grow well in Marin. It does not like the hard January frost.

The short, waist-high wall is blocking the rear passenger door, preventing Leyla from exiting from her side. She sits, still fuming and waiting for Aurora to open the door on the other side.

The fuming between mother and daughter has evolved over the years into a series of *oju malus*—evil-eye looks. Leyla narrows her eyes and exhales audibly with her mouth closed, her lower jaw set just in front of her upper jaw. Then she grabs a small bite of inner cheek with her molars, always on the left side of her face. Aurora's responsive fuming display includes the wave-off, where she raises her right hand and swats it toward Leyla. If one didn't know what the gesture means, they might easily confuse it with swatting at some persistent insect or offensive smell. It is Aurora's way of waving off Leyla's disapproval.

They do not fight. When Leyla was a little girl, she learned not to argue. If she tried to communicate with her mother, she invariably received the wave-off, followed by silent treatment. Silent treatment is something her father did too. Then he left for good. The parental shut down of communication was terrifying as a child, and she learned not to encourage it. She developed the art of the silent fume and endured Aurora's retaliating wave-off.

Leyla nods and darts her eyes back and forth from the door handle to Aurora, indicating with her chin for her mother to open the car door on her side. After an aggravating interlude of Aurora's audible respiratory resistance and more glaring, nodding, and eye-darting from Leyla, Aurora concedes and reaches for the door. Her lavish claws are an obstacle to obtaining an effective grip. The sound of Aurora's nails scraping at the faux metal of the door handle triggers Leyla. She snaps and abruptly reaches across Aurora to yank at the door, but there's not enough clearance between the back of the driver's seat and Aurora's velour-sheathed bustline.

"Lean back," Leyla finally speaks.

"I am leaning back."

"Lean back farther."

"It's these tiny little back seats nowadays," Aurora says.

"Jesus, could you just not start with the nowadays routine!" Leyla's chill bliss from yesterday is now a faint memory. She reaches across her mother again, extending her right arm in an angry, unintentional hug. Leyla wrenches the lever and flops back to her side of the car. She gives Aurora one more hard glare and emphatic reverse-nod to get out. The driver is staring at them in the rearview mirror.

The car dips as Aurora rocks backward in preparation to lift her girth. The accumulated momentum propels her forward and boosts her heft up and out of the seat; the car bounces back up again.

The vaudevillian car-exit performance takes a full five minutes. Leyla finally slides over and gets out.

Aurora marches off toward the gravestones, in vigorous forward motion without discussion, directions, or uncertainty.

Their recent outing to the shoe department at Macy's resulted in Aurora's sturdy new footwear. Leyla threatened her mother with an end to their sweatsuit-shopping sprees unless she agreed to wear them with sensible shoes. Aurora's sequined mules broke a heel, and Leyla demanded they be retired. To Aurora's delight, they found a pair of hot-pink, high-top Skechers.

Her feet measure a size seven double narrow, but Aurora is

adamant that she is only comfortable in a nine and a half wide. Therefore, her new Skechers are two-and-a-half sizes too big. Her reasoning is that as an ex-dancer, or "ex-hoofer," as she likes to say, she requires a lot of extra room in her shoes (she never danced professionally). When she got home from Macy's after shoe shopping, Aurora went straight to her craft table and glitzed the Skechers up with her stockpile of beads and baubles.

Off she stomps now through the cemetery in her oversized, sparkly, Day-Glo trainers. She looks like a member of a hip-hop dance group for seniors. Leyla hasn't seen her mother move like this in a long time. Leyla thinks Aurora's probably still avoiding her daughter's ire, just trying to keep her distance, but it becomes clear that Aurora is familiar with this place. She knows exactly where she's going.

Leyla hears Aurora say, "Papa is over there." She follows Aurora as she clomps along the rows of gravestones, lumbering and mumbling. Leyla jockeys up next to Aurora to hear what she is saying.

". . . and that's auntie Rica, and there is Uncle Victor next to her. That was papa's sister, *la madre de* Eleanora i Djoya. That's my cousin Eddie, oh I loved him so. Oh, there is Papa!" She marched up to her father's gravestone and stands in front of it. She turns around and puts her hand on it.

"Take a picture of me for the kids," Aurora commands.

The carving in the stone reads: *Leonard Bohar Hmans. 1886–1995. United States Army.* There is a little American flag in the grass in front of it.

Leyla had never really believed it. So, he really did serve in the cavalry.

"A hundred and nine? Eight 'known' wives! What a guy." Leyla shakes her head, but she is impressed. "Son of a gun."

Leyla is still reading it when Aurora moves on, continuing her audio tour for no one.

"There is Aunt Matilda Menashe, and there is Uncle Morris, Papa's youngest brother," Aurora continues. "Oh, there's Mama's brother, Chilibee; her sister, Serena; and Nissim, Serena's husband. Papa brought Serena and Rica over. They came through Cuba."

"Richie's brother, Raphael, lives in Beverly Hills with his wife and kids. Regina lives in Bel Aire with her twins, Allegra and Morris." On and on she goes, jabbering full names and relations with flawless recall. Aurora connects all of them with details both convoluted and simple, evoked with perfect clarity. Leyla is astonished.

All these names Leyla reads on the gravestones were her relatives. With each recounted relation, there is a connection to another, still living. Aurora knows where they live and what they do for a living. They are dentists, doctors (*all* the Benvenistes are doctors, Aurora adds), realtors, attorneys, florists, actors, stay-at-home moms.

The different quality of the monuments was reflected in their materials, marble versus granite, posthumous indicators of wealth and stature. They all have different views, angles and orientations based on social hierarchy. How ridiculous. Who cares about the view if you're dead, Leyla thinks.

Aurora knows who has been moved to be near someone else, who they left behind, who their children married. She remembers every disagreement between siblings and spouses, who wanted this view or that spot. Whose *borekas* were the tastiest, whose *boyus* had the flakiest dough. Aurora is a database of Los Angeles Rhodeslis burial genealogy.

This cemetery in Los Angeles with all these relatives isn't an ancient gravesite filled with long-lost ancestors in the old country on some Jewish heritage summer tour. Some of the years of death are within the recent decade.

Leyla is stricken. Why did Aurora, Floru, and her sister

Reigna live up north in San Francisco when there was so much family down here in LA? They were always so isolated and separate.

When her father and Branan left, Leyla and Aurora were so alone, so bereft. Leyla felt separate, different, always watching from the outside looking in, at the large, happy, loving families around her. She craved connection and belonging long before she was able to articulate the feelings.

Holidays were excruciating—the songs, cookies, storefronts, and Christmas trees. She was the only Jewish kid in her entire school. She attended Hebrew school with other Jewish kids outside of school, but even there she was an outsider as a mixed Sephardic/Ashkenazi. With her dad gone, Leyla was more Sephardic than Ashkenazi, which made her different in her Jewish world.

She hated the way the whole world was so quiet on Christmas mornings. Leyla and Aurora never had anything to do that day. They had no Christmas celebration, but no December Chanukah celebration to fill the void, either. Once Branan and R.H.F. left, Aurora stopped making an effort. Leyla was never worth any effort-making on Aurora's part.

They had no money, no family, no delicious kitchen aromas from the baking and roasting of delectable, traditional recipes that could be counted on year after year. She had no family to squabble and potluck with. Leyla pined for a family to cook and bake for, to exchange gifts, quarrel, and gossip with.

Here in the cemetery, as Aurora pointed out aunties, uncles, and cousins, Leyla is shocked to see the evidence of all this family.

Leyla's father took his family with him when he left and gave them to his new wife. Vicki was gifted the Feldenburg clan in its entirety, immersed in and welcomed by it. Leyla was siloed. Vicki made it clear she was not inclined to share Robert H.

Feldenburg and his family. That wasn't a deal breaker for R.H.F. He was not compelled to fight to have his daughter in his life, a concession he repeated with each successive wife.

But the Feldenburgs were all around her. Leyla was constantly running into them—her cousins, aunts, uncles, and grandparents. They were all living around her in the community. She saw them at High Holy Days services and Hebrew school. She saw them, but she couldn't have them. She could only watch them all from afar.

Why had Aurora kept her from all of this? Why hadn't she packed up the two of them and come down to LA when R.H.F. skipped out? All these sweet, generous people, who casseroled, simmered, and stewed their extravagant recipes from the old country. They'd been here all along—these strangers who automatically loved her upon introduction, the way Eliezer and Estrella did when she'd walked in the door with Josh and Simon. Why didn't Aurora gift all this to Leyla?

Leyla realizes she technically had what she'd always dreamt of—family—a big, giant, gorgeous, weird, interesting, loving mélange of people to belong to. She just didn't know it. Why had Aurora chosen to stay up in Tiburon, broke among the wealthy, alone among the togetherness of everyone else all around them?

She hates Aurora more than ever right now. She wants an answer. She wants to know why. Leyla could have known these people. She could have loved them and maybe been loved in return. She could have had all of that. Why did she end up overlooked in the empty crack left over between the worlds of the Feldenburgs and Rhodeslis? She looks up, and Aurora is still chattering on, "Oh there is Auntie Rosalie and Uncle Rahamim, and over here is Cousin Salvatore."

"Why didn't you tell me about all these relatives?" Leyla asks.

Aurora is still walking ahead of her. Either she does not hear or she is ignoring the question. Leyla moves toward the side of Aurora's good ear and repeats herself, louder.

"Why didn't we ever come down here to visit? Why did you keep all of this from me?"

Aurora stops, turns around, and faces Leyla. She levels her eyes at her daughter.

"*Ija, la mejor vida es asigun lo hazes tu y asigun ti ajustas*— Life is what you make of it and how you adjust."

"Don't call me *ija*, and don't answer me in proverbs. I want to know why."

"Fine, I am a terrible person," Aurora gives her the wave-off, turns around, and starts walking again.

Leyla's lifelong quest for answers from her mother had always been met with the same vexing response. Today, for the first time in a long time, she is inclined to push. But she knows, deep down, this is all she's going to get. Aurora wanders ahead, continuing her ramble.

Leyla's had enough.

"It's time to go, Mom." She orders an Uber. She wants to get back to the kids, find her husband, rejoin her family. The family that she made all on her own. When the Uber arrives, Leyla collapses into the back seat, exhausted and heartbroken—two feelings that accompany any time spent with her mother.

"I bet Acacia would be able to help me with the cemetery plot," Aurora says.

"Go for it, Mom," Leyla answers.

The woman Branan married, Acacia, is a high-level manager in the U.S. Foreign Service. She is smart and accomplished. Leyla knows that Aurora is throwing Branan's wife (or ex-wife) at Leyla to bait her. She doesn't fall for it.

"Go ahead. Why don't you call her right now on your cell phone?" Leyla knows it's a mean dig. There is no way in hell that Aurora can manage an international call on her cell phone.

Aurora gives her one more "Fine, I'm a terrible person" wave before Leyla, lulled by the hum of the car engine and the emotional exhaustion from an afternoon with her mother, slides into a deep sleep.

CHAPTER SIXTEEN

Mas vale poco ke nada.
Better a little than nothing.

★ ★ ★

Aurora and Leyla walk up the path to the front door, entrenched in their silent fumes. Eliezer is standing in the open garage. His truck is sitting in the driveway. He's moving the bags of bags around and writing things on his clipboard. Aurora heads toward the garage.

Leyla goes into the house. She's had her fill of Aurora for the day, and she just wants to pack up the kids and get out of here. It's time to call Stephen and speak with him, voice-to-voice. No more hiding behind cryptic, manipulative texts. She needs to have a real conversation with her husband. This day had been so transformative, she just can't bear to strategize anymore. It's too exhausting, and her heart is no longer in it. It's otherwise occupied, full to overflowing with love and appreciation for Stephen and her boys.

She came down to LA for information and got it. She wanted to catch him and did. Not in the manner intended or suspected, but rather caught him thinking about her, loving her. The need to tell him everything, come clean, and share it all, was welling up inside her—the conference, the edibles, the Cartier store, the feelings.

She felt love—not strategy or concern for power—but true, deep, desperate, pure, abiding, urgent love. Stephen was her home, where her heart lived. Leyla wanted to go home. Being perfect wasn't making him love her. Being perfect was keeping him and the kids at a distance. Her quest to be worthy of love was rendering her the opposite. Stephen, Josh, and Simon were everything—her world. All her life she had thought that perfection would keep her safe, but it is the pursuit of perfection that is putting everything and anything of any real value in her life at risk.

When Simon presented her with the Creamsicle, he was afraid she wouldn't take it. He'd wanted to make her happy. She had to learn to allow them to try to make her happy. When she had discovered Stephen jewelry shopping at Cartier, it wasn't the jewelry that had torn her heart open. It was that he was thinking about her. She wasn't even there, and he was thinking about her. All these years together, yet it was something Leyla had never considered.

Simon had bought that ice cream and saved it because he was thinking about her, and Josh had waited to perform his blessings for her first, for the same reason. She saw and felt this today and cannot recall why she didn't before. Perhaps she'd known it but did not *feel* it. She was feeling everything suddenly. Feeling big feelings, *tasting* food like the Creamsicle and Estrella's *borekas*, *smelling* flowers, and *seeing* colors like the gorgeous bougainvillea all around her. Her senses were awakened and acting on them now felt like an emergency.

She pressed dial on Stephen's number.

He picked up on the first ring. "Hey!"

"Hi, you mad at me?" Her voice was weak, trembling.

"'Bout my mom?"

"Sorry, I just couldn't leave them."

"I know."

"I thought I could, but I couldn't. I tried to, but I, I should have said something, explained. It was wrong to just leave like that. I was wrong."

"I know. It's okay, I talked to my mom; she understands."

"You did? She does? How did you? What did you?"

"I don't know, I just figured you had something going on. I trust you. The boys are happiest when they are with you. She knows how you are."

"How I am?" Leyla bristled a bit at the comment, ready to jump on it with the old defensiveness and resentment of the controlling judgmental mother-in-law. But she stops herself. Instead, she swallows the words, editing her reaction. His answer, "I trust you," had stopped her cold.

Trust was another intellectual construct that Leyla comprehended but somehow never actually felt. All the angling, strategizing, and striving for perfection, the attempts to control and maintain attachment, seem strange now. She doesn't remember why being perfect seemed so critical, why that had anything to do with love. Trust and love were things she had not truly believed in; they were just words before.

Now it seems like feeling is all there is, she's feeling everything now. Her nerve pathways are open and activated.

Things were always on the edge of a cliff for her before, balanced precariously on the edge, ready to fall off and crumble to catastrophe. Unless she was perfect, in control of her feelings, her body, unless she withheld, constrained, maintained her power over others, all would be lost. This was the paradigm she lived by, since that night she heard her father walk out the door.

"So, Bunny is cool? What about Sean?"

"Sean's fine; as long the young princes are fine and his Queen Bunny isn't displeased, Sean couldn't care less. Apparently, he and my dad ate the popcorn and cookies while watching the game together," Stephen laughed.

"How was the conference?"

"Okay. The usual. Lots of good contacts, some panels, meetings with clients." Leyla's attention rests on the word panel. "So, where are you guys?"

"Here."

"Here? Where is here?"

"LA"

"So, *you* are in LA? With the kids?"

"Yeah, we're here."

"What are you doing down here? I didn't believe the message when you said Los Feliz."

"Um, well," she sniffles.

"Wait, let me guess, it's an Aurora thing. I figured the way you took off from my mom's had to have something to do with your mother."

She stifled feeling offended. Her mother was draining, she knew all too well, but Leyla's knee-jerk reaction to the rest of the world was always to defend and protect Aurora. Aurora was the only thing that had separated her from total aloneness in the world for all those years; shielding and guarding was automatic. This time she let it pass.

"Yeah, it's partly Aurora. I mean the kids are with Aurora, but the thing is, something happened . . . see, you know how I went to the opening of the kindergarten building, and then I heard this conversation with Hallie Monrowe."

"Hallie?"

"And then I thought, maybe, that you and Hallie . . ."

"Me? And Hallie Monrowe? Are you kidding me? She's a shrew."

"Then I had to find out," she says, and begins to weep. "So, I asked your mom to watch the kids, and then I just couldn't leave them, and then I went to the conference."

"You were at the conference? My conference?"

"Yeah, I found . . . well, I stole, a pass."

"Stole a pass?"

"And I went in, and I went to the panel."

"The panel?"

"And then I met Buzz, and he thought I was Anupal."

"Buzz? Who's Anupal?"

"And then I ate the granola bites."

"What?"

"Well, I didn't know they were ten milligrams each."

"Ten milligrams each? How many did you eat?"

"And then I made these friends, and they were so sweet and kind and joyful and accepting, and then they came home with me."

"Home with you?"

"To Estrella's."

"Estrella?"

"She was so generous, so welcoming, and she baked, and we ate and laughed. She told us stories from the Judería in Rhodes." Her nose was now full and running.

"You made friends?"

"We ate *borekas*, so many *borekas*, and then I slept through the night." She was full-blown crying.

"You ate? You slept?"

"And the kids were so happy there, and I took Aurora to the cemetery and saw all these relatives," Leyla says, and begins to bawl. "She never told me. So many of them—aunts, uncles, cousins."

"Cemetery?"

"Family, Stephen, so much family, and then when I got back to the house . . ."

"The house?"

"Estrella's house!"

"Right, Estrella's house."

"And Simon bought me an ice cream from the ice-cream truck." She is wailing. "He saved it for me in his pocket because he remembered I said I always wanted one as a kid. He remembered." Leyla is hysterical now. "It was melted, and I ate it. It was so good, creamy and sweet, orange just like I imagined."

"A Creamsicle, your favorite."

"But he was so afraid that I wouldn't want it. Oh Stephen, I'm sorry. I'm just. I'm so sorry."

"Leyla," he says. He raised and somehow also lowered his voice, calm, even, and reassuring.

"Uh huh?" she says through tears, snot, and hiccups.

"I love you, Leyls." He hadn't called her Leyls in so long.

"Really? Still?" She sobbed. He laughed. She slobbers the words, "I love you, too." Wet, blubbery, heartfelt. "Are we okay?"

"We're okay. Why don't you guys come get me at the hotel? I am just about ready to check out. I'd love to take the kids to Nate n' Al's. Ya know? I was thinking about them when I walked in the neighborhood yesterday. A real Jewish deli. They boys have never been, and we have nothing like that in Marin. Would you do that with us? Would you let them? I know it's not local, organic, sustainable, low carb, protein balanced, grass fed. But how 'bout it, Leyls? It would be fun."

Leyla begins to bawl again.

★ ★ ★

"*Bueno primo. Ke haber?*—Hi Cousin, what's going on?" Aurora asks.

It's obvious that Eliezer is moving the purses around. He does not look up from the clipboard when she walks in.

"*Ke vengas en ora buena, prima*—You got here at the perfect time. I am organizing for you, to get you ready to sell your purses," he says, still not looking up.

"*Merci muncho*. But you don't need to do this," Aurora says.

"No problem, *kerida*. It is my pleasure."

"I am going to leave tomorrow. I will take them back home with me in my car," Aurora says.

"*Kerida*. All this won't fit in your car. You can sell them here. I will help you," Eliezer says, and looks up at her now. He makes direct eye contact.

"They will fit." Aurora thins her lips and rolls them back and forth.

"Bueno. As you wish. But, since I already started counting, I will finish for you."

"Thank you, but that's not necessary. I will do it when I get home," Aurora says.

Eliezer kneels to straighten one of the stacks. When he stands back up to his full six feet seven inches, his head hits the light hanging from the rafter. The bare bulb swings back and forth as he ducks away from it.

He is his usual shiny, aromatic, well-groomed self, elegantly attired in one of his vintage-cut suits. This one is blue, enhancing the intensity of his aquamarine eyes. But today he is perspiring, probably from working in the garage, she thinks. Aurora has not seen Eliezer perspire, even when they cleaned out Esther's apartment with all the trips up and down the stairs. He kept his suit jacket on the entire time. Not once did he break a sweat.

"Of course. As you wish," he responds. He pulls at his blue silk tie, loosening it from his neck. He removes his jacket and rolls back the sleeves of his white dress shirt. This is the first time she's seen him adjust his idiosyncratic and formal daily attire.

"You moved your truck, I see." She notices the bags of bags are now organized in order of size. The yellow legal pad attached to his clipboard is filled with handwritten lists. Though Aurora's "good" eye isn't all that great for distance vision, she can see that multiple pages of the legal pad have been filled with loopy, elegant cursive columns. "*Primo*, come inside with me. We'll have coffee and *echar lashon*—chat. I want to spend time with my dear family on my last night before I leave." Aurora's friendly words do not match the scowl on her face and the rolling of her lips.

"Mama will be so sad for you to leave, Allegra. Yes. Okay. I will pull my truck back in and come inside. Would you like for me to pack your car for you?"

She feels oddly apprehensive, but it would be impossible for Aurora to refuse an offer of assistance with manual labor. Especially with Leyla still in a deep fume. This would not be a good time to ask Leyla for assistance, and Leyla would never allow Josh and Simon to have anything to do with Aurora's flea-market enterprise.

"*Merci muncho, primo*," she answers. Aurora reaches into her purse and pulls out her car key. She hands it to Eliezer. "Please do tell your friend Craig thank you, anyway."

Eliezer stares back at her. He opens his mouth slightly as if to speak, but then doesn't. He closes his mouth, shakes his head, walks to his truck, gets in, and starts the engine. Aurora peeks into the flatbed as he pulls past her into the garage. It is empty.

Now she feels guilty. How can she have been so sinister as to suspect her darling *primo* of ill intentions with her bags? She's not sure exactly why. He was only counting everything, but the vibe in the garage made her uncomfortable. He's done so much for Aurora. He helped with Esther's apartment, and he gave up his room for her. He'd handed out crisp five-dollar bills every day for her darlings Josh and Simon. Now here she is with the gall to mistrust him.

"*Es verwenza*—What a shame," Aurora mutters.

She can't deny that her witch's intuition is vibrating for some reason. Her attention turns suddenly as she smells a fresh plume of warm, sizzling garlic coming from Estrella's kitchen. Aurora decides that she just can't, or won't, think about the purses anymore today. She turns and walks back to the house, following the aroma and the possibility of fresh warm *borekas*.

As expected, Estrella is in the kitchen, presiding over her flour sack. Josh is standing on a stool at the kitchen table. He's wearing Estrella's red checkered apron, the one with the ruffled shoulder straps; the wide red belt is tied around his waist. There are two large ceramic bowls in front of him. One is filled with a grassy wet batch of cooked spinach. The other bowl is filled with musky green water. Josh has a fistful of spinach in his hand, squeezing it over the second bowl, releasing the excess moisture from the wilted warm greens.

"Squeeze, *mi alma*. Squeeze like I told you, with a fist *ija*, like this." Estrella calls out the directions over her shoulder. She demonstrates by raising her small, puffy, jewel-adorned fist.

"Hi Grandma. We're making *borekas*," Simon calls out from his spot next to Estrella when he sees Aurora enter.

"I see that, my darling," Aurora answers. He is wearing another one of Estrella's aprons, this one with a large black-and-white velvet appliqued face of Minnie Mouse on the chest. Simon has flour in his hair, on his ears, eyelashes, and all over his shoes.

"Okay. Now take some dough in your fist." Estrella demonstrates again.

"How much?" Simon asks.

"Like this, *mi alma*," Estrella says. She grabs a clump of dough to show him. "Like a fist," she says.

Aurora knows Estrella will never concede to a conventional unit of measurement. Rhodeslis know their recipes by heart and gut, learned in the kitchens of mothers, grandmothers, and aunties, always with recipe directives of "some of this" or "this much" or "like a fist." They never have any use for measuring cups or teaspoons. Their recipes always turn out perfect.

Simon takes fistfuls of dough and places them on the parchment paper. Estrella kisses the top of his head repeatedly, adding, "*Mashalla, mashallah*," between kisses.

"Okay, *iju*. Now roll them out until you have a circle."

"Oh, my darlings. My little *nikucheeras*—those that are good in the kitchen and home. Just like your mama and my mama."

"How come you don't make *borekas*, Grandma?" Josh asks.

"Yeah. How come you don't make *borekas*, grandma?" Leyla enters the room behind Aurora.

Aurora turns to Leyla and gives her the wave-off.

"Because I am a terrible person," Aurora responds, displaying her sarcasm and lack of accountability to the next generation.

"Come on, guys. Clean yourselves up. We are going to get dad at his hotel," Leyla directs the kids.

The boys go to the sink and begin to wash up.

"*Gracias, Estrella, para todos.*" Leyla says.

"Here, *mi alma*, take some with you." Estrella takes some of yesterday's *borekas* from a Tupperware container. She pulls a white bakery bag out of a drawer and stuffs it full. She hands the bag to Leyla.

"Thank you, Auntie." Leyla takes the bag

"What's your plan, Mom?" she asks Aurora.

"Allegra. Stay, please, to eat, and then sleep." Estrella begins to cry and pleads with Aurora.

"*Sí, sí, sí,* Auntie." Aurora needs no convincing.

"Call me before you hit the road, Aurora." Leyla says, not waiting for a response.

"Got it," Aurora answers.

"Bye, Grandma," Josh and Simon say simultaneously.

"Bye, my darlings," Aurora responds.

"Okay, guys. We are outie. Got all your stuff?" Leyla says.

Leyla takes the white bakery bag. Estrella hugs Simon and kisses his head. She reaches for Josh next, gives him a squeeze, and adds more rapid-fire head kisses.

"*Pu, pu, mashalla,*" Estrella says over his head.

Leyla reaches for Josh and yanks him toward her, in anticipation of the forthcoming squall of saliva. Estrella begins to cry again. She reaches for Leyla next. Leyla hugs her.

"Watch your mailbox for the Bar Mitzvah invitation," Leyla offers.

"I'll bake!" Estrella says, wiping her tears with the corner of her apron.

"How did I go my entire life and not know you?" Leyla says and hugs Estrella again.

The boys go to Aurora for more hugs, kisses, and *mashallahs*. The three of them leave.

Aurora picks up her phone and manages to find a previous call from Acacia's number. She isn't sure what time it is in Thailand but takes a chance and hits the call button with her knuckle. To her surprise, it rings.

"Hello?" Acacia answers, irritated.

"Acacia? It's Aurora."

"Yes, I know. Everything okay?" Acacia asks.

"Yes. Everything is just fine, dear. Why do you ask?" Aurora answers, wanting to sound cheerful and nonchalant. "And how did you know it was me?" Aurora was amazed.

"Because your name comes up on the phone screen," Acacia responds with exasperation.

"I'll be darned," she says, impressed by the magic of technology.

"I thought maybe it was an emergency because I don't know why you would call your son's ex-wife at work. Unless, perhaps, you didn't check for the time difference? But that would be rude. And you wouldn't be rude, would you Aurora?" Aurora notes that Acacia sounds annoyed.

"Ex-wife?" Aurora asks.

"Branan hasn't told you that we're divorced? Figures. National security and all that," Acacia responds.

"Oh, yes, of course national security, well. Anyway, I was wondering if you might be able to help me with something, since you have such a knowledge of things," Aurora continues without acknowledging Acacia's divorce reveal. Now is not the time to pry. She needs something.

"Knowledge of things? What is it, Aurora?"

Aurora explained the scenario of Esther's cemetery plot.

"You called me in Thailand, in the middle of my workday, because you want me to help you find a way to sell your dead stepmother's burial plot? That you can't prove you own? You're kidding me, right. Good luck, Aurora."

"Fine, thanks for nothing!" Aurora hangs up, disconnecting the call with a stab of her knuckle.

I never liked that girl. She was stumped. She had tried Leyla, who wouldn't help. And now that "no goodnik" Acacia refused to help. She was never good enough for Branan anyway, so good riddance. Branan could not be reached and would no doubt give his usual, "Don't call me, I'll call you," response if she were able to reach him. Right now, she thought her children were both selfish and unhelpful. Young people nowadays had no respect for their elders. What she needed was an attorney. Some real legal help.

Of course, she knew Eliezer was an attorney-of-sorts. She can't remember what that fishy old story was anyway—was he fired? Did he commit a crime? She didn't know, and she didn't care. He would never say no to her. He'd already demonstrated how skilled he was when he showed her all the information about the burial plots. He was obviously very connected, with his powerful friends like Craig. He could probably take care of this lickety-split. She had a feeling it would cost her, but once she was rich, maybe fifty thousand dollars, as he'd said, she'd give him a little gelt for his trouble. There just had to be a way.

She walks through the kitchen, opens the door to the garage, and turns on the light switch. The garage is empty except for Eliezer's blue truck. She's confused. Eliezer said he would load the purses into her car. Of course, that must be where the purses and Eliezer are. She turns out the light and walks back through the kitchen.

Aurora walks to her Saturn at the curb, puts her face to the glass, and looks in the window. The interior is empty, except for her collection of Baskin-Robbins plastic mudpie containers and several crumpled packs of More cigarettes she'd tossed in the back. There was no way those purses would all fit in the trunk. She opens it anyway to be sure. The trunk is empty, too.

Eliezer's truck is in the garage. Estrella is napping in her lawn chair, snoring in the sunshine. Where is Eliezer, and where are the purses?

CHAPTER SEVENTEEN

Kada kavesa es un mundo.
Every head is a world.

★ ★ ★

When Leyla and the kids arrive at the hotel, it looks like a different universe. There is no effervescent crowd at the entrance, no swarm of cars, no herbal, woody scent permeating the air. The hotel's no longer teeming with people buzzing with energy on the ballroom floor, bouncing from booth to booth, their lanyards hanging on their necks, cellphones out, texting colleagues, making connections, negotiating deals, with security guards gatekeeping the enthralls of the magical whirl of the wonders of CannabizCon.

Stephen was standing at the entrance of the hotel when they pulled up. He looked like Jack from *Titanic*—a Jewish Leonardo DiCaprio. His hand reached out to receive them when the Uber came to a stop. He opened the door—her, their, Prince Charming. The kids exploded out of the car and monkey-climbed their dad, crawling all over him in that annoying, delicious, unbridled expression of adoration that young children express, assuming eminent domain to the physical bodies of their parents.

Watching them together, Leyla feels saved. It's a faintly familiar feeling. It had been a long time. But it came back. She remembered describing him to a friend when she realized she was falling in love all those years ago. Her friend asked her what it felt like. Leyla had answered, "It feels like being saved." That was the best Leyla could come up with when describing the feeling of finding the one, her *Beshert*. Stephen made her feel saved.

He takes the boys up to his hotel room to get his things and finish checking out. He couldn't have unglued from them if he wanted to at that point—Simon was wrapped around one leg while Josh swung from his bicep. Leyla said she'd wait down in the lobby, wanting to get the three of them ticketed on Stephen's flight before they reach the airport. She confirms their seats on the SouthWest app, and then strolls toward the ballroom—pulled to the epicenter of her recent adventure, the interview with Buzz, her new, now lost, friends, and her vision quest with the magical baked goods. She approaches the main hall and gives in to the urge to push on one of the large double doors. It opens easily. She steps into the room.

Yesterday, it was swarming with people, electric with motion and music, hundreds of booths filled with products and promises of happiness and laughter, an end to aches, pains, anxiety, insomnia, loneliness, and writer's block. The array of products and businesses was like Alice in Wonderland—eat me, drink me, rub me on your lower back—all legal, seductively packaged, lab-tested, available for resale.

The fantastical scene and the people that filled the space had been erased. The café where Leyla had sat with Buzz Baruch and their troupe of joyous comrades had been deleted from existence. She tries to remember which side of the hall it was located, attempting to recall the feeling.

She just isn't sure how much of it was real. She wants to

access it again, to put it into words, somehow solidify the emotional imprint, so she can reach back and dip into it.

Leyla has spent her lifetime prepping for every and any eventuality. She preps her children for school, her face for wrinkles, her body for menopause, her health for decline, herself for her husband leaving her. But nothing prepared her for unintentionally consuming forty milligrams—give or take—of cannabis edibles, opening her heart to strangers, meeting her own family, and catching her husband *not* cheating on her.

She hears a high-pitched motor. Workers with hard hats are navigating a motorized ride-on crane. They're removing signage from the wall. It's a violet-blue mylar psychedelic tie-dye patterned banner for BUDdy LOVE brands THC Wake n' Bakes. They yank at it.

"Hey, can I have that?" Leyla calls up to them. They shrug and toss it down to the floor. Reaching for it where it lands, she spots some crumbs on the carpet. Maybe some magical remains of BUDdy LOVE's free treats? She wonders if anyone else's life was changed yesterday. After rolling up the banner and stuffing it into her bag, she walks out of the ballroom to wait for her guys in the lobby.

Hungry now, Leyla regrets leaving the bag of *borekas* Estrella packed for her. She put it down at the front door and forgot to retrieve it. Stephen and the kids are probably hungry, too. They are headed to Nate 'n Al's. He wants the kids to experience the classic spot.

The elevator opens. Stephen and the kids walk out.

"Shall we?" Stephen says as he approaches Leyla.

"Are we going to deli? Dad said we're going to deli?" Josh says as he walks up.

"I want egg cream, and pickles . . . is that okay?" Simon asks his mom.

She never realized how afraid they all were of her. She feels a twinge of guilt. She can't remember now why she had cared so much. They walked out of the lobby together toward the front entrance to order an Uber. The kids and Leyla sit in the back, three across, as always. Stephen sits in the front. He reaches back and puts his hand on Leyla's knee. She puts her hand on top of his.

When Stephen had told Leyla that he wanted to take them to Nate 'n Al's, he did the usual nutritional negotiation windup before making the ask. He pitched it on the phone while she was blubbering. He asked twice just to be sure.

"I was wondering, if just this once, if we eat only vegetables and tofu for the rest of the week, and we keep the portions small and share, would you be willing to take the kids to Nate 'n Al's?"

He was shocked when Leyla stopped crying enough to answer and said, "Sure, sounds fun."

They have a family game they play when they drive to ski weekends in Lake Tahoe. It's in one of Leyla's "conversation tools for road trips with kids" kits, little strategies and tactics for keeping your kids off their devices and initiating rich family conversations. It was on the "Get your kids college-bound early" workshop recommendations list.

In a peer-reviewed study, it was documented that kids who verbally generate original fiction score higher on standardized tests. She signed both boys up for an after-school improv workshop immediately upon learning this. They call the game: "How would you know if I was replaced by an alien?" You have to think of something that a person would do or say, so out of character that your family would know that an alien had replaced you.

Stephen continued when they were all in the car, "You don't mind? Fatty pastrami, thick carby rye bread, coleslaw with globs of mayo, chocolatey, sugary cream sodas, eggy potato salad, heavy on the salt, all washed down with rugelach, and blintzes?" he teased her.

"Nope, don't mind a bit." She responded.

"Hey guys, it finally happened. Mom's been replaced by an alien." They all laughed. He smiled at her and asked, "Who are you, and what have you done with my quasi-anorexic, uncompromising, health-guru, wife?"

Leyla laughed, confusing him even more, but he smiled at her in a way that she hadn't seen in a long time.

"You guys won't believe this place. Wait 'til you see the pastrami sandwiches piled with mountains of warm, wet, pastrami, loaves of fresh rye bread, chocolate egg creams, and potato knishes like you've never seen in your life," Stephen says.

"I've never seen an egg cream in my life," Simon answers.

"Are knishes like *borekas*?" Josh asks.

Leyla laughs. When they arrive at Nate n' Al's, the kids race ahead toward the entrance. Stephen holds the car door open for Leyla and gently supports her arm as she gets out. Her phone buzzes. She reaches into her bag to find it, rummaging past the large banner she salvaged from the show.

"Why do you have a BUDdy LOVE's banner in your bag?" Stephen asks when he sees it bulging out as she digs for her phone.

"Long story. I'll tell you later."

She finds her phone. It's Aurora. She hesitates, not sure she has the strength to talk to her mother right now. She's so enjoying breathing Aurora-free air. But she answers just in case it's an emergency.

"Thank God you picked up! *Ah dio*, I've been robbed."

"Robbed?"

"Yes, robbed. My purses are gone. They are all gone, every single last one of them." Aurora is distraught.

"Gone? How is that possible? The garage was full of them. We were just in there a couple of hours ago. Calm down, Aurora. Tell me the details."

Stephen is looking at her with an expression of annoyed curiosity. He mouthed the word: "robbed?" She holds the phone away, covers it with her hand and whispers, "Aurora." He rolls his eyes. She motions with a wave of her hand, indicating for him to go inside with the kids. She holds up two fingers and whispers, "Two minutes. Order for me. I'll have whatever you're having."

Aurora is still talking, "I called Acacia. She was of no help, and rather discourteous, if I might add."

"What about the purses, Aurora? Get back to the purses."

"Right. Well, after that rude call with Acacia—apparently, she and Branan are splitsville, by the way, did you know that—Anyway, I went back out to the garage, and it was empty. I wasn't alarmed at first. Eliezer told me he was going to load my car. I went to my car to see how it could have possibly all fit, and my car was empty. Then I went back to the garage to check again just to be sure. They're gone, all of them, gone. Someone must have stolen them from my car."

"What did Eliezer say? Estrella? Did they see anything? Anyone?" Leyla asks. She's barely interested, exasperated, impatient, and hungry. She can see Stephen and the kids through the window. They are sliding into a booth.

"Estrella is napping in her lounge chair. I can't find Eliezer. He must have gone to run some errands. But his truck is still here," Aurora says.

"Call him," Leyla answered.

"I did."

"And?" Leyla asks.

"He didn't answer. I yelled his name for a long time, all throughout the house and in the yard."

"No, mother. On the phone, call him on the phone."

"Oh, right. I'll go ask Auntie Estrella to call him," Aurora responds.

"I don't know what to tell you, Mom. Not much I can do about it."

"He has been talking quite a bit about next door. I guess I'll go and see if he is there, since his truck is still here. But I don't know which next-door neighbor he was talking about. *Ah dio, dio, dio*," Aurora said.

"Mom, I don't think that's what he meant by next door. Nextdoor is an app." But the call ended. Fine by me, Leyla thinks. It's never that easy to get off a call with her mother. She does not have it in her to deal with Aurora today.

The entire scenario is ridiculous, a long-lost stepmother who was a hoarder of a very specific nature, a valuable cemetery plot in limbo, and the motherlode of cheap purses. Another day in Aurora Land, Leyla thinks.

She did recall feeling mildly suspicious when they returned from the cemetery fiasco and found Eliezer in the garage with that clipboard. He was clearly taking an accounting of the purse haul. But he had been super helpful to Aurora with Esther's apartment, and it was in Eliezer and Estrella's nature to be kind and giving. Last night's generous feast for total strangers was an example of their giant-hearted hospitality. Leyla was annoyed with Aurora after the cemetery and didn't focus too much on it, but now it feels like a clue to the missing bags and empty truck. Just her mother's good old bad luck, she guesses.

After she cuts off Leyla, Aurora walks back out to the curb. She turns around, faces the house to decide which "next door" to begin with. She chooses the one next to the garage, on the right-hand side.

She walks up their front path. It is identical to Estrella's front entrance. There is a screen door. It's closed, but the interior door is open. She pushes the button on the wall next to the door. The doorbell rings. She can see the silhouette of a human shape walking slowly toward her. It's either a child or a very small adult. As the figure gets closer, she can see it is a woman with short, grey hair, styled in a crew cut.

"Hellooooo," Aurora launches in without waiting for her to speak. "I am looking for my cousin, Eliezer. He mentioned to me he has a neighbor "next-door" that he is friendly with. I was wondering if he's here, or if you perhaps have seen him today. His truck is still in the garage, but I can't seem to find him, and some things of mine have gone missing. I wonder if you saw anything fishy going on in the driveway today." The figure gets closer. Aurora can see now that it is an older Asian woman.

"Eliezer left in a big truck," she says in a heavy accent.

"Oh, no. His truck is very small," Aurora answers.

"No, not his truck. Big truck. Big U-Haul came an hour ago. Very noisy. Eliezer filled the truck. Cleaned out garage. Put it in the truck and left."

"Oh my. Oh no. Oh my. Oh dear!" Aurora turns and rushes back to the house screaming for Estrella, who is on her lawn chair snoozing.

"Auntie!"

"*Ke es hadras I baranas sweetheart?*—What's the big fuss?" Estrella asks sleepily.

"He took my bags, Auntie! Esther's bags. I don't have his cell-phone number in my phone." Aurora was best at redialing. "Auntie, wake up!"

Who, *ija*, who took the bags?" Estrella asks.

"Eliezer did, Auntie. Why would he do that?"

"*Ah dio.* Eliezer," Estrella said, shaking her head.

"Call him, Auntie, and ask him where he is," Aurora pleads.

Estrella goes to the kitchen and calls Eliezer.

"Eli. *Mi iju. Ande sta?*—My son, where are you?" Estrella pauses, listening. "*Ah dio! Te vo dar los guesos en la mano*— You are going to be punished." Estrella clenches her pudgy, child-sized, gem-ladened fist and shakes it like a boxer threatening a punch.

CHAPTER EIGHTEEN

Al tinyoso, un grano mas.
Trouble follows trouble.

★ ★ ★

Leyla is wedged into one of the tufted, brown-vinyl, high-back booths at Nate 'n Al's drinking a Yoo-hoo, slurping the chocolatey-flavored water through a bent accordion blue-and-white striped paper straw. She has a forkful of pastrami, topped off with a balanced mountain of mayonnaise-drenched coleslaw, on approach to her mouth. She is indulging—but she did peel the rye bread from her half of the sandwich, unable to surrender her entrenched aversion to carbs.

"I like that scarf. Is it new? The bright colors look good on you," Stephen comments.

"Thanks." Leyla avoids his gaze, wondering how he would react if he knew this was purchased as camouflage for the purpose of stalking him. It was still a nice change to twist the vibrant-colored accessory around her black mock-turtleneck this morning.

Leyla's phone vibrates. Looking down into her bag at the screen, she sees that it's Aurora again. Hesitating, Leyla pauses—deciding whether or not to tap the side button and send it straight to voicemail, knowing full well the chance she is taking if she answers.

This family moment is so filled with delight, she doesn't want to ruin it. Executing a quick internal scan for "emotional inflammation," an exercise *E* taught her, Leyla decides that here, safely immersed in a joyful experience with her husband and kids, she is at a safe distance from her mother. Feeling loved and happy, the Aurora Risk Factor feels low right now. Depositing the dripping bite of pastrami into her mouth, she reaches into the bag, picks up the phone, and answers.

Ni el dushman de la mar—This shouldn't happen to my worst enemy," Aurora wails. "He stole my bags. The neighbor next door saw him. He took them in a truck, a big truck."

"Who, who took your bags? Which bags?" Leyla asks while chewing.

"Eliezer. He took all of Esther's purses."

"Call the police. I guess," Laila says, her mouth still full.

"Oh no. I couldn't possibly," Aurora responds.

"Why?"

"Leyla, he is family. *El sangre es mas espesa ki el agua*—Blood is thicker than water."

"If he stole your purses, he's a thief," Leyla says.

"Are you chewing? Lailiku? You're eating?"

"Stephen wanted to take the kids to Nate n' Al's," Leyla responds. "Then we're heading to the airport."

I am not going to get involved in this. She looks at Stephen and the kids happily chewing and slurping, thinks of *E*, boundary building and the expensive year of focused work in her therapy around this issue.

"*Aidi Vrey*—He is at his cousin's," Estrella says, out of breath. Laila can hear her in the background.

"*Ande sta?*" Aurora asks Estrella while holding the phone.

"You remember Joe Skenazi? His mama, Rivka, was your

Auntie Serena's sister-in-law. We used to go for Shabbat. He married Tzipi Capuya." Rhodeslis provide a complete Venn diagram of family structure, connections to you and each other. A simple reference by name will never do, no matter the level of hysteria or urgency in the moment.

"Yes, I remember," Aurora answers. Then into the phone she says to Leyla, "I'll be there in ten minutes," and ends the call.

"NO!" Leyla yells. She presses redial. Aurora does not answer.

Aurora walks out to her Saturn, hoping she has enough gas to get her to Nate 'n Al's. There's no time for an AAA con. She knows where the deli is. It's a Los Angeles institution, in business since the 1940s. She used to go with her cousin Eleanor when they were teenagers. They'd pool their change to buy a ten-cent egg cream to share and sip it slowly, hoping to see movie stars or maybe get discovered. Once they saw Carl Reiner eating blintzes with Dick Van Dyke. Another time, Doris Day showed up in her bathrobe.

"*Speda, speda*—wait, wait, take the *borekas, mi alma*!" Estrella is running along the curb with the bakery bag Leyla left behind. She rolls down the top of the bag, balls it up, and tosses it into the open window as Aurora pulls away, making a perfect "alley oop" through the passenger-side window.

Leyla says a silent, panicky, prayer that Aurora will not show up in ten minutes. She puts her phone back in her bag and returns her attention to the platter of pastrami. Stephen and the kids are staring at her, waiting for a debrief. Leyla looks from Stephen, to Josh, to Simon.

"Why don't you tell dad about your blessings practice?" she says to Josh, pivoting.

"Want me to do it for you, Dad?" Josh responds.

"Sure, buddy. Later, on the way to the airport. First, catch me up on what's been happening, guys. What's new?" Leyla's heart is full. Her family is together, her belly is full of pastrami, and Stephen is so happy, she doesn't want to wreck it by involving herself with another Aurora escapade.

Before anyone speaks, Stephen says, "Wait, let me guess what happened and how you wound up in Los Angeles. Some Aurora scheme that required you to risk life and limb, spend three days and three thousand dollars, and ditch my mother, so she can haul in a whopping twenty-five bucks this month."

"Esther died," Leyla says attempting a dramatic yet sympathetic change of topic.

"Right. You said that. Who is Esther again?" Stephen looks at Leyla from across the table.

She opens her mouth to explain but is distracted because past Stephen's shoulder, through the front window of the restaurant, she sees smoke.

"Oh, God," Leyla whispers. It's Aurora's Saturn.

"I'm just wondering. I mean, don't worry about it, I'll deal with my mom," Stephen continues. "I'm thrilled you guys are here; I just never got the whole story."

"Look, it's Grandma," Simon is sitting next to Leyla on the banquette. He has the same view. He points to the street. Stephen and Josh turn around and look.

They all say, "Oh, God."

"I'll be right back." Leyla shoves another bite of blintz into her mouth, grabs her bag, squirms sideways out of the booth, and runs out to the street. Aurora and her belching, smoldering Saturn are now the main attraction on Beverly Drive.

Leyla is baffled at how well Aurora remembers her way around Los Angeles. She can't find her Comcast bill five minutes after opening the mail, but somehow she navigates around LA with her gasping embarrassment of a vehicle without even a glance at a GPS.

Leyla opens the passenger side and gets in. She's beyond mortified. The plume from the front end is dark grey; the engine is hissing; the interior reeks of radiator fluid and burning oil. She turns around to place her purse in the back seat but changes her mind when she spots the Baskin-Robbins containers piled there, with the congealed residues of Jamoca Almond Fudge and whipped cream.

Leyla feels the same embarrassment she did when her mother finally pulled up to the curb for dancing school carpool, forty minutes late, car filthy, out of gas, engine smoking, a lit More cigarette between two fingers, and a can of Pepsi Light in the other hand. In Mill Valley 1973, the neighborhood driveways were full of BMWs (aka Basic Marin Wheels). Aurora had a fifteen-year-old burgundy Pontiac Grand Prix with a quilted t-top roof. Leyla would shrivel in shame.

"Drive, Aurora," Leyla seethes.

Aurora pulls away from the curb just as a bus person from Nate 'N Al's runs toward them. He is yanking the release pin on a large red fire extinguisher.

"When is the last time you changed the oil on this piece of shit, Mom?" Leyla is directing her gaze straight ahead.

"Oh, recently, I'm sure, can't recall exactly," Aurora answers, matching Leyla's icy tone.

"Mm hmm," Leyla responds.

"*Maz vale un azno ke me yeve ke de un kavayo ke me eche,* sweetheart—A donkey that carries me is better than a horse that throws me. By the way, how is your housekeeper enjoying that cute little Mini Cooper that you and Stephen bought her?" Aurora snaps.

Leyla texts Stephen:

Sorry. It's an Aurora thing. I'll meet you guys at LAX.

She forwards him the flight confirmations.

Stephen answers:

K

"Estrella said Eliezer is at Joe Skenazi's in Santa Monica. I have the address here." She hands Leyla a Post-it with the address Estrella wrote down. "Joe is Rivka's son. Rivka was my auntie Serena's sister-in-law. We used to go for Shabbat. He married Tzipi Capuya, but he always had such a crush on me."

"Stop. I don't need to know the 23andMe of your thief's accomplice,"

"He took my purses in a U-Haul. What on earth is he going to do with them in Santa Monica?" Aurora asks.

"Did you put the address in your Google Maps?" Leyla asks.

"Huh?" Aurora responds.

"Never mind, stupid question."

"I know how to get there," Aurora answers.

"I have no doubt," Leyla says.

Leyla maps it on her phone. It's a straight shot to the beach.

Twenty minutes or so of tacit rage later, they see a sign for the beach, followed by another sign for the Santa Monica Flea Market. Aurora turns to look.

"Eyes on the road, Aurora. We are not stopping at the flea market," Leyla knows her mother and the tantalizing draw of a rummage sale.

"Well, had I known, I could've set my table with the purses up right there. The table is in the trunk right now."

"Of course, you have a table in your trunk for emergency garage sales. That makes perfect sense. Jesus, what am I even doing here?"

"I'm just saying. I could sell the purses right here."

"Yeah, I heard you. I get it."

Then they both see it on the outside perimeter of the flea market lot as they drive by. In a U-Haul truck, standing at the back, pulling the rope attached to the rear gate, stands Eliezer in his dark blue suit. He locks eyes with Leyla.

"That son of a bitch. Pull over, Mom," Leyla says.

"But . . . ," Aurora responds.

"Pull over now. Let me drive."

Aurora pulls the car over. Leyla jumps out, runs around the front, and pulls on the driver's side door. Aurora starts her usual slapstick grapple for the handle, her nails complicating the everyday task of pulling a lever. After several attempts where Leyla pulls and lets go, and then Aurora pulls and lets go, they succeed in opening the door.

Aurora gets out. Leyla jumps into the driver's seat. She taps her hands on the steering wheel while waiting for Aurora's version of hurrying around the front of the car to the passenger side.

As she trudges past the windshield, Leyla can hear the velour chaffing from inside the car. Aurora yanks the door handle, hefts herself into the passenger seat, and closes the door. Leyla makes a U-turn across Airport Boulevard and heads toward the entrance of the flea market.

They both see Eliezer jump into the U-Haul. He pulls out of the driveway as they get close, maneuvering out on to the boulevard in front of them. Leyla follows. The rear gate of the U-Haul is not secured. It's bouncing open. The bags of bags are visible, sliding to and fro in the back of the truck.

"*Ah dio*. My bags!" Aurora cries.

"I see them," Leyla responds.

Eliezer turns the truck around and heads toward the beach. Leyla pursues. Bags bulge out of the gap at the bottom of the rear gate. A few fall out as he turns the truck sharply.

"The bags!" Aurora yells.

"I see them. We aren't stopping. I am going to get the son of a bitch."

More bags slide out, spilling on to the road. Aurora watches out the window as they go by. Cars are swerving to avoid the bags.

Leyla is trailing close behind the truck. The Saturn is emit-ting a foul grey column of steam and making a loud sound, a cross between a mule and a helicopter.

Eliezer turns right when the street dead-ends at the beach. They're now on the Pacific Coast Highway. He speeds up. The unsecured rear gate of the U-Haul bounces open higher and higher with each forward lurch of the truck. The mountain of purses surges back and forth with every acceleration and brake. They're detaching from their plastic shopping bags, which are swept up in the vortex of wind and begin to fly out of the rear gate. A flurry of them whips around in front of the Saturn. Other drivers are honking, swerving, and signaling at Eliezer to let him know he's losing his load.

"This is nuts," Leyla says.

Leyla accelerates, pressing the gas pedal to the floor, but she can't get the Saturn to go past thirty-five miles an hour. She falls two cars behind. The smoke from under the hood is drafting back inside the car, and they both begin to cough.

"I've got to pull over, Mom. This is insane. I'm not going to get us killed for some stupid purses. I don't know what came over me with this crazy chase." Leyla returns to her senses.

Aurora reaches into the back seat behind Leyla.

"What are you doing?" Leyla asks without taking her eyes off the road.

"The *borekas*. You want one?" Aurora says.

"You need a snack? Now? That's what's on your mind?"

"Where is that bag?" Aurora mutters.

The Saturn is shrieking. Leyla looks at the dash and every red light is on—oil, water, battery, engine, brake. She looks past her right shoulder to pull over.

Aurora's left arm is behind Leyla reaching and rummaging.

"Mom, leave 'em."

"I know they're back here."

"Leave them for now."

Aurora reaches back farther. She puts her right hand out and places it on the steering wheel.

"Mom, keep your hand off the steering wheel."

"I almost got 'em."

"Aurora."

Aurora grabs the wheel for leverage for her reach into the back seat. "Got 'em." When the *borekas* are just about within her reach, she yanks on the steering wheel.

The car begins to spin. Leyla stomps on the brake. Aurora still holds on to the wheel. Leyla tries to remember what she is supposed to do in a spinout. Do you go with the spin or against it, brake or accelerate? She loses orientation as they twirl out of control but has enough presence of mind to attempt to put her hand on top of Aurora's and try to pry it loose. They continue to rotate and spiral until they are onto the other side of the highway, facing into oncoming traffic.

There is so much smoke from the Saturn that Leyla can barely see. Through the smoky haze, plastic bags from Esther's purses are visible swirling in the whirlwind of energy swept up and around them.

Reflected in the rear view, the U-Haul truck is receding into the distance in the opposite direction. Horns are honking. Leyla looks up to see a white Tesla. It's heading straight at them; no one is in the driver's seat. It slams into the Saturn, head-on.

The impact halts the endless rotations. The cars are now attached at their front ends. She sees flames.

Leyla opens her door, jumps out, and runs around the front end to the passenger side to get Aurora. The door won't open. Aurora is hitting the window with her hand. People are running toward the Saturn. Leyla rushes back to the driver's side, climbs in, and tries to pull her mother out.

Two good Samaritans see her struggling. They grab Leyla,

forming a human chain, and pull. Someone smashes the passenger window. Aurora's Skechers are pinched in the crushed metal of the foot well. The flames are growing higher. Firefighters finally arrive and slice off Aurora's shoes. The good Samaritans and Leyla give one more heave-ho and free Aurora, pulling her through the driver's side.

More emergency vehicles arrive. The responders push everyone back from the smoke, flames, and swirling, melting plastic bags.

CHAPTER NINETEEN

La madre kon la ija, komo piedra en aniyo.
Mother and daughter, like a stone on the ring.

★ ★ ★

The sun hangs low above the horizon line, shining directly in Leyla's eyes. She squints. There's a balmy breeze.

She breathes in the cool air blowing off the Pacific Ocean, consuming it in large gulps, cleansing the taste of blood and vomit, a blessed reprieve from the reek of burnt oil, gas, and rubber on her clothes, skin, and hair. Her feet feel hot. She looks down and sees the soles of her favorite black-and-white Nike Airforce sneakers are soft and slightly melted.

She's fuzzy about how she arrived here on the beach. Did she run toward the water? Did she walk? Was she carried? She remembers being in the car behind the wheel and seeing Eliezer in the rearview. He was going the opposite direction in the U-Haul. Her comprehension of the violent force of the crash, wrenching Aurora out of the wreckage, the confusion, all the people who helped in the mayhem is slowly emerging.

The sound of the metal collapsing and glass exploding replay in her mind. She has a sense that someone or something lifted her and tossed her away from the pandemonium.

She knows Josh and Simon weren't with her, and she feels calmer once she has clarity about that. The faces of her boys were her first and last thought when the force of the impact convulsed through her small frame.

"My babies!" She thinks she might have screamed it, but she isn't sure.

She looks down at her jeans. There is a sparkling iridescence, which is strange and unfamiliar. She brushes her hand along the top of her thigh; it's sharp on her fingers. Realizing it's glass dust from the crash, she pulls her hand away. It's all over her.

Aurora is catching up, lagging as always, trudging toward where Leyla sits at the water's edge. In her stupor, she dropped herself at that narrow border of the beach where it's not dry, but it's not wet either—that firm, level spot left behind when a wave draws back to its mother, the ocean. It's a stable base to sit on, in opposition to the nauseating vertigo she is suffering. She hears an ambulance and begins to recall the police officer trying to interview her, insisting she be examined. No doubt they will find her here after they put out the fire. She gags when she turns back and, out of her peripheral vision, sees all the foam.

Leyla heaves; it's dry and unproductive. There is nothing left in her stomach. The pastrami, coleslaw, Yoo-Hoo, and blueberry-cheese blintz are up the beach behind her where she drenched the Pacific Coast Highway with her lunch after extricating Aurora from the snarl of hot smoking metal. She now realizes she was at the center of the embarrassing spectacle.

Aurora is struggling without her shoes, barefoot on the unstable sand, lumbering in the side-to-side and forward roll that some fat old people develop after years of excessive weight-bearing.

Leyla reaches up with her right hand without bothering to look. Aurora arrives, takes Leyla's hand, and holds on tight as she harumphs her girth down beside her daughter. The stretchy velour of her sweatsuit is mercifully forgiving as she wrangles her bulk down onto the sand.

After an inelegant landing, she rebalances herself, spits on her hand, reaches over to Leyla, and gently wipes some of the oil and blood from Leyla's cheek. She pulls a shard of glass out of Leyla's long brown curls that blow back with the breeze. Leyla takes her mother's hand from her head and holds it.

They sit together on Santa Monica beach, where the west coast meets the ocean, the edge of the continent, end of the earth.

The Saturn and Tesla continue to shoot flames behind them. Emergency-vehicle sirens are drowning out the sound of the breaking waves. First responders continue to hose the scene with foam. The combination of rubber, fuel, lithium-ion battery, and flame retardant creates a rank plume.

Surfers in the water face back toward the beach, floating on their boards, gazing like Zen zombies at the environmental havoc of the collision. The surfers stare at Leyla and Aurora as they bob up and down with the motion of the swells.

Leyla wants to call Stephen and the kids, but she doesn't have her phone or purse. Both are back in the incendiary ruins of the Saturn. She wants to hear their voices, thinking they might quell the high-pitched ringing in her ears.

She looks down, sees blood on her hands, and follows its trail with her eyes, up her arm to her shirt, onto her stomach and chest. It's hard to see at first because of her black turtleneck; it's shiny and wet. Her first thought is that it's Aurora's blood because she feels no pain.

Leyla puts her hand up to her forehead. She feels a broad open gash beginning at her hairline. Tracing it gently with her finger across her scalp and down around under her eye, she is certain that she needs stitches. Her hand appears to be positioned at an unfamiliar angle where her arm connects to her wrist. It is grotesquely larger than usual. As her awareness intensifies, her collarbone begins to sear. Touching it reveals that it's not in the spot she expects it to be—more like three inches higher and protruding in a strange way.

Leyla looks over at Aurora's bare feet. The toes of her oversized pink high-tops were caught in the metal of the Saturn's crushed front end. The oversized nine-and-a-half double Ds that Aurora insisted on saved her feet. If the shoes had fit her properly, her toes would have been pulverized in the collapsed metal when the impact compressed the front end. It would have been impossible to extricate her from the car with her legs and feet still connected. Her beloved, sparkly high-top trainers are now melting in the combusted tangle of metal.

Regretting that she didn't think to pull out her phone or purse after liberating Aurora and vomiting her brief but glorious Nate n' Al's feast, she scolds herself and thinks she could have done better. She continues to trace and retrace the gash in her forehead with her free hand.

Becoming more aware of the blood and grit in her mouth, she spits and runs her tongue across her teeth. They're all there. Three years of Invisalign and twenty thousand dollars' worth of bonding—she would have been pissed to lose one of those.

Aurora has a purple, egg-shaped lump growing on her forehead. Leyla hopes her mother doesn't have a concussion, though she isn't sure what difference it would make in her cognitive abilities at this point. Aurora's left eye is swollen shut. It's the one that she can't see out of anyway. That was lucky. Leyla looks down at her mother's hand as she holds it. Aurora broke a nail.

In her free hand, Aurora is clenching the crushed, greasy, smoldering bakery bag filled with Estrella's *borekas*.

She pulls one out, bites off half, and passes it to her daughter.

Leyla accepts the offering and bites into the soft, yielding dough full of spinach and salty seasonings, cleansing her palate and bringing her back to life a bit.

"Stephen didn't cheat on me."

"You are lucky, *ija*."

"Yeah. I am lucky," Leyla responds.

"*Todo va bien ki eskapa bien*—All's well that ends well," Aurora responds, nodding and staring out at the ocean. "I must be a mess." Aurora reaches over and takes the Tory Burch scarf from Leyla's neck, where it's flapping in the breeze, and wraps it around her own head, magically knotting it into a turban reminiscent of Gloria Swanson in Sunset Boulevard.

Leyla looks at her in disbelief.

"Well, one needs a little pizzaz. Look at all these handsome firemen."

"*Firefighters*, Mom."

"When I was a little girl, Papa took me here on Rosh Hashanah. All the Rhodeslis came to Santa Monica for Taschlich. The aunties did the blessing for all of us. It was always the women."

Aurora begins to hoist herself up. The process is slow and impressive. It requires a bit of rocking, hands first down on the sand in front of her, then on all fours, as if she's planning to crawl. It progresses to a kind of downward-dog where she places her feet down in an inverted triangle, then walks her hands toward her feet. Finally, in one powerful swoop, she is upright.

She ambles toward the water, bends down, and rinses both of her hands in the ocean break that's washing over her feet. She turns around and walks back to Leyla. She places her left hand, dripping with ocean water, on Leyla's cheek and looks her in the eye.

"*Todo mal de se vaiga*—Everything bad should go. What bothers you, worries you, or harms you—any sickness, illness, fright, or discomfort—all this should be swept away to the very depths of the ocean." Then she puts her right hand on Leyla's other cheek. "*Todo bien ki se venga*—Everything good should come. Everything now will be good, your pain will go away, illness will leave your body, healing will come to you. Every worry is now gone. Your heart will be content."

She reverses her geriatric yoga gymnastic technique and reorganizes her position on the sand next to Leyla. They hear a scrunch, squish, scrunch behind them. It's the sound of large rubber boots navigating the sand of the beach. The first responders are coming toward them.

They both stare straight ahead. Leyla reaches across Aurora into the bag for another *boreka*. Aurora takes one, too. They sit side by side and stare out at the impending sunset, bloodied, battered, bruised, together.

CHAPTER TWENTY

Si no sovra, no abasta.
If there is none left over, there is not enough.

★ ★ ★

Aurora is drinking her coffee and gazing out the kitchen window at the view of the carport. Her perfectly burnt Thomas' English muffin is on a plate in front of her, though she is thinking about Estrella and her endless supply of mouthwatering *boyus* and *borekas*. Someday I'm going to try to make one of those recipes. I swear. Maybe Leyla will make some for me.

She misses Estrella, the sunny, flour-drenched kitchen, and her auntie's joyful commitment to waiting on her hand and foot, though she is happy to be back in her own apartment with the morning Chronicle and a full pot of Medaglia d'Oro in the Melitta.

Having spread the last remaining glop of margarine onto her English muffin, she sees that the white plastic tub of Fleischmann's is empty. She needs to go to the grocery store. It's hard enough to find her favorite brand in the health-conscious, local, organic, sustainable, grocery-store culture of Marin. How is she supposed to do it now without her Saturn?

Leyla is always willing to take her to the market. She'll pay for the groceries, too—an added incentive, but Leyla gives such a lecture on ingredients, it isn't worth it. Scolding about soybean oil this and hydrogenated fat that. Aurora just wants to be able to go buy her damn margarine without the dissertation on nutrition and longevity.

On the way home from the airport last night, Leyla informed Aurora that she had "no intention" of buying her a new car to replace the Saturn. It's so like Leyla to be hung up on the legal driver's license issue. She told Leyla that her license was "perfectly legal," except for the date, but Leyla was unwavering.

Since Leyla was the one driving the Saturn when it crashed, Aurora felt that she should really be the one to replace it. After all, she's the one with the Rothstein bucks. After a futile, yet heated, back-and-forth, that is where they left the issue of Aurora's lack of wheels last night. So for now, Aurora is stuck up on this hill.

Leyla has advised, nagged, and pestered her many times over the years about needing to move, trying for eons to get Aurora to consider other options.

"Something where you can walk to town and wouldn't need a car. Somewhere warmer with some sunshine, out of this fog. A nice community where you can make some new friends and find community." Leyla has made versions of the same speech again and again, driving her crazy with her relentless research and suggestions. Aurora refuses to discuss it. Tiburon is her home. What's the difference if Leyla writes a check for this apartment or another? Leyla's bossiness wears her down.

The speeches are always the same. There was an assisted living facility in Petaluma to tour. Aurora refused to consider it, claiming she did "not need assistance, thank you very much." Leyla reminded her that the Rothsteins had been generously supporting (the new health and wellness building is named the Bunny and Bob Rothstein Family Center) the Reformed

Jewish Senior Residences in San Francisco for decades, hint, hint. Her response when Leyla repeatedly mentioned it was, "I am Sephardic and not Reformed. It is enough that I married that fat-faced *shumechu* in a Reformed synagogue. I won't spend my twilight years with them, too."

"Your twilight years?"

Last year, Leyla found an affordable housing development for seniors in Novato that had a spot open. Aurora pretended not to hear her, though Leyla intentionally spoke into her good ear when introducing the idea.

Leyla tries every few years to get Aurora to engage in a discussion of alternatives to the steep, moldy, isolated apartment with the desolate view.

"Mom, you've been lucky up until now. Eventually, one of those falls is going to result in a fracture. Waiting for catastrophe is not a good aging strategy."

Aurora falls frequently, a tumble down the stairs here, a trip on the driveway there. So far, her mishaps with gravity have only resulted in bumps and bruises.

"*Ija*, not everyone lives life preparing for disasters like you do. Since you were a little girl, you have always been a *spantosa*—one who is easily afraid."

"Discussing your living conditions and attempting to plan for you to age in place does not make me a *spantosa*. It makes me responsible."

"Age in place? *Qualu dishu* age in place? Where else would I age?"

"*Ah dio*, Aurora"

With a father who lived to 109, Aurora prides herself on her "good genes." Leyla has made no progress on the relocation topic, other than to get Aurora to agree to trade the sparkly mules for the hot-pink Skechers, which did end up saving her life.

Aurora stopped answering the phone until Leyla stopped bringing it up. She gave her daughter a large dose of silent treatment that lasted for three months.

Knowing how much Leyla wants her to move, Aurora figures it's another reason Leyla has for not buying her a new car—as that would facilitate making life on the hill easier for her, and Leyla would not want to do that.

Aurora refuses to give up her beloved Tiburon, with its one block of shops and restaurants she can't afford. Most of her old friends are dead or in assisted living facilities of their own.

She could try to hit up Branan for the new car. She's pretty sure she knows what the answer will be. And now that he's going through a divorce, his ex-wife Acacia, who had been warm and generous with Aurora in the early days of her marriage to Branan, is off-limits. So, for now, Aurora is stuck on the hill in the fog with the view of the dumpster, dependent on Leyla.

She has a couple of new ideas brewing on how to improve her circumstances and rectify the car situation. She plans to discuss it with Leyla later.

The phone rings.

"I knew it. I knew it was you. I'm a witch."

"Hi, Mom. You know, powers of sorcery are no longer required to find out who's calling. The screen on your phone displays names and numbers nowadays, just saying."

"I'm sorry. I can't hear you. I've got a banana in my ear." Pause for laughter. "*Ke haber, ija?*"

"Stephen pulled a string and got me an appointment with a plastic surgeon at UCSF at 11:00 a.m. to look at these stitches. He's a world-renowned expert in facial reconstruction. They itch like crazy. How are you doing?"

"*Kaminando y havlando*—I still walk and talk," Aurora sighs.

"I'll pick you up at one, and we can get you a new pair of Skechers."

"One? Will you have enough time? What about carpool and all the afterschool *bavajathas* for the boys?"

"It's fine. They don't have any afterschool 'nonsense' today. They're going to their friends' to play after school. They'll walk home."

Aurora sputters. "Walk home? Play with friends?"

"*Experiencia es una maestra ki se haga pagar kare las lessiones*—Experience is a teacher who makes you pay dearly for her lessons." Leyla replies.

"I thought you hated proverbs?"

"Estrella taught me that one," Leyla laughs, perplexing Aurora even more. Laughter and Ladino, she doesn't recognize her daughter.

For Aurora, the trip to Los Angeles was a draw. She lost her car, shoes, and flea-market table, but the firefighters saved her purse with the deed for the plot, launching it to the sidewalk before it was consumed in flames. She still has hope that she can find a way to cash it in. Maybe I'll go to the Santa Rosa DMV. I haven't tried that one yet. If I can just get past that darn vision test, I can get a new license, and maybe I can convince Leyla to take me back to LA, and to the cemetery. I can bring it to that tall beige woman. She was such a darn stickler. And voila, I'll sell the plot! Off she goes, her imagination taking her as always to ridiculous plans, ever hopeful in her habitual, foolish, clever strategizing about ways to score a miniscule fortune.

The impact of the collision knocked out her upper denture. An emergency responder spotted it on the front seat. Aurora gave it a quick rinse and popped it right back into her mouth. Her mink survived, but not without significant smoke damage. She is inclined to think Leyla should replace that as well but knows it is a futile hope.

Aurora has a doozy of a black eye and a lump on her forehead but, other than one badly broken nail, she is remarkably intact. She left her hardback cosmetic case back at Estrella's when she went to pick up Leyla at Nate n' Al's, so it and all its contents are safe and sound. She's upset about the flea-market table, but she has nothing to sell now and no car to get her there on Sunday anyway.

Leyla suffered worse. Her purse was not rescued, and the BUDdy LOVE's banner that she salvaged from the conference was lost. Aurora doesn't understand why Leyla is so sad about that. She guesses the bag was valuable, some fancy-shmancy designer bag.

Aurora knows it will all be replaced. Stephen, Leyla's Prince Charming, will no doubt gift her another lavishly expensive "it" bag of the moment. He treats Leyla like a princess; he always has. Aurora doesn't understand why her daughter won't just relax and enjoy what she has. It's never good enough for that girl. She doesn't see how much she is loved and adored by her boys, always on edge for some unseen threat around the corner.

"Okay. I'll see you at one." The banana is tucked into the crook of her neck while she talks to Leyla, Aurora's version of hands free. She rummages through her purse, looking for an emery board to smooth out her rough broken fingernail. At the bottom of the bag, she finds the letter opener from the desk at Esther and Papa's. She forgot she had it. The clean out at Esther's apartment seems like a long time ago now. So much has happened since then. She takes it out and holds it in her hand. Well, now she has both this and the cemetery plot to show for her expedition to Los Angeles.

She needs to find a way to cash them in. If she can figure out a way to get herself down to the flea market on Sunday, she can ask her coin-dealer friend if the letter opener is worth anything. It's shiny; maybe it's silver, and she can sell it right there. Maybe she'll make enough for a new Saturn. Her mind commences its involuntary pattern of hopeful reasoning, her childlike ability to muster faith in the ridiculous possibilities of miraculous windfalls.

"Mom, did you call Estrella and ask her about Eliezer and the purses?" Leyla asks now.

"No, *ija*. I don't want to bother her." After the accident, back at the house in Los Feliz, she had only enough time for a quick goodbye with Estrella, not even enough for a proper meal before Stephen, Leyla, and the kids came to get her and take her to the airport with them. She never saw Eliezer—or the handbags—again and didn't want to break Estrella's heart by telling her what a *shudula*—eccentric, unkempt, worthless person—her son was for stealing Esther's bags.

"How could I possibly bring myself to add to her *pena*—pain." Aurora says, shaking her head.

"You don't want to bother her? You are concerned about her *pena*? You drag me away from my husband and children on a foolhardy chase through Los Angeles in your derelict crap-heap of a car, put our lives in danger, but you don't want to bother her? You don't care if your daughter almost dies—"

"Oh, please, you didn't almost die."

Leyla continues. "—loses things of value—my phone, my bag—ends up with a gaping forty-stitch gash across the forehead, a dislocated collar bone, and a broken wrist. That's no problem for you. It's just Leyla, she can take it. But Estrella you don't want to bother, because, poor thing, she raised a *shudula*?"

"Forty stitches? I think that's excessive. These new doctors nowadays. Back in my day they weren't so precious about stitches, probably just wanted to pad your bill."

"Are you kidding me? It's the doctor's fault I have forty stiches in my face?"

"Look, *mi alma*. It was a nice visit. I don't want to ruin it."

"Ruin it? Nice visit? You went down to LA on a classic Aurora treasure hunt for the estate of your dead 'stepmother' (one of seven stepmothers, I might add.) You ran me around like a fool with your idiotic plan to liquidate a cemetery plot and risked my life chasing a couple thousand dollars' worth of cheap purses. That poor woman went to her death thinking she secured eternity at Forest Lawn Cemetery in her fully paid plot, which you disastrously attempted to sell. Now you'll never be able to, because you can't prove that it's rightfully yours."

"Leyla, *ija*. With you, *la aluenga korta mijor ke la tijera*— The tongue cuts better than scissors. What do you care? You were in LA anyway, chasing that *shumechu* and his floozy, may I remind you."

"That *shumechu* is my husband, the father of my children, and it was not his floozy."

"I don't know where all this anger is coming from."

"You don't care about me. You never have." Leyla surprises herself by speaking her truth.

"Fine, I'm a terrible person."

Leyla takes a deep breath. She brings her free hand to her temple and massages in a circular pattern. There's no point. Another scheme down the tubes, days and dollars wasted, hearts and bones broken, once again sucked into Aurora's messy intrigues, all for nothing. She has to let it go, must learn to let go of Aurora. She can't save her mother. Aurora is the one broken thing Leyla cannot fix.

"OK. I've got to go, Mom."

"Leyla, sweetheart, before you go. I want to ask you for a little help with something." Aurora's tone has changed to sweet, endearing, cloying.

"I'll see you at one, Aurora."

"Yes, *ija* okay, but just one little thing before you go. I was thinking that this weekend at the flea market, you could—"

"No, Mom."

"*Speda*, let me finish."

"No."

"I haven't even told you what it is yet."

"No, Mom."

"It would be so easy for you. You are so good at these things. I just need some help paying for—"

"No."

"No? Just like that? You won't help your mama?"

"That's right. I won't." Leyla is trembling, her heart racing, eyes welling with tears. She isn't sad. She is frightened and over-whelmed with adrenaline. A wife, mother, grown woman in her midforties with decades of therapy under her belt—yet she still struggles to stand up to her emotionally immature mother.

"I guess you're going to hold those forty stitches against me forever. I wasn't the one driving when the car crashed. Let me just remind you. I just need you to—"

"There is no point going over it. It's behind us. If you want new shoes, I will pick you up at one."

"Fine, I'll be ready at one."

"Wait, Mom, one more thing," Leyla says.

"What's that, *mi alma*?"

"You don't care about the bags, or Eliezer, and you don't want to hurt Estrella. Okay, I get that, but what about Esther?"

"Huh?"

"Where's Esther?"

"Who?"

"Esther. Your stepmother, you know, next of kin?" Leyla raises her voice.

"Oh, right, Esther."

246 | LISA F. ROSENBERG

"The entire goose chase began because Esther died. The phone call, the trip to LA, the apartment cleanout, the purses, the cemetery plot. Where the hell is Esther? Don't you have to get her from the hospital? Aren't they waiting for you to arrange for the remains? I mean, since you can't sell the plot, why don't you go ahead and bury her in it? Did you ever think of that?"

"Of course I thought of that. But it costs a lot of money to get her there, and well, I . . . oh this is all so unpleasant Leyla. This is very upsetting."

"Here we go. Whenever you need to deal with any kind of serious conversation, you start with the 'this is so unpleasant,' 'this is so upsetting.'"

"Well, I . . . I mean, I just, why are you so harsh?"

"You cannot sell that plot, Mom."

"You don't know that." Aurora's voice changes. It transforms to a powerful and direct tone that Leyla rarely hears.

"Yes, I do know 'that.' Aurora, she did not leave it to you. She did not leave anything to you. You can't prove any relation, so you can't even take it to probate, which would cost you a fortune that you don't have anyway. I know you, Mom. I know how this goes with you. The deed will sit in your purse or drawer for the rest of your life, Aurora. It does not belong to you, and you should not profit from it."

"Leyla, this is very upsetting."

"Right, it's upsetting. Hard conversations can be upsetting. But it was Esther's burial wish. It belonged to her. It was fully paid for, including an endowment supplement, as we learned when we visited the cemetery that you dragged me to, indicating that she hoped, intended, planned to be there for eternity. Maybe there is an organization or something we can reach out to that helps in these situations, to get her there, to her final resting place."

"*Ija*, sweetheart."

"Don't you think it's just a bit, I don't know . . . unethical, Mom?"

"Stay out of it," Aurora commands, reverting to the stern voice again.

"Excuse me?"

"I said, stay out of it. It's none of your business." Her voice deepens, sharpens.

"I beg to disagree, Aurora. When you take into consideration the forty, as you say, excessive, stitches I have running across my forehead from our most recent catastrophic expedition, which I add to a lifetime of disastrous escapades you have dragged me through, everything you do ends up somehow being my business. So, I am asking you, where is Esther?"

"What do you care?"

"I don't know how much I actually do care. I don't feel the need to quantify it. But I have a right to ask. I think it's, um, unscrupulous—that's the word, unscrupulous."

"How dare you. You and your fancy words. This is none of your concern."

"That's where you're wrong. You always make it my concern, Aurora. You need me to pay your rent because you could never get or keep a job."

"Oh, sweetheart, when your father left us, and took everything, we—"

"He left us over thirty-five years ago. Why am I still responsible for this? It's an old trope, and I am tired of it. You made me responsible for you when I was far too young. You were supposed to be responsible for me, Aurora, and I resent it. The least you can do is answer my question."

"Trope? Now you're going to throw around your fancy Rothstein words at me. Your big-shot words."

"Rothstein words? What does that even mean?"

"You have Stephen. He gives you whatever you want, and

your poor old mother is left behind, left out of it. After all I've done for you."

"Tell me, Mom, exactly what have you done for me?"

"You think it's easy?"

"No, I do not think it's easy. I guess that's something you and I can agree upon. It is not—has never been—easy."

"Fine, I'm a terrible person."

"Oh Jesus. Why do you have to go there? Why can't we just have it out?"

"What can I say? There is nothing more to say."

"You haven't said anything! You never do. It's always the same response. You never take responsibility for anything."

"This is all so upsetting, so unpleasant. I don't know where all this is coming from. Why are you so aggressive?"

"I don't know, Mom. I just have a lot of questions, and you never want to answer any of them. You just tell me you're a terrible person and then don't talk to me."

"I have to go."

"No, you don't have to go."

"I don't know where all this is coming from."

"Just answer me. Where is Esther? Just answer the question."

"Let's talk later when you pick me up. I need to go put my face on if we're going shoe shopping."

"Tell me where Esther is. Just answer me. Please tell me you didn't just steal her plot, and purses, and leave her at the hospital."

"I can do what I please. I'll see you at one."

"No. You won't. I don't feel well. My face hurts. The one with the excessive stitches, and my collar bone is throbbing, and my wrist is killing me."

"This is so unlike you, Leyla. What's come over you?"

"Come over me? Did you even hear me? My FACE HURTS, you know, that face, the one that was horribly disfigured in the car accident when you grabbed the steering wheel because you suddenly had an appetite for *borekas* while we were chasing Eliezer, the *shudula*, who stole the purses that you stole first."

"I am the next of kin."

"The face that you haven't even asked about, or said you were sorry for, and now you won't answer a simple question. I'm sick of your stupid, passive-aggressive, repetitive answers, your 'I'm a terrible person' fallback response to anything I ask. Why don't you ever act like a mother? You are my mother! Why don't you ever act like it? I'm the daughter! You're the mother! You know what, never mind. I'm tired, I'm angry, and I'm sad. Get your own shoes."

Leyla disconnects the call. She isn't going to pick Aurora up today. Something has come over her. All the years of therapy and exercises in setting boundaries have somehow finally kicked in. She checks her watch and realizes it's time to go to the plastic surgeon. She doesn't need to rush home since the kids have plans after school.

She calls Stephen. He picks up on the first ring.

"Hi babe. Want to meet me for lunch after my appointment?" She asks.

"I'd love to."

"Okay. I'll pick you up at one."

CHAPTER TWENTY-ONE

Al entiendedor pokas palavras.
He who understands needs few words.

★ ★ ★

"My god those barbarians, did they use pliers and yarn to sew you up? You're lucky I was able to see you, I was on my way to a conference in Barcelona when your father-in-law called. We got to those stitches just in time. Could they not see that it was the middle of your forehead? Those ER hacks have zero regard for optimal cosmetic outcomes. Such a pretty face too." It is? Leyla thought.

She couldn't help it. It was automatic whenever someone said something complimentary, always that knee-jerk feeling of disbelief—*who me?* The imprint left by her father's early repugnance was so deep as to be cavernous.

"Keep it moist, covered, and no sun!" Dr. Morgenthal handed her the round handheld mirror. She studied her reflection, still in shock. She could barely see the delicate fresh sutures.

It was such a relief when he pulled out the original stitches. He was right; the ER in LA had sewed her up like upholstery. The itching, redness, and tenderness had driven her crazy. He removed them, resutured her, and prescribed a series of laser treatments to address the inflammation and mitigate scarring. Her father-in-law sat on the board of City of The Bay Hospital. He made the call to Dr. Morgenthal personally. She was grateful for the Rothstein influence, but even more she felt appreciation for being part of a family who cared for, took care of, her.

Home now after her third laser treatment this morning, she stared into her bathroom magnifying mirror. Leyla's mirror was the maximum 20X and had a bank of LED lights surrounding it. She liked to be able to see into every individual pore. The gash made a jagged path across her forehead and down around her eye. Shiny and pink, it was a glaring reminder of her lack of boundary-setting with Aurora. A metaphorical border fence tattooed across her scalp.

"It's cool, Mom. You're like Harry Potter." Josh said yesterday. It was healing well, smaller and less horrifying with each day and laser treatment. Leyla was not as anxious about the scar as she thought she would be.

"I think it's hot." Stephen said this morning when he kissed her forehead on his way out the door.

She switched off the light on her mirror, walked to her closet, and reached for the orange Tory Burch scarf that was softer and less irritating than the hats. She had found a TikTok video that demonstrated how to tie it in various chic bandana styles to cover her forehead. She looked at her reflection over the sink and pulled a few curl tendrils down around her face to soften the look and camouflage the mark. She had been wearing her hair loose since she got back from LA. She was supposed to keep the stitches dry, so Dr. Morgenthal discouraged washing, drying, and straightening it. She was becoming accustomed to feeling it in its natural state of wild, rebellious curls, and not flattening and smoothing it every day was saving her hours of bathroom time, not to mention hundreds of dollars in styling products.

Last week, while she was still under concussion protocol, Stephen had come home with the most extravagant assortment of Hermes scarves. It was such a sweet Stephen extravagance, but she was attached to the garish Tory Burch mantilla.

Readjusting the velcro of her wrist splint to allow her wrist room to turn, she wrapped the corners of the scarf around the back of her head. She had transitioned to a removable splint, so she had the full use of her hand for daily tasks now. Still not allowed to bear weight, Yoga and Pilates remained out of the question until her hand could bear weight. Looking at her reflection in her closet's full-length mirror, she was softer and less toned as a result of the work-out hiatus, but she was sleeping better.

The sleep-reset app did say that extra body fat helped with sleep. The fact that she was sleeping at all was a welcome change. She and Stephen had cuddled this morning, something she never had time for before the accident. Leyla knew about the oxytocin released with the practice of hugging. She always made sure to hug her boys the minimum of twenty seconds, so they would have the added benefit. But she'd never actually considered it as a therapeutic strategy for herself.

After tapping the dimmer switch in the dressing room, she turned and walked to the office. The rubber ball that the physical therapist gave her to rebuild her grip strength sat on her desk. She picked it up, squeeze-release, squeeze-release. She opened her laptop and saw the document that remained open from last night. Her attention paused to take in the view from the window in front of the desk, and the fog seeping through the redwood forest below.

She had started to sit at her desk again—well, not really again.

Leyla had never really sat here much. She had selected the white acrylic console for its minimalist chic, appointed it with the perfect accessories, and then never used it. She had not wanted to scratch it, but since the accident she had been sitting here daily, appreciating the Kent Woodlands view in a way she hadn't before. She can't remember now why she never just sat here and enjoyed this stunning view. Always running from some appointment or other, she never realized how wonderful it is to simply sit and stare at something with no agenda. The fog today was a soft blue-grey. The deep-green canopy of the ancient redwood giants hovered above the cool moist billows.

Leyla had been more than a little surprised when Branan messaged her the details of the funeral. She hadn't spoken to or heard from him in so long, she can't even remember when the last time was. He was a stranger to her, a name Aurora complained or bragged about in equal parts over the years, depending upon her mood and whether or not she'd received his check on time each month. The message said he was coming to town to preside over the memorial for his father. Well, it was *his* father much more than it was Leyla's.

There would not be a graveside service as there was no grave to be beside. RHF died as broke as ever with nary a pot to piss in. Branan's financial situation was apparently not much better than his father's, so it was back to the Neptune society for cremation and scattering at sea, cost-effective and respectable enough.

Why in the world would he think I would want to be there? Their family had been surgically and permanently bisected when her father and brother went their own way all those decades ago. She had barely communicated with Branan since. Why would he contact her to give her the details? No doubt he received a personal phone call from a family member with notification of his father's passing and did not have to accidentally discover the news via Cousin Sam's social-media spectacle.

He's probably just trying to fill out the room. She did not respond, but she did not delete it either. She'd read and reread it since it arrived in her inbox.

Neglecting the Jewish custom of twenty-four hours in the ground after death, Branan had taken weeks to make the arrangements. He had been deeply imbedded in a war zone in Ukraine when his father passed, and it had taken him this long to get back. He mentioned that Acacia was bringing their kids, a generous act of civility, post-legal separation. No doubt it took a lot of logistical maneuvering to arrange it all.

Does he want me to meet his kids?

Of course, Aurora was going, wouldn't miss it. All funerals are compelling affairs to Aurora. Though she had spent the past five decades of her life spitting on the floor at the mere mention of his name, she was off today, swathed in her finest sequined velour, to take her place as the pious first wife done wrong. Probably just to rub Kathy's (Mrs. R H Feldenburg number three) nose in her presence. Either that, or she was going for the spread. Aurora never passed up a free lunch.

Leyla still hurt, her forehead and wrist for sure, but mostly her heart. It was the same hurt that was always there. She can't remember a time when it wasn't. The big hurt lived in her core since the night Robert Henry Feldenburg walked out the door of twenty-nine Bay Veranda Way. The night he left so quietly, gently walking out on his family. Leaving behind a little girl with a big sadness. He never was much of a dad, but children love their parents in a way that defies logic, even abusive parents. Leyla's festering ache lived within her from that day; the hurt had never left her, never resolved, or healed. She had masked, denied, repressed, and, in her teenage years, medicated it. But it was always there, probably always would be.

She never got to have her say, never had the chance to tell him what she thought. As long as he was alive there was always that idea of a chance of a someday. She might run into him and finally tell him to fuck off. All that therapy, all those years of CBT, analysis, past life regression bootcamp, dialectical behavior strategy, EMDR trauma counseling—what was the point now that she could never confront him?

Her last *E* had suggested letter-writing exercises. They were supposed to be effective with the processing of painful estrangements, encouraging healing when actual dialogue and direct communication weren't possible. Leyla followed directions, writing and rewriting her missive many times, composing and deleting draft after draft. Some versions were long and verbose, detailing every act of cruelty, every degrading insult and infraction. Some angry, disjointed, foul-mouthed; others eloquent and poetically wordsmithed—all ultimately deleted. Something about putting it all in words, on paper or screen, wrenched by text out of her heart and head, made it dangerous.

There was no guarantee that he would even read it if she did send it. It might be intercepted by wife #3, Mrs. Devolay-Feldenburg. It might be shown to others in a cruel violation of privacy, laughed at, ridiculed, villainized, and gossiped over.

Something occurs with words when they are birthed into the world, when narrative gives trauma material form. One cannot control for interpretation. Gravity may be interpreted as humor, sarcasm as levity, or vice versa. It is impossible to know if people receive communications in the manner intended. Leyla continued this practice of composing and deleting as a therapeutic exercise.

On her screen now was this one final draft. She had written it the week before LA. She hadn't deleted this one, not because the words were more exceptional, meaningful, or descriptive, but because of the way she felt when she read it.

There was something her father said to her when she was a

FINE, I'M A TERRIBLE PERSON | 257

little girl. He said it all the time, pretty much for everything and anything she did. It wasn't even the worst thing he said. But it was the one she most remembered. It stayed with her and played daily on a loop in her head for most of her life.

He used to say: "You ought to be ashamed of yourself."

When Leyla brought home an achievement that wasn't enough, when she cried too much if she fell, when she came in second—not first—in the swim meet in the eight-and-under category. When she got a ninety-nine on a reading quiz instead of one hundred. When she wanted him to come in and turn out the light at night, too scared to get out of bed and walk to the light switch herself. He would say: "You ought to be ashamed of yourself."

That was what she wrote, just that. Now he was dead. What was the point? It was too late for a showdown with RHF.

★ ★ ★

"Will you be able to drive us? Or will Stephen drive?" Aurora inquired.

"You've got to be kidding me?" Leyla was still surprised every now and again by her mother.

"What? I told you. Branan needs me."

"Then tell Branan to come get you and drive you. Because I'm not going."

"*Ija*, he was your father."

"Have you lost your mind?" Stupid question.

She was slightly tempted to go, just to spy, maybe hide somewhere at a safe distance and watch the maudlin speeches for a laugh, for the comedy/drama of it. It was tempting, but Leyla was too well-behaved. She would not want to be a distraction for those who mourned, would never want to make a spectacle for those in pain.

Branan's kids would be there. Maybe someday she might

meet them. Maybe they would like her, and she could be someone's aunt. The boys could have cousins.

Oh, for fuck's sake, like that would ever happen.

What would it solve anyway? There was no way she was going to walk into that room with Aurora. Sitting here now, she was feeling it strongly, happening around her. It was just like the old days, when she was little, and the family was all together somewhere for some holiday or one of his damn weddings. They were all together, and she was left out, ever the Feldenburg outsider. It was all the old ghosts dancing in the aura around her again.

She looked back at the document on the screen with its one simple sentence:

You ought to be ashamed of yourself.
Your Daughter,

Leyla

It felt so perfect. She could not bring herself to delete it. No graphic details of his beatings and humiliations, his rejections and insults, no dissection of the interpersonal dramas, or accusations about the food insecurity and forlorn holidays, just his own words used against him. His ethos was the most perfect description of the life he lived. She was still hurt and angry. That would probably never go away, but this sentence felt empowering and rang so true. Maybe writing was healing after all.

She hated the son of a bitch, didn't care that he was dead. But she resented that she was denied the chance to grieve a father. You can't mourn someone you loathe, can't lose someone you never had. In reality Leyla had been grieving to some degree since she was a kid. She was robbed of the experience of having a father, the feeling of going through life with an unconditional presence, someone always having your back. The damage he wrought on her soul and psyche was vast. Why didn't he want her? Why didn't he value her? Why was he so kind and charming to everyone but her? Why was she such a disappointment to him? She will never get the answers.

She clicked *print* and looked out the window. The fog was now thinning and lifting as it crawled up the canyon. The sound of the printer had a welcome finality to it. Unprinted, it was eligible for revision. Printing it ensured permanence. The one single complete sentence, lacking substantive detail, names, dates—the lack of specifics eliminating the threat of anyone accusing her of lying or making anything up. There was no risk of her children finding it one day and asking her about the salacious minutiae of her past.

Leyla lived in fear of her children finding out the sordid details of her parents, childhood, younger years. It was one of the reasons she resisted journaling. Whenever an *E* suggested therapeutic writing exercises, encouraging the healing power of journaling, all Leyla could think was: What if my kids read it after I die!? *E* responded with "You'll be dead? What do you care?" No way would Leyla take that risk. She could not bear the thought of wounding her children, ever, in any way, even in death.

The printer finished. The room was silent again. She pulled the single white sheet from the tray. She had no one to send it to. RHF was dead, would never read it, and no one else really mattered. She carefully folded it in thirds, then ran her finger across the creases, rendering them crisp, distinct, refined. She stuffed it into a plain white envelope, took a pen from the drawer, and wrote: DAD on the front of the envelope.

She got up from the desk and walked toward the sliding glass doors that led out onto the deck. The view from their home was spectacular, sloping sharp canyons stacked with the primeval titans of the redwood forest tiering up the steep ravine, a creek running gently down the slope. The sound of the water was soothing. She took a long deep cleansing breath.

She pulled the slider open with her good arm and walked out onto the deck holding the envelope in her bruised hand. Her scarf blew in the cool moist breeze. The air washing over her warm, inflamed forehead felt soothing. She crumpled the envelope, squeeze-release, squeeze-release, compressing it in the method her physical therapist had prescribed for her rubber-ball exercises, finally crushing it into a small tight wad. She opened her hand and began to tear it with both hands. First in half, then in half again and again, until she held fistfuls of the tiny scraps of her words.

She put her hands up and opened them one final time. The wind caught the bits and pieces of her heart and letter. They swirled in the wind away from the deck and down the deep chasms of the forest floor below. She leaned over the railing and saw some of the pieces floating away in the creek.

Leyla looked at her watch. It was time for carpool pick up, Friday. She and the kids had started stopping for ice cream after school. It was Simon's turn to choose. His favorite was gas-station ice cream; she did not want to be late. She wiped the tears from her cheeks before they made a mess of her new white t-shirt, The black turtlenecks were too tight to pull over her head past the stitches.

Her phone buzzed back on the desk. She could see the screen from here. It was Aurora. "Pick up when I call later, *Ija*. I'll tell you everything," Aurora had said this morning when they spoke. Who got fat, who got old, who was using a walker now, who in a wheelchair, how many sandwiches there were on the buffet, how much she hated that awful *Shumechu* noodle kugel that her ex-sister-in-law was "famous" for. It always took Aurora several heaping portions for her to be able to give a full review of how truly awful it was. Leyla let it go to voicemail. She gave her scarf a tug, glancing at her reflection in the glass of the doors on her way past. She brushed her curls away from her face and walked back into her home.

ABOUT THE AUTHOR

LISA F. ROSENBERG has a B.A. from U.C. Berkeley in Art History, a M.A. in Graduate Humanities, and MFA in Creative writing from Dominican University. Her early professional career was in the blue-chip retail art world as a Gallerist for several prominent San Francisco art dealers including Crown Point Press and John Berggruen Gallery. After transitioning to museum education, she was most recently a public guide at SFMOMA and Museum Educator on staff at the Contemporary Jewish Museum in San Francisco. Her writing until recently has been in her professional life, primarily non-fiction, essays for exhibition catalogs, art criticism, tours, and public talks. Her fiction has appeared in Amaranth: a journal of food writing, art, and design, and she was recently a quarterfinalist in the Driftwood Press in house short story contest. *Fine, I'm a Terrible Person* is her debut novel.

ACKNOWLEDGMENTS

For Peter, who has generously indulged me with infinite support and unquestioning encouragement. In thirty-five years, you have never once uttered a single word of discouragement, questioned my abilities, goals or aspirations, however impractical. For Jake and Cyrus, my tireless sounding boards. You never fail to wildly inspire and steadfastly support me. You both are wondrously generous in your straight-faced belief in my abilities. I would also like to acknowledge and thank the faculty, staff, and peer community in the Low Residency Creative Writing MFA program at Dominican University of California, in particular Judy Halebsky, Marianne Rogoff, Claudia Morales, Kim Culbertson, Thomas Burke and Bobby Bradford. I am indebted to them all for their guidance, feedback, patience, wisdom, and support in the process of writing and publishing this book. I would not have been able to sit at my desk and write at all without the support of Dr. Darcy Oikawa DC, Cinda Van Lierop, L.Ac. and Avidan Graller CMT, CNC. It is my good luck that the universe placed you and your compassionate brilliance in my path to hold my body together so that my brain may have a healthy vessel to allow it to produce this book. There are others that I must thank by name: Karen Lansill the best cheerleader a friend can have, Michelle Beare for her big giant ears, loyalty and support, Melanie Field for her stalwart belief in me, my very first readers Meg Neville, Erika Smith, Mary Rosenthal, Marianne Vernachia. Reneé Marie; my beta reader Claudette Cruz (Theeditingsweetheart) who came through with generous referrals and a reverence for editing emergencies. Finally, my earnest gratitude goes to Vicki DeArmon, Maureen Jennings and Julia Park Tracey at Sibylline Press.

I am indebted to The Jewish Museum of Rhodes and the

Kahal Shalom Synagogue, whose scholarship I used in the writing of this book and the personal histories of my fictional characters. I also referred to documentation in the archives of the Jewish Community of Rhodes at the United States Holocaust Memorial Museum in Washington D.C.

BOOK GROUP QUESTIONS

1. Which character did you relate to or empathize with the most and why?

2 Who would you cast to play each role for the movie version?

3. What was the most satisfying or disappointing part of the story and why?

4. Can you think of any real-life people who share traits with the characters in the book?

5. How, if at all, did this book relate to your own life?

6. Who was your favorite character and why?

7. What do you think happens to the characters after the novel concludes?

8. If you could ask the author one question about this book, what would it be?

9. Which character in the book would you most like to meet in real life?

Sibylline
PRESS

For other great titles from Sibylline Digital First, please visit
www.sibyllinepress.com or online retailers.